I absolutely loved the book! I literally couldn't put my phone down while reading and finished it in under a day. I highly recommend it! It's soooo good I loved it. I read it at least three times, and I'm so excited that it'll be published!
Can't wait to buy a copy!
–Shreya, *Goodreads*

I don't even know how to express how much I love this book in words. I just connected to it so much, and I felt as if every scene was real, right in front of me. IDK, the author's just really good at writing. That's all I've got to say.
–Alex, *Goodreads*

This was a beautiful story with great characters. I simply could not stop reading it and was always waiting for new updates on Wattpad. I highly recommend it and am excited to know that it will be published!
–Jonathan Kim, *Goodreads*

This book is amazing! I found it on Wattpad, and I was so happy to find out it is being published. It deserves a lot of attention because it can change someone's life, like it did to mine. I've read it three times and once it finally gets published, I am going to buy it and read it many more times. And of course, tell my friends how awesome it is. The best part of this book is that every chapter makes you smile!
–Monique Bueno, *Goodreads*

An amazing adventure, where two broken pieces unite.
–Eva Jain, *Goodreads*

Typewriter Pub, an imprint of Blvnp Incorporated
A Nevada Corporation
1887 Whitney Mesa DR #2002
Henderson, NV 89014
www.typewriterpub.com/info@typewriterpub.com

ISBN: **978-1-68030-952-2**

DISCLAIMER
This book is a work of fiction. The characters, incidents, and dialogue are drawn from the author's imagination and are not to be construed as real. While references might be made to actual historical events or existing locations, the names, characters, places, and incidents are either products of the author's imagination or are used fictitiously, and any resemblance to actual persons living or dead, business establishments, events or locales is entirely coincidental.

SAVING GRACIE

TALESHA MITCHELL

type writer pub

This book is dedicated to my mother with love.
You've always inspired me, made me laugh, and feel loved.
And because of that, this is for you, Mum.

FREE DOWNLOAD

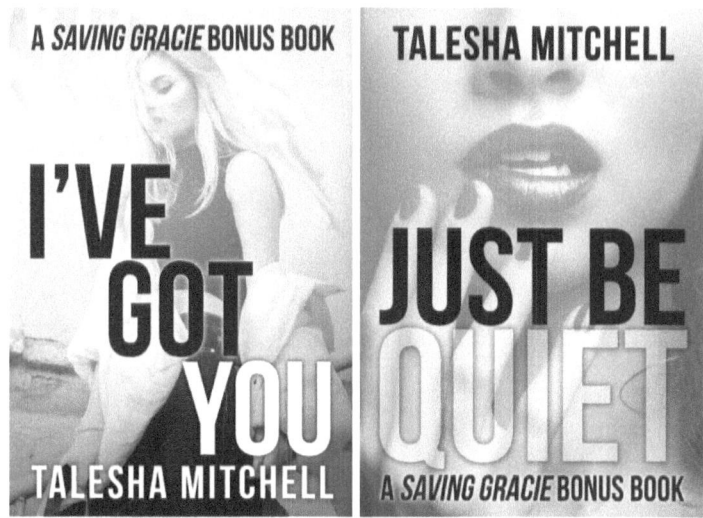

Get these freebies and more when you sign up for the author's mailing list!

talesha-mitchell.awesomeauthors.org

CHAPTER ONE
Just Leave Me Alone

"Have a great day, sweetheart!" Mum says happily as she leans over to kiss my forehead.

I send her a small smile before getting out of the car. Feeling the raindrops on my head, I breathe out a sigh and head into the building.

Let me introduce myself. My name is Grace Leigh Parkinson, and I'm not your usual seventeen-year-old school student. You see, instead of having basic brown, blonde, or black hair, mine is dark purple. Instead of applying makeup like most teenagers nowadays, I put in my nose and lip piercings. And instead of wearing nice dresses or jeans to school, I wear my usual baggy pants and oversized jumper.

Oh, and I am not one of those girls who just do not care about the school and its rules, because I actually do. The only problem here is the people who do not get that bullying is a crime.

For the past five years that I've attended this school, I have been bullied by at least half of the school's population ever since day one. Do not bother asking me why, because I have no clue. It may be my piercings or the fact that I have no friends.

Why don't I have any friends? Well, it's because the only one I had was dragged into my problems and bullied by everyone, and that's when she told me she could not be friends anymore. I do not blame her, but ever since, no one has wanted to be my friend or even be seen talking to me.

I feel more alone without friends. It hurts that I have no one to share my thoughts with, to talk about boys, school, and life. The usual people who talk to me are the principal or the school nurse only. That's it.

And what's worse is the fact that I cannot even talk to Mum about anything, because she is dealing with her own problems. Since she has cancer from secondhand smoke, I do not bother telling her about what happens at school. Mum is fighting her own battle, and hopefully—for everyone's sake—she wins. Because if I lose her, I won't know what to do.

You see, Mum and I are inseparable. We always hang out when we can and are usually in the same room, except for when it is time for bed. I think we are close because we look alike—or maybe it is because I am an only child.

If we were that close, you might ask, "Why wouldn't you tell her about getting bullied at school?" Well, like I have said, she is dealing with her own problems. Once she gets through them, I will tell her everything.

"Excuse me, you're in my way."

The voice of the girl in front of me pulls me out of my thoughts, and I look up at her. Realising I am in the middle of the hallway with my books clutched to my chest, I apologise and move to the side, only to bump into another girl, making my heart race.

At this exact moment, I know she had planned this.

"Ew! You just touched me!" the girl whom I bumped into screeches, making me apologise.

I try to step away, but nearby students block my escape. The crowd surrounds me along with the two girls, making my heart race even more. That's when I see Nicole.

Remember the friend who left me because she was getting hurt too? That's Nicole—the girl who's now one of the popular kids at school. She's on the cheerleading team, and some students say that she rules the place.

"Hello, Grace," Nicole says. The look of disgust is clear in her eyes.

Before I can speak, she kicks me to the ground, and my head slams against the lockers. I wince. The three girls stand over me, all glaring down at my thin, fragile figure.

"When I first met you, Grace," Nicole begins, placing a hand on her hip, "I thought you were a strong, independent girl, but I guess I was wrong."

The girl to Nicole's left slams her heel into my stomach, making me bite my lip. If you think the word *kills* describes the pain, you're dead wrong—the pain is excruciating!

"P-please . . . ,'" I plead, choking out the words, but this only makes the girl slam her foot a second time. I groan loudly, clutching my stomach.

Nicole smirks, crouching to meet my green eyes as I stare into her cold blue ones.

"You're just a little girl—just like everyone said," Nicole whispers menacingly.

I gulp.

As she stands, the girl to her right drives a kick into my stomach, knocking the breath out of me.

When the bell finally rings, everyone, including Nicole, begins to walk away from me, leaving me groaning and struggling to sit up. I rest my back against the lockers, exhaling a deep sigh as I let my head hang low.

"Would you like some help?" a guy says, standing in front of me.

I slowly look up at him—someone I never expected to come near me.

"What are you doing?" I ask, my voice raspy. I narrow my eyes at Luke and cough as something tickles my throat.

Luke crouches down, furrowing his brow. "Trying to help. What does it look like?"

I stretch out my leg, trying to look away, but I fail and sigh, deciding instead to focus on my hands resting on my stomach.

In a few sentences: Luke is the school's player. You know—the blond hair, blue eyes, and the face of a model? Yep, that's the famous player. Luke is known for sleeping with girls and breaking their hearts the next day, just for fun. Everyone says he's trouble, but to me, he's just a pig.

"It looks like you're either trying to get yourself into trouble or trying to trick me," I mumble, meeting his blue eyes.

Luke raises an eyebrow. "Trick you?"

"Yeah. Like, you offer me a hand, and when I go to take it, you pull away and run off laughing," I explain.

He chuckles, holds out a hand, and smiles.

"I won't do that," he says.

I roll my eyes. "Just leave me alone."

The boy simply shakes his head.

"I'm just going to take you to the nurse," Luke says, and I stare at him for a few seconds, searching his face for a hint of humour.

Without thinking, I reach out and grab his hand, breathing out a sigh.

"Ow!" I groan as a sharp pain shoots through my stomach.

Luke wraps an arm around my waist, and I cling to his shoulders to hold myself up. As we begin the slow walk to the nurse's office, I cannot help but ask myself: *Am I dreaming?*

My heart flutters as the realisation hits me—I'm not dreaming. Someone is actually helping me, walking me to the nurse's office.

Am I happy?

More like ecstatic.

CHAPTER TWO
I Think You Have the Wrong Number

Dear Diary,

Today was surprisingly different from my usual days at school. Actually, today was different from all the events that have ever happened at Jacksonville High! Yes, there was the usual abuse, but something else happened. After Nicole made a scene and left, I was leaning against the lockers when a boy with bright blue eyes and blond hair approached me.

I would've never guessed it would be the player. I mean, out of all people, the player was the one who approached me. What I also found shocking was that he offered to help me and walk me to the nurse's office. Like, when does that ever happen to a girl like me? People would kill just to get a wave back from the player!

Some people would call it pathetic that I was happy about Luke even walking in my direction, but they don't understand me or what I'm going through.

After Luke took me to the nurse's office, I never saw him for the rest of the day—and I understood why. He didn't want everyone coming at him because of what he did, just like Nicole did. Luke was only there to help me get to the nurse's office. That's it. He didn't want to get involved in my life, and I don't blame him.

I don't know, but I hope tomorrow goes just like today, since today wasn't as bad as any other day of

the week. I'm just praying it won't be as terrible as every
other week, because it's really messing me up. All I do is
ask myself: Why me? I just have to cross my fingers . . .

Grace Leigh Parkinson xxx

"Grace! Dinner's ready!" Mum calls.

I sigh as I close my diary and leave it in the drawer. I throw both legs off the bed and walk out of my room, heading down the stairs towards the kitchen.

When I enter, Mum is placing a plate of food on my placemat.

"Where's Dad?" I ask, watching as Mum sits in the chair next to me and places her own plate on the table. I notice the sad look in her eyes, but she quickly masks it with a forced smile.

"Working late again," Mum says.

I nod and begin eating the vegetables on my plate.

Ever since I was young, I have always gotten the vibe from Mum that she loved having everyone at the dinner table. She said it was the one time she could get everyone together in one room. But ever since Dad got promoted, he has been working more—much more.

Dad says he tries to come home as quickly as he can, but coming home at two in the morning almost every night only makes me doubt him.

I find it hard to believe that Mum tries her very best to let everything slide, because I know Dad is cheating on her. Ever since he got promoted, not only has he been working late, but he has also been getting phone calls in the middle of the night from his "partner" at work.

Little did he know, I knew everything from day one.

Dad is in love with *another* woman.

*   *   *

After saying goodnight to Mum, I lie in bed, holding my phone. I grab my earphones, plug them in, and scroll through my playlist. When my eyes land on Phoebe Ryan's song *Dead*, I sigh wearily.

> *I've made mistakes . . .*
> *been dishonest . . .*

As the song plays, I stare at my ceiling decorated with glowing stars. I know—I'm such a child.

It is weird how you think about the life you are living now and remember the past. You see, when I was younger, I did not care about anything. Nothing bothered me at all. But of course, as I got older, everything had to change.

I mean, does not everyone think about the time when they were younger? How you wish you could still live the same lifestyle? Like, we did not have to worry about what to wear, how we did our hair, or what people were saying about us? Yeah, life was perfect back then.

Sometimes I think the whole change might be a challenge for us—one meant to test us and push us through life's obstacles, making us stronger. And sometimes I think all of this is just a dream, that every obstacle is a way of telling us to wake up. But if it is a challenge, I hate it so much. If it is a challenge, why do I have to deal with everything life's throwing at me? Why me?

Suddenly, a ping goes off, pausing the music, and I frown in confusion. Who would be messaging me? I have no friends, and I have not given my number to anyone except my parents.

> *Hey, how are you feeling?*

I furrow my eyebrows in confusion at the unknown number. I have no idea who this is. Wait—do they know me? Oh God, do I have a stalker?

> *I think you have the wrong number.*

I get a reply almost instantly.

> *This isn't Grace? Oh damn. Sorry.*

My eyes widen in horror. My name is Grace! Whoever this is, they know my name. What else does this person know about me? Do they know Mum? Do they know about my school life?

Can I ask who this is?

Only if this is Grace.

It is.

Prove it.

How the hell am I supposed to prove that it is actually me? Do I send a picture? Wait—I do not even know who this person is. They might be a murderer! And if I send them my face, they will know what I look like—and they might come after me and kidnap me in my sleep!

Wait . . . I have an idea.

I exit out of my messages and click on the sound recorder, clicking the red button.

"Hi, stranger," I say in a quiet voice, and quickly press the red button again. I go back to the messages and send the recording of my voice.

Okay, it's you.

Now, tell me who you are.

Guess.

Wait, what kind of game is this person playing? I do not want to play any guessing games—they're such a waste of time.

Wait . . . Is it Nicole?

Oh God. What have I done?

. . .Is this Nicole?

I'm a male. We spoke today.

Suddenly, the events from today enter my mind, and I realise that I have only talked to one boy. It cannot be him, can it?

How did you get my number, Luke?

Ding, ding, ding! You got it, Gracie!

Please don't call me that.

Okay, Gracie. Anyway, just a little advice—you shouldn't leave your number on your Facebook information. You don't want random people messaging you at any time of the day, do you?

The sudden urge to reply with *Like you* flashes through my mind, but I push it away. Still, I feel so stupid. I might as well deactivate my account—there is no point in keeping it. All I ever see are Nicole's constant posts about me anyway.

How are you feeling, by the way?

Good.

Great. Just checking up. Good night, Gracie.

As if trying to drive me insane, a small tingling begins in my stomach, making me smile. Instead of another hate message, it was only Luke, checking up on me. Well, I guess I was wrong about that boy. He is actually nice.

Turning off my phone, I place it on the dresser. I wonder if I will talk to him again. I really hope I will.

CHAPTER THREE
Well, That's Helpful

Some people would say that teachers are amazing, that they are our guides to future careers. Others would say that teachers are nobodies who could not find anything better to do with their lives, which is why they became teachers: to make themselves feel powerful, to feel like somebody. I, on the other hand, say that teachers are just people who want to help kids get a better education, or a better shot at life, and achieve great things.

When Nicole yelled out that our English teacher, Mrs. Dargen, is an old hag a few minutes ago, I could not help but pity the teacher.

You see, she is an elderly lady, probably in her fifties, or sixties. And even though she can be mean when she has to be, the students in our class always treat her like a nobody. All she is trying to do is help us, but some people would rather be on their phones than pay attention to her. I'm not some weird nerd with a passion for school, but I think students should at least pay some respect to Mrs. Dargen, who is only trying to help us.

I watch as Mrs. Dargen sighs loudly. "Class—"

"Just go home, lady!" one of the boys, who thinks he means something to everyone, screams out—only proving my point.

I shake my head in disapproval before resting my forehead on my arms, realising that we are not going to learn anything in this class because of how disrespectful the students are.

But suddenly, before I can drift off to sleep, someone knocks on the door. I quickly raise my head, afraid that Mrs. Dargen will put me in detention for not paying attention, and watch as she walks over to the door. She swings it open, revealing Christopher James.

Christopher James is one of the scariest people in our school. If someone looks at him the wrong way, you can expect him to approach and start throwing insults—or worse. He has not done this to me, but I have seen it happen once in the cafeteria.

"You're late, Christopher," Mrs. Dargen scolds him, but Christopher just smiles at her.

"At least I came, right?" Christopher says, and I mentally nod in approval. He hardly ever comes to class, and when he does, everyone immediately starts being nice to Mrs. Dargen. Some people say Mrs. Dargen is actually Christopher's grandmother, but then again, it is just a rumour.

Mrs. Dargen sighs but steps aside to let Christopher walk in. He takes his usual seat in the back row, where I am sitting.

When no one says anything, Christopher decides to speak. "So, are we going to learn today or what?" he asks, knowing how rude everyone is when he is not around.

I guess that is why Mrs. Dargen can never be angry at Christopher, because he helps her shut everyone up.

I notice Mrs. Dargen smiles and begins talking about the book we have been reading in class, and how we have an assignment on it soon.

But, because I hardly got any sleep last night, I bow my head back into my arms again, hoping to get at least a few minutes of sleep.

*   *   *

It's lunchtime, and I have not seen Luke at all today.

Hey, you cannot blame me for thinking about him. He has been running through my mind all day. I do not know why, but a part of me is relieved that I have not bumped into him, while the rest of me is a little disappointed.

Today, I thought I would have someone to talk to, to spend my lunch with, but I guess I was right about him not wanting to get involved.

Suddenly, out of nowhere, a familiar voice is calling me.

"Hey, Grace!"

Before I can turn around, something cold runs down my back, followed by Nicole's laugh.

"C-cold . . . ," I mutter, a shiver running down my spine as the cold liquid soaks into my sweatpants. As all eyes are on me, I glance up to see Nicole starting at me for the second time this week.

"Oh, really? I thought it would've been hot," Nicole sneers, prompting laughter to fill the cafeteria.

I bite down on my lip, tears welling up in my eyes.

Before I can stand up, Nicole's hand presses firmly on my shoulder, holding me down.

"I haven't dismissed you yet," Nicole whispers in my ear, her voice echoing inside my head.

Then, something hard hits the back of my head, and my forehead slams against the table. I whimper in pain.

"Have a lovely day, Grace," Nicole spits.

My head slams into the table again.

Nicole bursts out laughing, prompting another wave of hysteria from the crowd. The tapping of her heels echoes around the room, and I squeeze my eyes shut, waiting for the bell to ring.

When it finally does, I wait a few minutes until I am sure everyone is gone.

After the last person leaves, I jump up and run as fast as my legs can take me until I reach the school parking lot. The tears in my eyes blur my vision, making me bump into someone.

Please, please, don't be Nicole.

"Gracie . . . ," a male voice says, making me look up to see the blue eyes.

Luke looks down at me, taking in my now-soaked shirt and pants, the confusion clear on his face.

"Please—" Before I can make my escape, I try to move around him—only for him to latch onto my arm, pulling me back.

Luke's eyes narrow as they stare into my green ones.

"What happened?" he asks.

The question makes me try to pull my hand out of his grip, but he just shakes his head.

"Don't worry. You can come to my house, have a shower, and then tell me."

As we walk towards his car, Luke's words circle my mind until I finally grasp what he just said. I am shocked I did not react to his words quickly enough—my eyes widen.

Wait—I'm going to Luke's place?

*   *   *

"No one is home, so I don't know why you're just staring at the door like that," Luke says, pulling me out of my thoughts as he opens the door. His right hand is placed on my back as he begins to guide me into his house.

Just as Luke starts to walk into a room that might be the kitchen, he glances over his shoulder and smiles faintly.

"The bathroom is upstairs to your left."

When he disappears into the room, I look around, not moving from my spot.

Before I can even take anything in, Luke reappears with a can of Coke in his hand. His eyebrows furrow in confusion as he looks at me, still standing.

"Why aren't you moving?" he asks, his eyes staring into mine, making me a little uncomfortable.

The question I have been trying to figure out appears in my mind again, and I look down at my shoes.

"Why are you helping me?" I ask, my voice soft, fragile.

Luke chuckles. "Because I want to," he says, popping open the can. "Now go take that shower. You look like you need it."

Sighing, I walk slowly towards the stairs, dragging each step. At the top, I turn left as he told me, spotting the sign that reads Bathroom.

Well, that is helpful.

I step inside and close the door behind me, locking it. At the sink, I let out a sigh and grip the edges before looking up and meeting my reflection in the mirror.

God, I'm such a mess, I think to myself as I take in my appearance.

Large bags hang under my green eyes—clear proof that I have not been getting any sleep. And to top off the whole look, my lips are dark purple, making me look like I just took a dip in the Antarctic Ocean for a few days.

I sigh, blinking the tears away. It will be okay.

*   *   *

After a quick two-minute shower, I find the clothes that Luke told me to wear—a pair of black shorts and a white tank top.

Now, I am wandering the hallway in search of the blue-eyed boy.

"Luke?"

Suddenly, he appears from one of the rooms, heading in my direction.

"There's food downstairs on the table. Make yourself comfortable, Gracie," he says, taking the towel from my hands, with a faint smile.

I nod, then head downstairs.

I spot the coffee table—and the food—and sigh in contentment.

I've never been treated like this by anyone other than Mum, which makes it surreal. I do not even know Luke that well, yet here I am, taking showers and eating his food.

Smiling, I grab the container of fruit from the coffee table. Inside are watermelon slices, grapes, apple slices, star-shaped pieces of pineapple, and chunks of rockmelon.

I stab a piece with the fork and pick up the remote, switching the TV from a documentary to the news. The reporter on the screen continues talking until she passes the lead to someone else, then the topic instantly grabs my attention.

"A man in his late thirties has been found dead near Jacksonville College. Jacksonville police report that the man died from fatal stab wounds. Witnesses say he was attacked by four men for his laptop."

A photo of the man appears on screen, making me shake my head in disappointment.

Suddenly, a voice from behind interrupts me.

"What are you watching?"

"News," I reply, trying to calm my racing heart.

Luke nods and sits next to me on the couch.

When I catch him glancing at the container of fruit, I turn to him and offer it. "Do you want some?" I ask.

He shakes his head, pushing the container away.

"I wasn't looking at your food, Gracie," Luke says.

His words confuse me. Then what was he looking at?

I continue staring at him, hoping he will explain. Instead, he just points at my arms.

I look down and instantly know what he was looking at. I fold my arms, resting the container of fruit on my thighs.

"Uh, they aren't—"

I'm cut off by the sound of the front door opening, making both of us glance over to see who is at the door.

A woman with blonde hair steps inside, her blue eyes locking with mine.

CHAPTER FOUR
Mum, My Friend Is a Boy

"Hey, Mum," Luke says, greeting his mother.

I quickly drift my eyes away from his mum.

"Hey, honey," she says, looking tired. "Who's this?"

When I realise that she is referring to me—the girl who is currently sitting on her couch—I feel my heart race in fear for making myself comfortable in her house. I glance over and watch as she puts her handbag on the table, before walking over to us. Luke turns to me, a small smile on his face.

"This is Grace," Luke says, and his mum looks at me. "She's a friend from school."

"Hi . . . ," I trail off, not really knowing what to do in this situation. I'm a really socially awkward type of girl, if you have not noticed already.

Luke's mum smiles at me, making my heart continue to race. Suddenly, she pulls me into a hug, taking me by surprise.

"Hello, Grace. I'm Bree." When Bree lets go of me, her smile only grows. "Are you staying for dinner?" she asks, but I shake my head.

"N-no, I have to leave," I stutter, watching as Bree nods, and brings me into a second hug.

"Well, it was nice to meet you, Grace. Hopefully, you can come around for dinner another time."

Her instant kindness towards me makes me smile shyly as I stand up.

Suddenly, Luke grabs my hand, but before I can say anything, he pulls me towards the stairs.

"We aren't finished talking about . . . ," Luke trails off, hoping that I know what he is talking about—and I do. When nothing comes out of my mouth to protest, Luke continues, "We'll talk tomorrow."

All I do is nod.

"What about the clothes?" I ask, pointing down at the white tank top and the shorts. Luke glances down before smiling.

"Keep them," Luke says.

Before I can thank him—or even say anything, for that matter—he grabs my hand as we walk out of the house.

"I'll drop you home."

*   *   *

After Luke drops me home, I walk into my house to see Mum sitting on the couch, her sketchbook in her hands. Smiling, I close the front door behind me, catching her attention.

"You're home . . . ," Mum trails off.

I nod as I walk over to her. After giving her a quick hug, I sit next to her and glance over at the unfinished drawing.

It is a picture of a man. Perfectly shaped lips. Sharp jaw. Curved nose. Neat eyebrows. Freckles. Blue eyes. Taking in the drawing, I immediately recognise the person Mum has drawn.

Uncle Christian.

"Would you like something to eat?" Mum asks, closing the sketchbook and placing it beside her.

Nodding, I stand up at the same time she does and follow her into the kitchen. As she begins making me a snack, I think about the drawing.

Uncle Christian—or Chris, for short—was the most amazing man I had the chance of knowing. Although I had first met Uncle Chris when he was in the hospital, trying to fight the cancer, he was still pretty amazing. According to Mum, he was the best older brother you would wish for—protective, funny, and caring.

Mum always told me stories about Uncle Chris. When her father was never around, he would help her with her homework until the early morning hours; when a few boys at school texted rude, sexual comments to her, she showed Uncle Chris, and he set them straight.

From everything Mum had told me, I knew even then that if she lost her older brother, she would be devastated.

Three weeks later, after I met Uncle Chris for the first time, Mum received a phone call from the hospital. As I had predicted, she was crushed. She stayed in her room all the time, never ate, never went to work. She did not even check up on me. Mum was a mess, and even though Dad tried to help her, she did not acknowledge his presence.

Mum had shut everyone out—including me.

That was until Aunty Carol decided that Mum needed to stop the way she was acting. So, she came over and stayed a few nights, helping Mum—even if all Aunty Carol managed to get her to do was eat something. She continued staying over until Mum finally fixed herself up.

If it had not been for Aunty Carol, I do not know if Mum would be here now.

This is why Mum started drawing—to express her feelings. It is what her mother, my grandmother, used to do too when she was in a mood, so I guess that is where she gets it from.

"So . . . ," Mum begins, her voice pulling me out of my thoughts, "where did you go after school? You usually come home quicker."

She takes a seat next to me and hands me a plate with a sandwich on it. She has made one for herself too, which makes me smile.

"A friend's place," I say, watching as Mum nearly jumps from her seat. Since she knows I do not have any friends at school, this is obviously a surprise to her. I glance over to see her wearing a wide smile, pleased that I have a friend.

Wait—is Luke even my friend? Can I classify him as that?

"Really?" Mum asks, and I nod.

"Oh, well, I must meet this friend. I hope she is nice and—"

"Mum," I say, cutting her off. "My friend is a boy."

I bite into my ham and cheese sandwich. Out of the corner of my eye, I notice her grin.

"A boy?" she asks. I nod slowly.

Suddenly, she pushes her plate away, placing an elbow on the table as she looks at me.

"Tell. Me. Everything."

*   *   *

"So, he's one of those . . . playboys?" Mum asks, a small frown beginning to spread across her face.

I nod.

She sighs before composing herself, taking in the information.

"Has he . . . touched you?" Mum asks.

I shake my head almost instantly.

"No," I say, watching as the concern begins to drift away from her face. "I actually see a whole different side to him when it's just the two of us. It's reassuring."

She smiles.

"That's so good to hear—"

"What's so good to hear?"

Suddenly, Dad's voice fills my ears, making me nearly jump out of my seat. Mum glances over at him, her smile still on her face as he walks towards her.

When Dad kisses her on the forehead, Mum's smile seems to grow.

"Hey, you came home early," she says, watching as Dad walks over to the fridge and grabs a beer.

"I finished things early," Dad says, popping his head out of the fridge. He glances at me before speaking again. "What's so good to hear?"

Mum glances over at me, her smile turning into a grin.

"Grace made a new friend." She wraps an arm around my shoulders. "And it's a boy," she adds, kissing me on the cheek.

Dad glances between Mum and me before raising an eyebrow in question.

I nod slowly, and he returns the nod.

"Well . . . I'll have to meet him soon," he says before exiting the kitchen.

Mum looks at me and wraps her other arm around me, hugging me.

"I'm really happy for you, Gracie," she whispers. "I love you so much."

She stands up after breaking the hug and grabs both our plates. As I start to walk out of the kitchen, she calls my name.

I look over my shoulder. "Yeah?"

I get the feeling she is about to say one of those inspiring quotes she secretly steals from Tumblr. She always does this when we part ways. Mum thinks it's good luck. That's why.

"Don't ever give up, because there's always someone out there you inspire," she says, proving my prediction right.

I smile at her, and she returns it before leaving the kitchen.

I love you too, Mum.

CHAPTER FIVE
That's a Little Creepy

Some people say that every new day is a fresh start. Well, as much as I would like to believe that, today is definitely not one of those days. Why? Because as I walk into the school building, I spot Nicole standing beside my locker.

Grumbling, I mutter, "What could she possibly want now?"

As I make my way over, I tug at my jumper, trying to calm myself—or at least brace for the worst.

"Good morning, Nicole," I say, trying to start on a good note.

But judging by the way she looks at me, I doubt being nice will help me at all. I chew on my bottom lip as I shove my books into my locker. I feel my legs begin to shake.

After I slam my locker shut and turn to face her, I am ready for whatever she is about to do to me. But instead, she places a hand on her hip and frowns—not the sad kind.

"You see, Grace, I'm not very fond of people who try to steal my boyfriend," Nicole says.

Her words spin in my head. Boyfriend? I did not even know she was dating anyone. So how could I be stealing him? And even if I had known, I would not do something like that, even if I do hate her.

I furrow my brows, just staring at Nicole. When she narrows her eyes at me, I force out a response.

"I have no clue what you're talking about," I say quietly, already wishing I could walk away and just get on with my day.

Nicole points a finger at me.

"Look, I'm just going to make this easy for you. If I catch you with Luke, I will ruin your life."

Like you have not been doing that already, I think bitterly, but I just nod.

Wait—Nicole and Luke?

Ugh. I was just starting to befriend him.

*   *   *

"I want all of you to do five laps around the field. If I catch anyone cutting corners or stopping, I'll make you run another five. Got it?" our sports teacher, Mr. Peters, says.

We all nod and begin running.

After running five laps, Mr. Peters sends me a firm nod. "First again, Grace," he says.

I smile and head up the hill to grab a drink.

That is when I see them—Nicole and Luke.

"Come on! Just one kiss! If you won't go out with me, at least kiss me," Nicole begs, clutching his shoulders.

I furrow my brows at the sight.

Luke pushes her away. "No, Nicole. No dating. No kissing. No anything," he says and turns to walk away.

I frown in confusion as Nicole runs a hand through her brown hair.

I thought they were dating.

Nicole suddenly yells, "It's because you have a thing for that little slut, isn't it?"

I glance over to see that Luke has stopped walking. He turns around slowly, walking back to her.

Luke points a finger at her and narrows his eyes.

"Grace is not a slut. You are," he says, then turns and walks off again.

My heart races. My mind spins.

Luke defended me. But why?

As Nicole storms off in anger, I take the chance to run up the hill and grab my drink from my bag.

I sip, then splash some on my face to cool down.

"I saw you running . . ."

The voice makes me jump and spill my water. Luckily, it was just on the grass. Looking up at Luke, I furrow my eyebrows at him.

"That's a little creepy," I say, putting the lid back on the water bottle.

Luke raises an eyebrow at me, crossing his arms over his chest.

"So is watching Nicole and me." He smirks, making me nervous as I look down at the ground.

How the hell did he see me? I ask myself, biting my bottom lip.

"S-sorry . . ." I stutter.

All of a sudden, he gently holds my chin.

I cannot help but look up at him.

"It's fine, Grace," he says, his smirk now turned into a small smile.

All of a sudden, Nicole's words from earlier enter my mind, making me step away from him.

"I . . . I have to go," I say before running off, leaving him with that stupid smile on his face.

*   *   *

I smile as I walk up the pathway. I'm excited to tell Mum about school today and everything that happened—most importantly, what Luke did. She is going to be so happy, since I can already tell that she likes him.

You are probably wondering why I'm in such a happy mood—and from what happened today, I guess it is obvious. But it is not just because Luke and I talked again today or because he defended me—it is because school is done for the day, and I'm going home, which is my favourite part. I feel like home is the only place I can get away from the drama at school and be free from everyone there, especially Nicole.

I smile, spotting Mum's parked car in the driveway.

Quickly, I make my way up the stairs and take a deep breath, trying to calm myself down, but the smile on my face probably is not going to fade, so I do not bother.

I unlock the door with my house key, step inside, and close it behind me.

"Mum, I'm home!" I call, hoping that she is not sleeping.

When I do not get a response, I furrow my eyebrows in confusion.

"Mum," I call again, a little louder. "I'm home!"

I walk around the living room, but she is not there. Walking into the kitchen—she is not there either.

I wonder if she is out in the garden, fixing up the flowers.

Yeah, maybe she is doing that.

I walk down the hallway leading to the backyard.

"Mum?" I call again once I find myself standing out in the yard.

When I don't see her outside, I begin to worry as my heart starts to race.

The bedroom.

I run back inside and up the stairs.

When I push the door open to find an empty room, I gulp.

Maybe the bathroom.

I walk down the hallway to the bathroom. I grab the handle and push the door open—but she is not there either.

"Mum!" I scream, my hands clutching my hair.

As I pace the hallway, I suddenly stop by the mirror on the wall. I look how stressed I am, so I take a deep breath and drop my hands.

Calm down, Grace, I tell myself as I reach into my pocket to grab my phone.

I click on Mum's contact and press the phone to my ear.

The song *Dear Life* by Delta Goodrem plays, making me lick my lips in irritation. Mum did not take her phone with her. I walk down the hallway to grab Mum's phone.

I walk into her room and sit on the bed, holding her phone in my hands.

"Where are you?" I ask quietly, trying to keep myself calm.

All of a sudden, a thought pops into my mind about calling Dad. I mean, maybe he knows where Mum is, right?

I grab my phone and click on Dad's number, pressing the phone to my ear. But I immediately groan in frustration when the phone goes straight to his voicemail. Because of this, I throw my phone at the wall, smashing it.

"Grace?"

The voice calling me makes me turn around and see a man wearing a dark leather jacket and jeans.

I step back, alarmed that a stranger is in my house.

"Who are you?" I ask, watching him take a step forward.

He grabs my hand and guides me out of Mum's room.

"I need you to come with me."

CHAPTER SIX
Don't Get Lost

Throughout life, good things happen. Like on your birthday, you open presents and finally unwrap the gift you have been wanting—whether it is a phone, clothing, or a gift card for your favourite store. Or maybe you start to realise how great your life is beginning to turn out. What I am trying to say is that sometimes life brings good things, but bad things come too.

And right now? I'm dealing with the bad.

"No! I want to see Mum!" I cry out as tears fall down my face.

The doctor reaches out his arms to grab me, but I push him away in anger and storm down the hallway. Babies crying and patients groaning in pain echo around me, but I keep ignoring the noises and continue to look for my mum.

"Grace!" the doctor yells.

But I ignore him and walk up to the reception desk.

"Where's Mum?" I ask, looking up at the lady.

"Name?" she asks, slightly smiling.

"Rose Parkinson," I say without hesitation.

The lady nods as she types into the computer. When she finds it, she grabs a sticky note, writes down the information, and hands it to me.

"Don't get lost," the lady reminds me, but I do not bother to reply. I just want to find Mum. I look down at the sticky note, reading the level and the room number:

Level Three, Room 218.

I fold the paper, place it in my pocket, and walk up the stairs, hoping that Mum is okay.

*   *   *

After walking around the hospital for about ten minutes, I've concluded that I'm lost, because I swear I have been around this part of the hospital already.

"Excuse me," I begin, looking at the person holding a sleeping baby in front of me. "Do you know where this room is?"

The guy looks at me before glancing at the paper in my hand. He purses his lips before pointing down the hall.

"Should be over there somewhere," he says.

I smile slightly, thanking him before walking down the hallway.

Finally, I'm getting somewhere.

I look at the numbers on the doors above me, counting down . . . Room 216, Room 217—" I'm cut off when I bump into someone. I groan and rub my head.

"Sorry—" I say, but I freeze when I see Dad staring at the door.

"Dad?"

"Hello, Grace," Dad mumbles, not bothering to look at me.

When I realise he is standing at Mum's door, I point at it while staring at him.

"Is Mum in there?" I ask.

Dad finally looks at me. He stoops down and holds my hand.

"I don't want anyone else to tell you this . . . so I'm just going to say it," Dad says, breathing deeply.

I frown in confusion, waiting for him to continue.

"Your mother . . . she . . . the cancer . . ." he says.

His hand shakes a little. Still, hope rushes through me.

"She got through it?" I ask, smiling.

He takes in another deep breath, his hands moving to my cheeks.

"Please believe me when I say this, okay?" he says.

I bite my lip, the hope slowly fading with every second that passes.

"She . . . she didn't make it."

CHAPTER SEVEN
Curse You, Stupid Hair

It has been a week since Mum passed away, but nothing has changed.

Nicole is still bullying me at school, and Dad still comes home late from work.

What about Luke? Well, that's the one thing that has changed.

I have not seen Luke. And I'm starting to think that maybe he has finally gotten it through his head to stay away from me if he does not want trouble with Nicole. I mean, I won't lie—I like Luke's company. But it's for his own good that he keeps his distance from me, even if it hurts.

Today is Sunday, and I am alone in the house.

I'm sitting at the table by myself, thinking about everything.

Dad does not work on weekends, but I know where he is. And let me just say, he is not sorting out Mum's funeral. Oh no, no. He is with that *girl* from his work.

Sometimes, when this happens, I question why Dad married Mum.

I mean, Mum told me enough stories about her and Dad—how they met, what they got up to, and how much she loved him.

But what I do not understand is why she said he chased her.

One: If that were true, would that not mean he loved her?

And two: why would he go through such trouble to get Mum in the first place, only to cheat on her later?

It just does not make any sense to me.

Mum was such an amazing woman. I bet she had all the boys chasing after her—Mum was gorgeous! So why did she choose Dad out of all the other guys? Why Dad? I'm not bagging on Dad. I'm just trying to understand what made him so special to her.

Well, I guess I will never find that out anymore, will I?

As I question Mum's choice, a tear slides down my face, and I quickly wipe it. I've cried enough this past week. Why do I have to keep crying? I have had enough sleepless nights crying about everything. But the tears keep coming, making everything feel so real:

Mum is gone.

Dad has not changed.

And I am alone.

I have to be strong, I tell myself, breathing out a sigh.

And just then, Mum's last words enter my mind:

Do not ever give up, because there is always someone out there you inspire.

I close my eyes tightly, trying not to sob.

Opening them, I look towards the picture of Mum on the counter.

I stand up, walk over, and hold it in my hand.

"I love you so much, Mum," I whisper, rubbing my thumb over her face.

Her green eyes sparkle in the sunlight as she smiles at the camera.

I remember the time I took the photo. It was on her birthday, and we were at her favourite ice cream shop. She looked so happy that day, so I took a photo.

I walk out of the kitchen with the photo still in my hand and head towards my room. I close the door behind me and place the framed picture of her on my desk, weakly smiling as the memories flood my mind.

Dad does not deserve Mum. If anything, I am the only person who deserves her because I truly loved her. Not him.

*   *   *

"Wake up, sweetheart," a soft voice whispers in my ear.

I open my eyes and see Mum.

She is smiling down at me, and my heart practically jumps out of my chest as I pull her into a hug.

"You're here!" I exclaim, tears streaming down my cheeks.

Mum chuckles and lets go of me.

"It's nice to see you, too," she says, her smile making my heart race. "I've missed you," she adds.

I smile as she runs a hand through my hair.

"You don't know how much I've missed you, Mum," I say, tears streaming like a waterfall.

Mum kisses my forehead, holds my hands, and smiles.

"I have to go now, Gracie," Mum says. My smile fades instantly.

"Please take care of yourself," she adds, making me frown further.

Where is she going? Why is she leaving?

"Why, Mum? Please stay," I beg, staring into her green eyes.

She flashes me one last smile before releasing my hands, her body floating away.

*   *   *

I jolt awake in bed, looking around in hopes of finding Mum. When I do not see her in my room, I bite down on my lip.

It was just a dream. I wipe my eyes, realising that I have been crying in my sleep.

I throw my legs off my bed, walk out of my room, and into the bathroom.

Washing my face with cold water, I breathe out a sigh as I close my eyes. I look up and open them, staring at my reflection in the mirror.

I look terrible, I think to myself.

I grab my piercings from the edge of the sink. After putting them on, my eyes trail up to my hair. Running a hand through it, I find my fingers caught in the knots, which makes me sigh.

"Curse you, stupid hair," I mutter. I grab my brush and begin to run it through my hair, holding in my groans as I pull at the knots.

I let go of the brush, watching as it just lies in the knots, not bothering to fall—obviously, it cannot. I ignore how ridiculous I look as I stare at myself in the mirror.

Then someone knocks on the door, grabbing my attention.

"Knock, knock," Dad says, taking me by surprise.

I step back and cross my arms over my chest.

"Aren't you supposed to be at work?" I ask. He walks into the bathroom, coming closer towards me before pulling the brush out of my hair without a struggle. He smiles at me, looking into my green eyes.

"I just wanted to check up on you," he says. His response makes me shake my head.

"You don't need to. I'm fine," I say.

He looks at me for a few seconds, as though he is trying to figure something out, but my face is stone cold. He nods slowly before placing the brush on the edge of the sink. He then walks out, leaving me alone in the bathroom.

I would have been happy if he had checked up on Mum now and then, but obviously, he never cared. I would rather let Mum take my time with him than him trying to spend it with me, because Mum was the one who needed his love the most—not me.

Pathetic.

*   *   *

As soon as I walked into the school building, I instantly knew that everyone had heard the news about Mum. It was clear on their faces. The looks of sympathy were all I was receiving, and I hated it. I do not know how everyone found out, but that's not what I'm worried about right now as I stare at Nicole, who is looking at me the same way everyone else is.

Something about their looks immediately makes me want to explode.

I slam my locker shut—hard and loud enough to get everyone's attention, if they were not already looking at me—and send them the message that I do not need their pity. I glare at them, the feeling of anger rushing through my veins.

"Don't you all have anything better to do?" I shout.

My eyes narrow at Nicole. "Stop staring at me!" I snap, glancing back at everyone, who are still sending me the smallest bit of pity.

When I look back at Nicole, she looks away and walks down the hallway with her friends by her side, not bothering to do anything else. I roll my eyes and begin to walk to my first class.

I'm okay with the attention if Nicole is involved because I'm used to it—I have been for five years now. But if it has anything to do with my family, especially Mum, I'm not okay with it at all.

I will never be okay with it.

CHAPTER EIGHT
Fuck You, Haters

The school day flew by quickly, and, to be honest, I am still quite annoyed with everyone's staring. I mean, unlike every other day, no one looked at me at all unless it had something to do with Nicole. But now the unwanted attention is just irritating me.

I hate the fact that everyone knows about Mum's passing. I hate the fact that everyone is finally treating me as a human being instead of someone no one notices. I hate the fact that everyone is starting to care about me and what I'm going through because of Mum's death. Well, it took them so long to accept me. I mean, why couldn't they have done that before?

Why can't I have a simple, normal life? Why am I the unlucky one?

Tired and miserable, I slowly insert my key into the keyhole and walk into the house, closing the door behind me with a heavy sigh. Walking up the stairs, I step into the bathroom.

I take in a deep breath, looking into the mirror as I do so. I have to calm down. I don't want to do something stupid. But honestly, why do I get bullied? Is it because I am weird? Is it because of the way I dress? Is it because of my hair and the fact that it's purple? Why can't I just have a normal life?

You've lost everything. I still don't know how you're still here! Just leave. It's not like anyone will care, my inner voice says, making me groan in frustration.

It is true, though. No one will care. No one will even know that I'm gone. I am invisible to everyone, so obviously they won't notice that I've just done what they have been secretly wanting me to do for ages.

I flick the rubber band on my wrist, closing my eyes.

Ignore the thought, I tell myself as I try to stay strong and calm, but forcing down these heavy thoughts only makes them grow stronger. And next thing I know, I begin to walk down the stairs and out the door, heading to the one place where I know it can be done—the school.

*   *   *

As I walk towards the gates of the school, I notice that they are open, probably because of the ongoing after-school tutoring. I walk down the pathway and towards the back of the school.

When I reach the back doors, I walk through them, knowing that no one will be around this part of the building. No one is ever here.

I quickly make my way up to the highest floor and walk down the quiet, empty hallway. At the end, I see the stairs leading to the top of the building. When I reach the door, I look around to see if anyone is there before I walk through it.

I take a deep breath when I finally reach the top of the school's tallest building, the warm wind brushing past me. I rub my arm, breathing out a tired sigh before walking over and sitting down. I swallow at the height while my feet dangle.

I reach into the pocket of my large jumper and pull out my smashed phone, which surprisingly still works. I open the Facebook app and click the Live video, holding the phone in front of me.

"So . . . I'm finally here," I say, smiling weakly at the camera. I watch as the view count in the corner of the screen begins to rise, and before I can say more, it has already increased to fifteen.

"To everyone who wanted me to fall and finally break to the point where I feel like nothing, I guess you've got what you've always wanted," I say, and suddenly, two comments appear, both from the football team.

James Declan
You're damn right!
1s Like Reply

Michael Holt
Woo-hoo!
2s Like Reply

I breathe out a sigh, ignoring the comments. "You see, a week ago, my mother died . . ." I gulp, trying to keep myself together.

"And for those who knew my mother—like Nicole, who met my mother a few times—I know you all pity me. So just to let you all know, don't do that, because the way you've all acted towards me makes no sense with what you've all been doing recently," I say, standing up.

I look down at the ground below me and turn my phone to show everyone where I am.

"Now, I know you all hate me, and that doesn't make me the only one, but what you all have done to me does hurt. So, I won't hesitate to say"—I turn the phone back to me and smile—"fuck you, haters," I say before dropping the phone to the ground and listening as it smashes completely.

Breathing out a sigh, I sit down again, my feet dangling off the edge.

"I'm sorry, Mum. I'm sorry that I didn't tell you what was going on. I'm sorry I couldn't help you in any way. I knew that you needed Dad, and the fact that he wasn't always there for you makes me so angry. And to be honest, you didn't deserve him. You deserved a man who would've loved you forever," I say, looking up at the sky as tears begin to fall.

"I love you, Mum," I whisper, furiously wiping away the tears.

I stand up and look at the field, my vision still blurry from the tears.

"I'm sorry—" I say, choking up again, letting the tears fall down my cheeks.

My heart tightens as I look down at the ground below; my hands begin to shake. I close my eyes, preparing myself for the decision I've made to go ahead with.

Just as I'm about to let my body fall off the building, someone shouts, "Stop!" from behind me.

Biting my lip, I turn around to see who the person is.

"Don't do it, Grace," the boy pleads.

My eyes widen a little at the sight of *him* standing there.

"Luke?" I ask, trying to see through the tears.

Luke steps forward and holds out his hand towards me.

"Suicide doesn't take the pain away; it only passes it on to someone else," he says, his voice soft and gentle.

I look back at the field, blinking furiously.

"I don't deserve to be here, Luke," I say, bringing my hand up to wipe away the tears.

I look over my shoulder to see Luke, his hand still outstretched towards me.

"Yes, you do. You have so much to live for."

I scoff.

"Yeah. Mum is dead, my dad is cheating on her, and the whole population of the school hates me. Right, I have so much to live for," I say sarcastically, rolling my eyes.

"I don't hate you, Gracie," Luke says.

I send him a glare and point my index finger at him. "That's what you say now," I reply.

Luke shakes his head.

"Look, I don't want to see you like this," he says, a small smile beginning to stretch across his face. "Do you remember what our first conversation was about?" he asks.

The memory immediately pops into my mind.

"It looks like you're either trying to get yourself into trouble or trying to trick me," I mumble, my eyes meeting his blue ones.

He raises an eyebrow. "Trick you?"

"Yeah. Like, you offer me a hand, and when I go to take it, you pull away and run off laughing," I explain.

He chuckles, then holds out a hand and smiles at me. "I won't do that."

"Luke, leave me alone," I say.

His hand moves closer.

"I won't trick you, Grace. Just please don't do this," he says.

I look at his hand and then his face. His eyes stare into mine, waiting for me to make a choice. I know he is hoping it's the right one. A part of me wants to forget him and continue with my decision, but another part of me wants to step away from the edge and let Luke hold me.

Don't do it, Grace, my inner voice says. Suddenly, I feel myself grabbing Luke's hand, letting him pull me into a tight hug.

"Thank you, Grace."

No, Luke. Thank you.

CHAPTER NINE
Dance with Me

"Thank you for—you know."

"It's fine," Luke says with a smile. "I'm just happy that you listened to me."

I nod slowly, looking back at the view of the water crashing against the shore.

After he managed to get me off the school grounds, he took me to the nearby beach, just a ten-minute drive away. Now we are currently sitting on the sand, watching as the sun sets and waves continue to hit the shore.

"I have an idea," Luke says suddenly, making me look at him, confused but intrigued. He stands up, a small smile on his face, dusting himself off before holding out both of his hands. "Let's dance."

I immediately shake my head; the smallest smile spreads on my face. "No way."

He looks down at me, his smile growing. "Why not?" he asks. "It'll be fun."

I roll my eyes. "To watch me fall will be fun for you, but not for me," I say, narrowing my eyes at him.

He pulls out his phone, and a few seconds later, a song that I immediately recognise plays through the speakers.

He takes my hands and pulls me up, his smile widening into a grin.

I want you to show me how to get to know
Someone like you . . .

"Come on! Just ignore everyone and let yourself be free," Luke says.

I shake my head again as *Meant to Be* by Arc North continues to play in the background.

"Even if I do, you'll just end up laughing at me," I say.

Luke shakes his head.

"I won't—promise," Luke says, his words making my smile grow into a grin.

"Okay. Well, what do we do now?" I ask. I can't believe I've actually agreed to do this.

He lets go of my hands and moves back, kicking his feet to the rhythm, sending sand flying.

"Just move to the beat and let your body take over." He smiles as he twirls in the sand, stumbling a little before falling onto the sand.

I let out a laugh, nodding.

As the beat drops calmly, I smile and start to twirl in the sand just like how Luke has done, minus the falling part.

As he watches me, I notice him smiling again.

"There you go!" he says, his words making my smile grow.

As I walk towards him, I grab his hand.

"Dance with me," I say.

Luke nods, his blue eyes staring into mine. "Of course, Gracie."

*   *   *

As I enter my house, I notice that Dad is not home again. I close the door behind me, breathing out a sigh. I walk into the kitchen and grab a bottle of water from the fridge, not bothering to grab an apple like I usually do, since Luke had already bought me something to eat on the way home. I open the bottle and take a sip, walking up the stairs and into the bathroom.

I place the bottle of water on the edge of the sink and look at myself in the mirror, my smile appearing on my face once again.

"Wow. Would you look at that?" I mutter, flicking some of the sand out of my hair. I pick up a few strands of my purple hair and examine them.

I really need to brush my hair.

After I brush all of the knots out of my hair, something catches my eye, and I glance over to see that it is a pair of scissors.

Should I? I ask myself as I place the brush back down on the sink. I mean, would shorter hair even suit me? Tilting my head, I finally decide as I turn on the tap.

After wetting my hair and making sure that it is soaked, I grab the pair of scissors. "Good luck, Grace," I say to myself before cutting a huge chunk of my hair off.

*   *   *

Dear Diary,

> *Today I made the decision to kill myself. Obviously, since I am writing right now, it didn't go as planned. Do you want to know what happened? Shockingly, Luke practically stopped me, telling me whatever he could think of at that moment to make me not jump off the school's roof.*
>
> *I didn't even know what emotions were running through me at that time when I gave in to Luke's words and grabbed onto his hand. I was happy, but then again, I was angry—not with Luke, but with myself. I didn't go through with what I had planned, and this made me feel weak—a coward.*
>
> *But anyway, after we left school, Luke took me to the nearest beach, and we danced. We freaking danced! The last time I remember dancing was at my parents' wedding, and that was when I was truly happy. But even though I am in a bad state of mind right now, I felt just*

as happy as I did at my parents' wedding, which obviously means something, right?

I don't know why, but I just can't stop thinking about Luke. I may actually have a tiny crush on him, as much as I really don't want to—for his sake. But I like the feeling I get when I'm around him; it reminds me of the feeling I had when Nicole and I were still friends.

I don't want Luke to leave me like Nicole did because I get pretty attached to people if they start to give me the impression that they care. But since I have trust issues, I doubt everything, which makes it complicated because I can't admit to myself that I trust someone after what happened with Nicole, you know?

Anyway, I should be asleep now, but I can't fall asleep because of that damn Luke Peterson. Well, I guess I just have to try, right?

Grace Leigh Parkinson xxx

I close my diary and place it in the drawer beside my bed. As I lay my head down on my pillow, I cannot help but continue thinking about Luke.

Do I like Luke, or is it just an attraction?

Well, either way, I really do not care, because as long as I have him by my side, I am happy.

CHAPTER TEN
Once a Player, Always a Player

I stand in the shower, dreading the day that is coming faster by the minute. I mean, everyone thinks that I have actually done it—that I have jumped to my death. When they see me at school today, they will know I did not. The bullying is going to get worse, along with everything else I already endure at school. I can already imagine how today will play out.

Nicole is going to do the same thing she does every day—bully me and make me feel like crap. Just like a couple of weeks ago, Luke will show up right after Nicole kicks me to the ground. He will ask me if I am okay, take me to see the nurse, and then my day will end as badly as it always does.

Ugh, such a great life.

I close my eyes, letting the water splash down over my face. After a few more seconds, I turn off the shower and step out. I wrap a towel around my body, tucking in the end so it does not fall. I also wrap a towel around my hair so the water does not drip down my back.

As I walk out of the bathroom and into my room, I close the door behind me. Instantly, my eyes notice something on my bed. I furrow my eyebrows and look at the small box, a sticky note attached to it. Without giving it much thought, I immediately assume it's from my dad—maybe something to make me feel better.

But when I read what is written on the note, the initials "L. P." make me think differently:

I know this isn't great, but at least we can talk, right?
—L. P.

When I open the box, I am shocked to see a new phone. It is not one of those expensive ones, but it is sturdy enough to last me a while—if I decide to get something better, that is. As I look back at the note, I realise who the phone is from: Luke Peterson.

Wait—did he get me this so we could talk?

And how did he get into my house?

I take the phone out of the box and quickly switch it on. In less than a second, a message from someone named "Best Friend" appears on the screen:

I'm waiting for you outside.

Luke, why did you set your name to "Best Friend"?

Because you're my best friend now, duh. You're mine. Anyway, hurry up and get dressed if you don't want to be late.

I smile, placing the phone on my bed before walking to my wardrobe to pick out some clothes to wear for school.

I hope Luke does not end up leaving me as Nicole did, because, right now, I cannot lose anyone else.

*   *   *

"You cut your hair," Luke says as soon as I get into his car.

I glance over at him and give him a nod.

"You don't think it's too short, do you?" I ask.

He smiles before starting the car.

"I think it's perfect," he says.

His words make my own small smile grow. As he begins to drive in the direction of the school, the song on the radio catches my attention, and I turn up the volume.

"I love this song," I say.

My smile continues to grow as I listen to *Paris* by The Chainsmokers.

Luke nods when he stops at a red light.

"Yeah, it's okay," Luke says and looks at me.

I turn to him, my jaw dropping. As the song continues, I throw him a frown.

"You mean it's amazing," I say, raising my hands to prove my point.

He laughs, turning his head back towards the road.

"Like you."

"Huh?" I ask, playing dumb as I look at him.

He glances at me for a split second before waving me off quickly.

"Don't worry," he says.

I nod and look out the window.

Little does he know, I heard what he said, but I don't plan on telling him that. My stomach begins to tingle, and I can't tell if it's because I haven't eaten this morning or because of what Luke said. Either way, I know I'm definitely crushing on Luke.

*　　*　　*

"Are you okay?" Luke asks, standing beside me as he watches me take out my books from my locker.

I nod before slamming the locker shut.

"Yeah. Everything is perfect," I say, watching as he frowns at me.

"Is it because everyone is staring? 'Cause I can make them stop," he says.

I nod. "Yes, but even if you tried—"

"Take your eyes off my best friend, you bunch of gorillas!" he practically shouts.

My face goes a little red, but I try to hold in the laugh that wants to come out.

When he turns to me, I raise my eyebrow. "Gorillas?"

He shrugs. "I'm not much of the swearing type of guy," he says, earning a small nod from me.

"I can see that," I say as I start to walk down the hallway with him by my side.

When we stop outside my classroom, he places a hand on my shoulder.

"Don't let anyone start on you, okay? You're tough, Gracie," he assures me.

I nod as he gives me a quick smile before walking down the hallway to get to his class.

I walk into the classroom and quickly make my way to the back. I instantly notice Nicole shooting daggers at me, and I know she knows. But I ignore her as I take my seat.

When Mr. Jameson, our teacher, does not show up after five minutes, Nicole stands up and walks towards the table in front of me. She spins the chair to face me before sitting down.

"Do you need a reminder?" she spits, but I just watch her, not saying a word. "How many times do I have to tell you to stay away from—"

"He isn't your boyfriend, Nicole," I cut in, watching as she narrows her eyes at me.

"Neither is he yours," she snaps, obviously not liking the fact that I'm hanging out with her boyfriend.

I roll my eyes. "Just give me a break . . . please," I say, running a hand through my short hair.

Nicole shakes her head. "So, you think you're so cool now? You've finally got a friend? Wow, I won't be surprised if Luke tries to get into your pants anytime soon," she says, trying to mess with my mind.

I shake my head. "You don't know him like I do," I say, looking at the smirk forming on her face.

"Once a player, always a player," she says before standing up. "Remember that."

*   *   *

"So, Gracie, tell me about yourself," Luke says, making me smile before taking a bite of my sandwich.

"Well . . . my parents—"

"Gracie, I asked about you," he says, cutting me off before I can finish my sentence.

I stare at him, raising an eyebrow. "Why? I'm not interesting," I mutter, watching as he shakes his head, that cute smile still on his face.

Wait, what?

"First off, you are interesting. Secondly, to answer your question—because I want to know more about you. Is that such a crime?" Luke asks.

I shake my head, a smile forming on my lips.

"Okay. Well . . . I don't like cats," I say, watching his face instantly fall. "If you threw a cat in my face, I would either run or scream," I explain.

He raises an eyebrow at me. "What's wrong with cats?" he asks defensively.

I roll my eyes playfully. "They're scary."

"You mean cute," he says.

I shake my head, my face dead serious.

"No. They are honestly really scary, especially their eyes. I mean, they are cool, but at night, their eyes turn bright when light shines on them. It's just scary. And, to be honest, I wouldn't be surprised if, in fifty years, the world is no longer ruled by humans but by cats," I explain.

Luke laughs immediately. "I still can't believe you don't like cats. I pray for you, Gracie, I really do," he says with a faint smile.

I roll my eyes. "Well, I just did."

He, too, rolls his eyes before asking, "What else can I know about you?"

I shrug. "Uh . . . well, this is a little embarrassing, but when I was younger, I used to think that stars were cannonballs shot into the sky by circus men."

"Oh my God. Really?" Luke asks, laughing loudly.

"I'm dead serious," I tell him, staring down at the other half of my sandwich.

When he has calmed down, he looks at me with a small smile. "Tell me more," he says faintly.

"Uh . . . I like cheese," I say.

He rolls his hand, hinting for me to continue.

"I like . . . the colour yellow."

"What else do you like?" he asks, his face coming closer to mine, but I don't move away.

"You," I whisper, watching as his lips tilt into a grin.

"Likewise," he whispers back before pressing his lips gently onto mine.

CHAPTER ELEVEN
Would They Mind if I Throw Up in Here?

It's been a week since Luke and I kissed—well, actually, we had a really intense make-out session—and my mind has been going crazy about him. All the worries I have go away when I'm with him.

Right now, I am sitting on the couch, texting him about a party he wants me to go to tonight, but I keep telling him that I do not want to go.

Come on, it will be fun! Besides, you don't have to worry about Nicole because, according to everyone, she isn't going to be there.

I don't want to go, and you already know it's not because of Nicole. I just don't want to go anywhere near people who think I am a coward because I couldn't go through with my suicide.

Gracie, ignore them. They can go shove their opinions up their rear end because . . .

Because they are losers.

That's my girl. Now, get up and get dressed. I'll be at your place within an hour or so.

But I don't want to go!

Trust me, no one will start on you.

I'm not going.

Don't make me drag you into my car because I will do that, and I do not care if you're wearing your pajamas. Go get ready.

Nope.

Are you sure you don't want to go?

Yes.

Fine, but call me if you want me to pick you up if you change your mind.

That won't happen.

Sure it won't.

I place my phone on the couch and walk over to the kitchen to grab something to eat. I open the fridge, take out a chocolate bar, and walk back to the couch.

Before I sit down, though, I notice a pair of bright lights appear in front of the house. I walk towards the window and look outside to see my father's truck. I frown in confusion but go to the door anyway.

I open the door, but instead of seeing my father getting out of his truck alone, I notice that someone is with him. It appears to be a woman, and my heart sinks.

"Don't worry," I assure myself.

I let out a sigh and walk back into the house, leaving the door open. I sit on the couch and pretend to watch the television, even though the show is boring. Dad walks through the door and smiles at me.

"Hello, Grace," Dad greets.

I send him a wave while gluing my eyes to the screen.

He walks into the kitchen, opens a bottle of beer, and stands in front of the television, grabbing my attention.

"Yes?" I ask.

I notice the girl walks in. She places her handbag on the table and makes her way over to Dad, standing beside him.

"Grace, I would like you to meet Eve," Dad says.

I look at the girl, who seems to be smiling at me.

"Hello, Grace. Your father has told me so much about you," Eve says.

I nod. "I'm sure he has," I say before looking back at Dad.

"So, is she that girl from your work?" I ask.

Dad nods happily. I frown and narrow my eyes at him. As if he knew where this was going, he asks Eve to go to the next room so we can have a conversation—just him and me.

When Eve leaves, I look at him with a frown.

"Why is she here?" I ask.

His smile grows. "She is my girlfriend, Grace."

My heart clenches in pain.

I stand up in rage. "Your girlfriend? It hasn't even been a month, and you're already moving on from your wife? How dare you do this to her?" I growl.

Dad steps back in shock. "Grace, listen—"

"No, you listen! You think it's okay for you to cheat on Mum all this time and think that everything is still okay? You basically broke this family apart and made her think you were just working so hard for this family. Mum told me you're just working overtime, but little did she know that you were cheating on her! I knew, Dad!" I scream, tears forming in my eyes.

Dad's eyes widen, and before he can say anything, I raise my hand and slap him.

"You're a pig!" I scream before walking up the stairs and into my room. I pull out my phone from my pocket and dial Luke's number.

"Hey—"

"Pick me up now."

*　　　*　　　*

"You look amazing," Luke says as I enter his car.

I roll my eyes. "I'm just wearing jeans and a simple top, Luke," I say.

He sends me a glare. "What have we talked about? Stop bringing yourself down," he says.

I roll my eyes again. When he does not start the car, I turn to him and narrow my eyes.

"Why aren't we going?" I ask.

He frowns at me. "Why are you upset?" he asks.

I shake my head. "Honestly, I don't want to talk about it."

He nods and starts the car before driving off. I sink into my seat and let the breeze enter the car as I roll the window down a little.

*　　　*　　　*

"I'm scared," I say, sitting in the car as I look at the large house in front of us.

People are dancing around in the front yard, and from what I can see, some are even climbing out of the windows to do *whatever* on the roof. Red cups cover the lawn, and loud music from inside makes the floor vibrate. Even being thirty metres away from the house, I can feel the vibrations.

"Grace, you'll be fine," Luke assures me, placing his hand on mine.

I look over to him. "From what I can already see, I will not be fine," I say quietly.

He frowns. "Those people are a bunch of idiots. They will probably be too drunk to even recognise you," he says, a small smile forming on his lips as he tries to make me worry less.

But when I remember a certain person, I frown at Luke. "What about Nicole?"

Luke sighs. "I already told you she won't be here. Look, I'll be by your side the whole time, if that makes you feel better." He smiles, and I smile back at him.

"That actually makes me feel a lot better," I say.

He nods, the smile still on his lips, and he gets out of the car.

I take two seconds to breathe before stepping out.

He meets me by my side and sends me one last comforting smile before we walk towards the large house.

"You don't drink, do you?" Luke asks as we make our way to the kitchen. He grabs a bottle of vodka from the fridge before turning to me. I look at the shot glass in front of me and shrug.

"My dad did make me try some of his beer, but it was absolutely disgusting," I say.

He chuckles, grabs the shot glass, and takes a small sip before nodding. "This is only vodka. Try some if you want," he says, pushing the shot glass to me.

I look at the alcohol before picking up the glass and drinking it slowly. Almost instantly, I feel the urge to throw up.

Luke notices and grabs my hand, guiding me around the counter before standing over the sink.

"Would they mind if I throw up in here?" I mumble.

He shakes his head. "No, just go ahead," he says.

As I remember the taste of vodka, I feel everything in my stomach rise into my throat, and I lunge forward, holding the edge of the counter.

Luke rubs my back and moves my hair away from the sides of my face.

Once I finally stop, he grabs some paper towels and hands them to me. I thank him and wipe my mouth, throwing the paper in the bin.

Luke holds my shoulders and looks down at me with concern. "You probably shouldn't drink that again. Maybe water or Coke?" he suggests.

All of a sudden, the thoughts of Eve and my father appear in my mind, and I shake my head.

"No, let me try again," I say, and Luke furrows his eyebrows.

"Are you sure?"

"Yes," I say, walking over to the counter.

Luke pours me another shot. He pushes it to me, and I take a deep breath before drinking it again, but faster this time.

My throat burns at the taste, but I shake it away, trying to focus on something other than the taste.

"How do you feel?" Luke asks, narrowing his eyes at me in a concerned way.

As if to test me, the images of Eve and my father laughing on the couch appear in my mind again. I grit my teeth.

"More."

"What? Are—"

"I'll do it myself then," I say, snatching the bottle of vodka from his hand and pouring some more into the glass, filling it to the top.

"Stupid Dad," I mutter before drinking the alcohol fast, before my body can react.

CHAPTER TWELVE
I Will Never Leave

After the party started to calm down at three in the morning, Luke and I decided to head off. Right now, we are at a park, just talking, because I still do not want to go home.

"I want to fly," I suddenly say, taking Luke by surprise. I start to push myself on the swing, but he stops me.

"You're drunk, and you will probably throw up if you start to move your body—especially your stomach—so don't try to move for now," he says, grabbing my waist to stop me from swinging.

I let out a sigh and lean my back against him behind me.

"I feel like I'm going to lose everyone," I admit, looking down at my feet. "I mean, I've already lost my mum. Who knows who I will lose next?"

"You're not going to lose anyone, Gracie. I'm here," Luke says. He grabs onto the chains and swings me lightly.

"You say that now, but later on, you will leave," I say, bending my neck back to look at him.

He lets out a chuckle and walks around to stand in front of me. He sits down on the grass and pats the seat next to him.

I get off the swing and slowly make my way next to him, trying not to fall over anything since I am practically the clumsiest person alive.

"I will never leave," he says as soon as I sit down next to him.

My heart races when he places his hand on my thigh, giving me a reassuring smile.

"O-okay." I breathe out, and Luke nods.

When we sit in silence for about two minutes, just staring at the dark sky, he breaks the silence.

"So why did you change your mind?" he asks, his hand not moving from my thigh.

The memory of my father introducing me to Eve appears in my head, and I let out a sigh.

"Today just hasn't been my day, that's all," I lie.

He frowns at me. "You can tell me," he says.

I nod. "I know, it's just . . . hard to say."

He nods slowly. "You don't have to tell me if you don't want to."

I shrug. "But I want to. I mean, this is what friends do, right? Talk about things . . ." I trail off, and he nods.

"Yeah, I guess," he says.

I let out a sigh and run my hand through my hair.

"Okay, well, you know how my mum . . . ," I mumble, not really wanting to say the next word. "And you know how my dad has been cheating on her this whole time?" I ask.

Luke nods again.

"Well, he brought that girl home today and said that they are dating. I don't know what ran through me at the time, but all I could think about was my mum and what she would do if she were still here. I mean, it hasn't even been a month yet, and he thinks he has the right to bring in some new girl and just assume we are going to play like a happy family? Ever since I found out that my dad was cheating on my mum, we have never been happy. Nothing was perfect, and my mum knew that—she just didn't want to say it because she was still clinging to the hope of the perfect life she always dreamt of having. My dad ruined that for my mum, and now I won't get to see her ever again," I say slowly.

Luke frowns, grabbing my hand, but before he can say the whole "I'm sorry" thing, I speak again.

"I dreamed about my mum. She talked to me, but only for a few minutes before drifting off, and that's when I woke up. It's like she's watching me—then she appears in my dreams, where no one else can disturb us, and we talk about things," I say with a smile.

Luke wears his own smile and turns to me. "What did you two talk about?" he asks.

I shrug. "Life, basically," I say, and he nods.

"Well, you're lucky."

"Somewhat," I say.

After a few minutes of silence, I lean my head on his shoulder, closing my eyes.

"I should get you home," Luke says, and I raise my hand to cup his cheek.

"Not yet."

"Okay, Gracie."

*   *   *

"Maybe she will accept me later on if I start being friendly to her," Eve says from outside my room.

I roll my eyes and turn over in my bed for the fifth time. Dad lets out a sigh, but he does not say anything.

The fact that Dad still does not see what is wrong with him bringing his girlfriend home confuses me. How can he not even care about my feelings? He knows how close I was to Mum, but he still ignores my feelings and acts like Eve is going to make everything better.

Want to know what I think? I think he never loved Mum and only thought about his feelings, whatever they are. I think he introduced me to Eve because he believes it will make everything okay between us. I think he is trying to replace Mum with Eve because Mum was nothing to him.

I know I have questioned Dad's love for Mum before, but now I am actually eager to know what his true intentions were when he met her. Did he mean to go this far into their relationship? Was I someone who was never meant to be born? Maybe that was why he does not talk to me much. Maybe that was why he never actually cared about me like Mum did. Maybe that was why I could only depend on her to make me feel loved—because Dad could not do it.

Ugh, all of this confuses the hell out of me.

I take out my phone and earphones. When I put the earphones in my ears, the song *We Don't Talk Anymore* by Charlie Puth begins to play, and I let out a sigh, finally feeling a little calmer.

A few minutes later, I finally feel myself falling asleep with a small tear running down my cheek as the last memory of Mum appears in my head.

"Hey, sweetheart." Mum smiles, walking into my room. I look up at her and stand, pulling her into a hug.

"Hey, Mum," I say.

She pulls away from me and sits on my bed next to me.

"So, that boy you talked about . . ." She grins, and I let out a small laugh.

"Yeah. I think I actually have a thing for him." I smile.

Her eyes widen in surprise. "Really?" She places her hand on her heart and blinks away the tears forming in her eyes.

"You're finally growing up," she says, and I chuckle.

"I guess so," I say.

She grabs my hand, sending me a smile. "Be careful about the man you choose to be with, okay? It might seem right at first, but make sure you're ready," she says, and I frown at her.

"Were you careful? Did you actually love Dad?" I ask, and she nods, her eyes slipping shut.

"Yes, I did, but even though it seemed like a good idea to take the next step, I wasn't ready. I hardly knew your father, but I promised myself that I wouldn't give up just yet because he could be something special," she explains.

I nod slowly. "Okay. I'll make sure I'm ready," I say.

Mum nods. "Oh, and don't fall into things too quickly," she adds, and I nod.

"I promise," I say.

Mum smiles before getting up and giving me one last hug. "See you soon, Gracie."

I wave at her. "See you soon, Mum."

CHAPTER THIRTEEN
That Was the Foot-Eating Monster, Luke

The funeral is in a few days, and I cannot help but wonder about everything. I know I will not be able to keep it together, but hopefully, I can keep my crying and sobbing to a minimum and, hopefully, speak in normal sentences when I go to read my speech.

I have been preparing my speech ever since the morning Dad told me about Mum's upcoming funeral. I have not done much, but from what I have written down, it should be enough.

I start to edit my speech, crossing out unnecessary words and fixing mistakes. After five minutes of doing that, I set my book aside, get out of bed, and glance at the clock. I let out a sigh as I realise that it is finally noon, and decide to head downstairs.

I walk into the kitchen and see Eve sitting with Dad at the table, happily eating their food.

"Oh, good morning, Grace!" Eve greets cheerfully.

I just send her a wave and look into the fridge. I grab my salad, which I was supposed to eat last night, and pick up a fork, ready to walk back to my room. But Dad grabs my hand, stopping me.

"Grace, why don't you eat with us like a normal family?" Dad asks.

I hold back the thoughts that are screaming out.

"I'm fine, thanks," I reply, just wanting to go back to my room. But his hold on my wrist stays tight.

"Why?" he asks.

Before I can say anything, Eve places a hand on his free hand, which is resting on the table.

"Honey, why don't you let her go? She probably just needs a little time to herself," Eve says.

Dad looks at me once more before letting go of my hand.

"Fine, go. Do whatever you want," he says, anger clear in his tone.

I don't stay to say anything. Instead, I begin to walk out of the kitchen and up the stairs as fast as I can, not wanting to be anywhere near them.

I sit on my bed, placing my salad in front of me when my phone buzzes. I let out a sigh, grab my phone, and shove some capsicum in my mouth, unlocking my phone at the same time. It's my best friend.

> *You busy?*
>
> > *No, why?*
>
> *Okay, good. I want to take you somewhere on this beautiful Saturday afternoon.*
>
> > *Okay, I'll just need to get ready. Pick me up in ten?*
>
> *I'll be waiting.*

I smile to myself as I put the lid back on my salad and place it on my table. I walk over to my cupboard and decide to wear a pair of white skinny jeans and a blue-and-white striped singlet. I strip out of my pajamas and begin to get into the clothes, trying not to fall from excitement and happiness.

Five minutes later, my hair is brushed and tied into a small braid, and my piercings are in. As I am about to leave my bedroom, though, I decide to take out my lip piercing and leave just my nose piercing in. I need a change.

I smile to myself and walk out of my bedroom, skipping happily down the stairs.

I don't bother to say goodbye to Eve and my dad; I walk straight out the door. Since they are too busy talking to each other, they don't notice me slip out, but I don't care—at least I am out of that damn house.

"You look amazing, like always," Luke says.

I roll my eyes. "I've said this before, but it's just jeans and a top," I say as he opens the car door. I get in and look up at him.

"And I've said this before, but stop bringing yourself down," he throws back.

I shake my head, chuckling.

Once he gets in the car, I turn to him. "So, where are we going?"

"It is a surprise," he says with a grin.

I let out a sigh of annoyance. One thing you should know about me is that I hate surprises, no matter how good they seem in the end.

*   *   *

"No way," I mutter, looking at the large sign hanging above the centre.

"Yes way," Luke chuckles.

I squeeze my hands together in excitement, trying not to scream—but it's too late.

"I can't even speak!" I scream, holding my hands over my mouth.

He wraps an arm around my waist and pulls me closer to his side.

"Come on, you don't want to be waiting forever," he says.

I nod eagerly, walking with him into the Sea World Centre.

This is why I hate surprises—I always come unprepared, and I hate it. You see, I would have brought a camera or something, but no, Luke just had to keep everything a surprise.

"Oh my god, look at that!" I squeal in excitement, tugging at his hand.

He lets out a laugh and follows behind me as I run towards the arched walkway that has sharks and other fish in it.

Yes, a girl can love sharks. It is not a crime.

"Hello, big guy," I say, placing my hand on the glass as I watch the large shark come towards me. It bumps the glass and swims away in anger, probably trying to find its escape.

"Gracie," Luke calls, and I turn to face him to see him holding a camera.

"No pictures!" I immediately say, covering my face.

He takes my hands away with a chuckle.

"C'mon, just smile," Luke says.

I shake my head.

"Please? I'll buy you ice cream later," he adds.

At that, I smile, raising my hand.

"Just one," I say as I smile at his camera.

The camera beeps, and I let out a sigh before turning back to the sharks and fish.

"I'm in love," I say, smiling at the fish.

As we walk down the walkway, looking up at the fish swimming overhead, I notice Luke smiling—and my heart flutters.

This is so not a crush.

*   *   *

"Ugh, I wish I could stay there longer," I mumble, letting my feet dangle above the water.

"There is always a second time for things," Luke says.

I nod. "Yeah, I will bring my camera next time," I say.

He laughs. "You didn't bring your phone?"

"I did, but I would rather take pictures on my camera. It's just better," I say.

He nods and scoops another ice cream and eats it, watching the people walk past us on the dock.

I look in the water, eating my ice cream, and all of a sudden, a weird thing comes up to the surface, trying to grab my foot. I let out a scream and immediately jump back.

"What the hell?" Luke laughs.

I point in the water, my hands trembling. "There w-was a . . . foot-eating monster in the water!" I say in horror, but this just makes him laugh some more.

"Foot-eating monster? Please, Gracie, there is nothing—" he gets cut off by his own scream as he jumps back in fright.

"What the hell was that? It tried to bite my foot!" he says, looking at me in horror.

I grin at him and pat his thigh. "That was the foot-eating monster, Luke."

*   *   *

I walk back into the house after saying my goodbyes to Luke. Eve is sitting on the couch by herself, looking at the television.

"Wow, who would pay fifty dollars for an aging cream?" Eve chuckles to herself, and I let out a sigh.

"My mum," I mumble to myself as I walk up the stairs and towards my room.

The sound of the shower running probably explains why Dad isn't around and Eve is alone in the living room.

I close the door behind me and walk over to my bed. I notice that my phone is flashing, so I pick it up and see that Luke has sent me a message:

Don't ever doubt yourself because you are beautiful :)

As I read that, another message pops up. It is the photo he took of me today, and the little thing he wrote with it made me smile.

My beautiful best friend.

He basically claims me by adding "my" in his message— but let me get one thing straight: I am not complaining.

CHAPTER FOURTEEN
I Have to Keep It Together

I let out a shaky breath as I wipe my hands on my dress, blinking away the tears. I look at my reflection in the mirror and grip the bottom of my black dress.

The dress is sleeveless, a sheer material all the way down to my knees, where it stops. There is a thin layer under the dress, which makes it not see-through. Since the dress is sleeveless, I am worried that people will see my scars and think I am weak—but I guess that is what I am, right?

I am just a weak little girl who runs away from her problems because she is too much of a coward to face them like a real human being.

Although these scars make me—well, make me—that does not stop my heart from racing at the thought of people noticing them. I do not want anyone to see them because they remind me of the past—of the times that I was weak and needed to feel alive.

I guess that's why I do it. I need that sudden pain to feel alive, because without it, I would probably be that person who feels nothing at all.

Shaking my head, I look back at myself in the mirror, trying to focus on something other than my arms. My hair is brushed neatly into a bun, and some of the loose strands stay around the sides of my face, making me look somewhat nice.

My phone buzzes, and I let out a sigh. I walk over to it in my black flats and pick it up, my heart suddenly stopping when Nicole's name appears on the screen.

I hesitate to read the message, but after mustering the small amount of courage I have, I click on the notification.

> *Hey . . . It's your mum's funeral today, and I just wanted to say that I will be there since my mum basically forced me. Don't get too distracted by me, as I'll only be there to pay my respects to your mum.*

I frown in confusion at Nicole's message. Why would she say that I will be distracted by her? I will be distracted by everything in that freaking room! Has she lost her mum? Of course not—so she obviously does not know what it feels like.

Also, how did she get this number?

I do not bother replying to her message, as I am too focused on the day ahead. I grab my speech and fold it in my hand tightly as I walk out of my room and down the stairs.

I notice Dad standing in the living room, glancing between the television and his girlfriend. I let out a sigh and grab onto my dress, trying to hide the scars from him.

"Hey," I mumble.

He looks at me with a small smile.

"I'm glad you took my advice when I said for you not to wear a cardigan," Dad says.

I just nod in reply.

As we walk out the door, Eve says her goodbyes.

I just wave.

But Dad walks back into the house and kisses her before meeting me back outside.

"Okay, let's go," he says.

*   *   *

I sit next to Dad as Mum's sister, Aunty Carol, comes up to the podium to say her speech. Only Aunty Carol and I are speaking today because my father said—and I quote—"I could not bring myself to it." I wanted to believe that he meant that, but the only reason he said it was because he never loved Mum. After so many years, it was all a lie.

Realising that the funeral will be quicker than I expected, I let out a sigh of relief. Hopefully, I will be out of here fast because, just by looking at Mum in the coffin, my heart is torn apart in pain.

"From the day I saw my baby sister in the arms of my mother, I knew that the journey planned for us ahead would be difficult. My sister, being the youngest, was the peacemaker in our family when my brother and I would argue. I guess my sister always seemed to find the good in anything, and that's why everyone loved her. When she told me that she had cancer, I knew that she wouldn't be able to fix this. This time, she knew that she couldn't solve this problem, and that is what broke us all."

Aunty Carol wipes a tear away from her eye and lets out a shaky breath.

"My sister would be laughing right now if she heard me say this, but when we were younger, she always asked me if I could smile for her. To this day, I still don't know why she always wanted me to pose for her, but I think I sort of have an understanding of why she wanted me to do that.

You see, my sister loved to see everyone happy, and every time she saw everyone in a good mood, she would pose to make everyone laugh. I guess that's why she asked me to smile—because she wanted me to cheer her up, to make her feel happy like everyone else. Rose Elizabeth Parkinson," Aunty Carol says.

Aunty Carol glances at the coffin. "Because we are all here for you today, I will do this once more for you, but this time, I want everyone to join in—for my sister," she says.

Everyone stands, even I.

She smiles and wipes another tear from her eye.

"Please smile for my baby sister," she asks weakly into the microphone.

Everyone does as told, pulling weak poses.

"Tell Christian I said hello, Rose. Don't have too much fun without me because one day, I will join you again. I love you so much, Rosie." She finishes.

I choke out a sob and sit back down as she begins to walk off the small stage.

Dad pats my thigh, and I let out a sigh and stand. My legs wobble as I make my way up to the podium, my hands suddenly sweaty. I place my small piece of paper on the glass surface of the podium and glance over at Mum, lying in the coffin.

It still does not feel real.

It still does not feel like she is gone.

"H-hello, everyone. As some of you may know, I had the great pleasure of being the daughter of the amazing Rose Elizabeth Parkinson—my mum. Some of you may even know the great bond we shared when my mum . . . when she was still here." I bite my lip, trying not to cry.

I have to keep it together.

"When I was younger, I was obsessed with taking photos of my mum—not because of her stunning looks, but because of her smile. Her smile was one of the many things I loved about her, and I'm pretty sure everyone can agree with me when I say that." I wipe away a tear and lick my dry lips, closing my eyes for a second to try to relax my nerves.

As I am about to continue, the doors open.

Nicole walks in, taking a seat at the back. She nods at me.

I clench my shaking hands, letting out another shaky breath.

"When my mum smiled, she made everyone feel amazing, and that's what she did to me. She made me feel like I was amazing in every way, and now her smile is etched in my mind—and I don't know if that is a good thing or a bad thing. All I know is that she loved me for who I was—not the person I was trying to be, which was her," I say.

The crowd says a soft "awww," making a slight smile fall on my lips.

"Mum, I never really told you this much, but you are my inspiration, and even though you're not . . . here . . . that won't stop me from reaching my goals. I love you, Mum, and I miss you already," I say, looking over at the coffin.

My heart clenches in pain, but I try to ignore it as I let the last tear fall down my cheek.

"The last words my mum said to me are the words that make me at least try to push myself to get out of bed in the morning. She said—I quote—'Don't ever give up, because there's always someone out there you inspire.' " I let out a painful whimper, looking at the coffin one last time.

"I will never forget you, Mum," I whisper, clutching my arm as I let the tear fall to the ground.

CHAPTER FIFTEEN
I'm Not Hungry

It has been one month since Mum's funeral, and I have never felt so alone. Even though Luke still takes me places, talks with me about anything, kisses me at random, and goes to a few parties now and then, his company does not come close to Mum's.

I miss Mum. I miss everything about her. I miss her smile, her laugh, that twinkle in her eyes when she sees me—I miss everything about her.

"Hey, you're zoning out again," Luke chuckles.

I smile at him. "Sorry," I say.

He nods. "It's okay. So, what are we watching tonight?" he asks.

I cuddle up next to him and smile when I see the movie *Bad Neighbors* appear on the screen.

He nods in agreement.

"I love this movie," he says.

I let out a laugh. "Who doesn't?"

He rolls his eyes at me and grabs my hand, rubbing small circles on my palm.

The movie begins, and we both watch in silence as the awkward sex scene comes on.

"Oh my God, can we skip it?" I ask, looking up at Luke.

He smiles at me, leaning closer to me. "I can distract you, if you like."

I smile back at him. "Yes, please," I mumble.

His lips touch mine, sending butterflies into my stomach and making my heart flutter.

Okay, I should explain. Over the past month, Luke has been sneaking into my room on Saturday nights, and we just watch movies. It is like a movie night for us, but he just keeps kissing me, which basically changes the whole movie night thing to *movie and kissing*—but mostly kissing—night.

To say that I have developed stronger feelings for Luke is a massive understatement.

I think I love him.

But then again, what is love? How do I even know what love is when Dad never loved Mum? Does he love Eve, or is he doing the same thing he did with Mum—cheating on her with another woman?

See, my life is very confusing. Since I don't know what love feels like, let me just put it this way—Luke makes me feel like I'm on top of the world.

Every time he looks at me, my brain just wants to freeze the moment and keep it forever locked in my head so I'll never forget it. Every time he laughs, I just want to record it and play it over and over again so I will never get tired of it. Every time his lips touch mine, I feel like he takes a small piece of my pain and turns it into happiness.

I feel like he is changing me, but for the better, helping me become this person I never thought I had inside of me. Even though I do not know who that person is yet, I feel like one day I will truly know, and I will never want to go back to the person I am now.

"Gracie . . ." Luke says, looking me dead in the eyes.

I stare at his blue eyes, trying not to smile from happiness.

"Yes, Luke?" I ask, my smile coming out.

He rests his head on mine. "It was only a month and a bit ago that I met you, and to be honest, you make me so happy," he says.

I close my eyes, breathing calmly. "Likewise," I say.

He chuckles, running a finger along my jaw.

I open my eyes and touch his nose, making him move away with another chuckle.

"I want you to be my girlfriend, Gracie," he says.

My face drops. The happy smile I wore on my lips a second ago turns to a straight face.

"Luke—"

"I mean, you don't have to say yes because, like I said, it was only a month ago, and I don't want to rush things because I really like you, and—"

"Luke."

I rest my finger on his lips to shut him up. Once he has stopped his ranting, I move my finger away.

He frowns. "What?"

"I really like you too, and that is the reason why I want to be your girlfriend," I say with a smile.

His face slowly lights up when my words hit him. "Oh my—"

Before he can finish his sentence, someone knocks on the door, taking us by surprise as we immediately separate from each other and end up falling on the floor with a loud thud.

"It's only me," Eve says.

I let out a sigh of relief.

"I just want to say that dinner is downstairs if you want it," she explains.

"No tha—"

"You're eating," Luke whispers, his hand resting on my mouth.

I roll my eyes and pull his hand away from my face.

"I'll be down soon," I say to Eve, pausing until the sound of her footsteps fades away. Then, I pounce on Luke.

"I'm not hungry," I growl in anger.

He laughs, resting both his hands on my cheeks. "You are."

"No I am n—" Just as I am about to finish my sentence, my stomach growls, making Luke smirk.

"Yes, you are. Now, I'll text you later, my beautiful girlfriend." He grins as he picks me up by the waist and sits me on my bed. He kisses me once on the lips before climbing out of my window.

"Bye, Luke," I whisper.

He throws me one last smile before disappearing out of my sight.

I let out a sigh and walk out of my room, trying my hardest not to squeal with excitement and happiness.

I am Luke's girlfriend.

Luke is my boyfriend.

God, I cannot wait to tell Mum—

I stop in my tracks at the last stair, biting my lip in pain as I blink away the tears. I pinch my arm—something I do to distract myself—and then walk into the kitchen to grab my dinner.

As I make my way to my room, I cannot help but let my mind wander to Mum again. The conversation we had in my dream appears in my mind, and I let out a sigh.

"Be careful about the man you choose to be with, okay? It might seem right at first, but make sure you're ready."

I know Luke asked me straight away, which took me by surprise, but did I make the right decision? Yes, Luke makes me happy, but am I ready to put my heart in his hands? Can I trust him not to hurt me?

He does act differently around me, yes, but does that mean he is a completely different person from the rumours that go around about him? Will his playboy ways come into this relationship?

No, he won't hurt me.

"Once a player, always a player."

Oh, look—now Nicole is getting into my head. I mean, she could be looking out for me, but then again, she could be jealous. Oh, I have no idea what that girl feels. One minute she hates me, and the next minute, she is all nice and civil with me.

I let out a sigh and begin picking at my food.

I hope I made the right decision, Mum.

CHAPTER SIXTEEN
I Warned You

"Oh, how I love school," Luke says happily as he wraps an arm around my shoulders.

I shake my head. "You hate school," I say.

He rolls his eyes. "And the moment has died," he says.

I chuckle, throwing his arm off me as I begin to grab my books out of my locker. "We didn't even have a moment," I say.

He leans against the locker beside mine, watching me with a grin. When I slam my locker shut, he holds out his hand.

"I'll take you to class," he says.

I smile, grabbing his hand as we walk down the hallway.

After saying my goodbyes to my boyfriend, I walk into the classroom to see someone in my seat. This person just happens to be Nicole.

"Great," I mutter, walking down the narrow aisle to my seat. When I reach my desk, I let out a sigh.

"Please get out of my seat," I say, looking into Nicole's brown eyes. She stands up and moves to the table in front of me, taking a seat.

"Since you said please," she mutters.

I walk to my seat and sit down, frowning at her.

"What do you want?" I ask, frustrated that I have to deal with her again.

She lets out a sigh and faces me completely, looking me dead in the eyes. "I'm sorry," she says.

I furrow my eyebrows. "What—"

"I said I'm sorry. I'm sorry for treating you like a bitch because you didn't even deserve it. You were getting bullied the time we were friends, and when I pushed you away, your life just became worse," she explains.

I run a hand through my hair. "No need to remind me."

"I am really sorry, though," Nicole repeats.

I nod slowly. "Okay."

"Are we cool now?" she asks.

I narrow my eyes at her.

"What makes you feel that I'm going to say yes? I've been through so many years of bullying from you and everyone else, and now you want to say sorry? I'm finally happy, and I don't want to go back to the same place I was just a few weeks ago. So, if you don't mind, can you just leave me alone? Thank you," I say.

Before Nicole can say anything, the teacher walks in, and I focus my attention on the teacher, ignoring Nicole's pleading stares.

*　　*　　*

School is finally done, and the bell dismisses us. Students begin to run out the door. I, on the other hand, take my time, walking out of the classroom at my own pace, not bothering to run out of the building.

Ever since Mum died, I have not been looking forward to going home. It's just not that happy place anymore. Dad has moved on faster than I expected and already let his new girlfriend move in to take Mum's place and live the life Mum was supposed to have.

I have nothing against Eve; it's just that Dad only seems to care about himself. Eve seems nice, and I am willing to get to know her, but she will never take Mum's place. I only have one mum, and even though she is gone, that does not mean the spot is open for anyone else. Mum is my one and only mother, and no one is going to change that.

"Hey, beautiful," someone says before pressing a kiss to my cheek.

I smile and bring Luke into a hug.

"Hey, Luke," I say.

Luke chuckles and wraps his arms around my waist, pulling me close to him.

I rest my ear on his chest, listening to his steady heartbeat.

How is he always so calm?

He lets go of me after five minutes of us standing in the middle of the hallway. He grabs my hand, leading me out.

Just as we are about to part ways, I hold onto his hand, making him spin in confusion.

"Yes, Gracie?" He grins.

"Do you think I can stay at your place tonight? I really don't feel like going home," I say.

Luke nods. "You didn't even have to ask, Gracie," he says.

I let out a laugh as we make our way to his car.

"Oh, so I can just jump in your car like a normal person and expect you to drive home without any questions?" I ask.

"Of course," he says.

I smile and get into his car, leaning into the comfortable seat.

I think I have finally found my happiness, and that is with Luke. I just hope he does not cheat on me like players do to their girlfriends, because if I lost him too, I wouldn't know what to do.

"Please don't give up on me, Luke," I whisper before he gets into the driver's seat.

He sends me a wink, and I feel my cheeks flush.

Yep, I can't lose him.

*   *   *

"Oh Grace, it's been a long time since I have seen you," Luke's mother, Bree, says.

I send her a warm smile, my heart sinking a little. I am still not used to Mum being gone, and since I will probably be seeing Bree a lot now, it makes me feel alone because I have no mother.

Breathe, Grace. You don't want to be crying in front of Luke's mother now, would you?

"Yes, it has been a while," I say.

All of a sudden, Bree pulls me into a hug, taking me by surprise. She wraps her arms around my small waist.

Luke clears his throat, and she jumps back, sending me an apologetic look. "Sorry, I got carried away," she smiles.

I chuckle, nodding. "It's okay," I say.

Luke grabs my hand, pulling me to him.

Bree turns to look at the two of us, and a small grin appears on her lips. "Am I missing something?" she asks, raising an eyebrow.

I turn to Luke with a small smile.

He pecks my forehead and stands behind me, wrapping his arms around my waist. "We are together."

Bree's eyes widen. "Oh my gosh—"

"We are going now before you start screaming the house down," he says, earning a chuckle from me.

But Bree grabs his arm, making him stop.

At that, Luke turns to me and nods at the stairs.

"I'll be up in a sec, okay?" he says.

I nod, making my way up.

As I reach the last stair, I can't help but hear Bree say a few words that make me start to worry inside.

"Don't hurt her, Luke. She is fragile, and I know how you work, young man. Please don't break this girl, okay?" she says, and Luke lets out a chuckle.

The chuckle sounds forceful, making my heart sink even more.

"I . . . won't," he says.

*   *   *

I throw a piece of popcorn at Luke's nose while he is on his phone, and he lets out a groan.

"That's the third time you've hit me on the nose. One more time and—"

I cut him off by throwing another piece at his nose again.

"Gracie—"

"Yes, Luke?" I ask innocently.

He places his phone beside him and pounces on me, holding my hands above my head.

"I warned you," he says.

"What are you going to do, Luke?" I ask, grinning, testing my boyfriend.

He smirks. His hand releases mine as he brings it to my thigh, running his fingers up towards my stomach.

I hold my breath and look into his eyes as he stares into mine.

All of a sudden, his fingers begin to tickle my side.

I let out a squeal and move under him, trying to get away from his touch. "L-Luke!" I squeal.

He grins, sending my heart racing. He lets go of me and moves off the bed towards the door.

"I'm going to go see when dinner is ready. Stay here," he says before slipping out the door and down the stairs.

I roll my eyes and cross my legs as I look around his room silently.

His phone buzzes, and my mind instantly urges me to check who it is, while my heart tells me to leave it alone. Sadly, my curiosity wins, and I reach over. I grab his phone and see a message from someone named Daniel:

So, how is the dare going so far?

CHAPTER SEVENTEEN
I Can't Lose Him

My heart sinks as I read the message over and over again. So many emotions run through my head as I stare at the word "dare" on the screen.

What has Luke got himself into? What kind of dare is Daniel talking about? Does it have anything to do with me?

At the sound of footsteps coming up the stairs, I throw the phone back to where it was and try to calm my nerves so I do not look suspicious.

"Dinner is going to be ready in a few minutes. So, what do you want to do?" Luke asks.

He sits on the edge of the bed, and I shrug, masking my emotions.

I mean, that's what I'm good at.

"Up to you," I reply, getting off the bed and standing on my feet with shaky legs.

He stands up after grabbing his phone, then takes my hand, leading me out of the room.

"Let's go watch some television," he says.

I nod.

Luke wouldn't hurt me, right?

He flashes me a small smile before heading down the stairs, with me closely behind him.

As I watch his back, I let out a small sigh.

Please don't hurt me, Luke.

* * *

"Leave the door open at all times, okay?" Bree narrows her eyes at her son.

Luke rolls his eyes but nods.

I lie down on the air bed, watching as Bree switches off the light.

"Goodnight, you two," she smiles.

I send her a wave while Luke nods.

When she is out of sight, Luke turns to me and pats the space on his bed.

I shake my head. "I'm comfortable here," I say with a small smile.

"Come on, cuddle with me," he says.

I let out a sigh before getting up and walking over to him.

He lies down and holds the blankets up so I can get in.

I lie down next to him and face him, my nose so close to his. "Luke?"

"Yes?"

"Can you promise me something?" I ask.

He nods with a small smile on his face. "Sure."

I look down at my hands. "Don't ever hurt me," I mumble.

He grabs my chin so I have to look at him. "Where is this coming from?" he asks gently.

I shrug. "I don't know. I just really like you—hell, I may even love you, so I'm just saying—"

He cuts me off by pressing his lips to mine, his hand resting on my face. "Gracie, I will never hurt you."

I nod with a small smile on my lips.

He wraps an arm around my side and pulls me closer to him.

"Now, get some sleep. I have a feeling that tomorrow is going to be a big day," he says.

I nod. *So do I, Luke.*

*   *   *

"Hey, Gracie, can I talk to you for a second?" Luke asks, standing at my door.

I nod and skip down the stairs towards him. As I wrap my arms around his neck, he grabs my arms, stopping me. "Please . . . it will only make it harder," he says.

I frown and don't say anything. Dropping my hands, I step out the door, closing it behind me so Eve won't hear our conversation.

"What's up?" I ask, trying to hide my emotions. I bite my lip nervously, and Luke lets out a sigh.

"I can't do this anymore. I . . . I feel like this is going to lead to something that we both can't handle. I do like you, but . . . I just don't want to hurt you in the long run," he explains, and my heart clenches at his words.

Is he breaking up with me?

"Wh-why?" I stutter, trying to blink away the tears.

I can't lose him.

I can't let go of him this easily.

"Because, like I said, I don't want to hurt you." Luke frowns, looking away from me.

I grab his hands and hold them in mine. "Then don't hurt me at all," I say, looking into his eyes.

He turns to me and places a short but gentle kiss on my lips before letting go of my hands and stepping away.

"Please understand," he says, and the first tear falls—my heart breaking more and more as another second passes.

"I don't want to," I mumble as I watch Luke's retreating figure. I fall to the ground and try to control my sobs, but it's useless.

"I don't want to."

"Gracie, wake up," someone says in my ear.

I let out a whimper and grip my hair.

"I don't want to," I say, and suddenly I woke up, my eyes widening. I look to my side to see Luke smiling at me.

It was just a dream.

Oh my God.

I rub my eyes and let out a yawn, stretching my legs. I lie back down to look at him, my eyes welling up.

He notices and pulls me into a hug. "Hey, what's wrong?" he asks.

I shake my head, holding onto him. "I'm just glad it was just a dream," I mumble.

He pulls away from me and presses his lips to mine gently.

"Do you want to go back to your place to change? I want to take you somewhere today, and I don't want you walking around in the same clothes as yesterday." Luke chuckles.

I nod, getting out of bed. "Okay."

*   *   *

I enter my house with Luke following behind me. I look around the living room to see Eve sleeping on the couch.

That's strange.

"Is that her?" Luke whispers.

I nod.

He slowly follows me as I begin to walk up the stairs. Dad is snoring as I pass his room, and I let out a sigh.

"He's asleep," I say.

"Good, because if he was awake, I would've put him to sleep," he says.

I sigh again sadly.

"Violence can't solve the problems inside my heart," I say as I enter my room. I grab a few clothes and hold them in my arms.

Luke sits on my bed.

"I'll take a quick shower. Just stay here," I say.

He nods as I walk into my bathroom. I close the door behind me and sigh, running a hand through my hair. I place the clothes on the bench and start the shower, feeling a little relaxed.

I strip off my clothes and step under the running water. After washing my hair and body, I wrap a towel around myself.

Suddenly, a familiar voice is in my room.

Oh no.

I quickly put on my clothes, trying not to slip. I tie my hair in a bun before stepping out of the bathroom to see Dad staring into Luke's eyes.

"Is this the boy?" Dad asks, not bothering to look at me.

I let out a sigh, and before I can say anything, Luke lunges towards my father, tackling him. He throws a punch, and I scream, running out of my room to get the only person who can help me—Eve.

I run down the stairs and start shaking Eve, trying to wake her. She lets out a groan and opens her eyes. When she sees me, her eyebrows narrow, and I grab her hand, pulling her off the couch.

"Luke and Dad!" I say, panic in my voice.

Eve instantly runs up the stairs and into my room. Our eyes widen when Dad throws a punch into Luke's face, blood already dripping from his nose. Eve and I rush to pull them apart.

I hold Luke in my arms, staring down into his eyes.

"Are you okay?" I ask softly.

He coughs, blood spilling from his mouth, and my heart clenches in pain. He snaps his gaze to Dad, sending him a hard glare.

"How could you . . . do this to your own . . . daughter?" Luke says, sucking in a few breaths.

Dad glares at Luke but does not say anything.

"You broke your family . . . apart. You cheated on your wife with someone else for years, and just when Grace's mum dies . . . you bring her here? Do you not care about anyone?" Luke says.

Eve's eyes widen. "You said your wife passed away ten years ago!" she screams.

My eyes widen.

Wait, what?

It has not even been a few weeks since my mum died . . . since his wife died. I cannot believe what Eve is saying. How could he do this—lie to both of them?

"I wouldn't have been in a relationship with you if I knew Grace's mother died recently!" she continues. "You're making me look like the bitch!" She pushes Dad out of her arms.

I stare between the two of them, my mind swirling with a million thoughts about what I've just heard. I stand up, helping

Luke to his feet and holding his hands. Once he is finally standing, I grab his hand and pull him out of my room.

Then Eve grabs my hand. "I'm sorry, Grace," she says.

No, I'm sorry, I think to myself as I stare into her eyes.

I nod slowly. "It's okay. My dad always has problems," I tell her. For once, a smile appears on my face as I stare into her eyes.

She nods and pulls me into a hug. "Please . . . if you need anything, just call me, okay? I'm here for you, unlike this bastard," she says, eyeing my dad.

And I find myself hugging her back.

She lets go of me before yelling at Dad again.

I turn around and grab Luke's hand as we head down the stairs.

"Do you just want to stay at your place for today instead of going anywhere?" I ask.

Luke shakes his head. "I'll be fine. I just . . . need to wash my face and change since my shirt is covered in blood."

I frown at him. "Are you sure?"

"Yes, Gracie. I'm sure."

CHAPTER EIGHTEEN
Stop Avoiding the Question

After Luke cleans himself up, we drive off to wherever he wants to go. I sit back in my seat and glance at him, taking in the bruise on his jaw. I rub my wrist, trying to avoid looking at it, but for some reason, I just cannot stop.

It's just like how I cannot stop thinking about that message Daniel sent him that night when I stayed over at his place. I have been pushing myself to ask him, and every time I want to, it's always a bad time. I feel like I will never get to ask him about it, and that kills me because I really want to know what that message meant.

And I also cannot stop thinking about what my father said. I thought he loved Eve deeply. The way they greeted each other in the morning said it all. But after hearing what Eve had to say, I have no words. I mean, I did not like what he did—bringing Eve home after Mum's recent passing. Right now, I do not even know what my feelings are towards him anymore.

I start to think about what would have happened if my mum had not died from cancer. If she were still here, maybe my father would not have turned into the person he is now. Maybe he was hurting so much—that's why he did it. Maybe he was scared to end up alone. But still, Mum's cancer is not a valid reason to cheat. People should not cheat. Period. No one could ever replace Mum. I do not want anyone to replace her.

After a few minutes, Luke pulls over to the side of the road. I look out the window, and my eyes widen at the scene.

A football field?

Luke gets out of the car, and I do the same, walking over to him as he runs a hand through his hair. I grab his hand and begin to walk towards the field. When we reach the middle of the field, we sit down, facing each other.

"Luke—"

"Please, let me speak first. I know I probably don't want to talk about it, but I'm curious about them," Luke says, and he grabs my wrist, sliding up my sleeve.

My heart clenches when I see the first white scar.

"Why do you do it?" he asks.

But I don't answer. I look away. I cannot look at the scars because they haunt me every day. The scars remind me of the bad memories I want to forget.

"Gracie . . . ," Luke says. He leans over and grabs my chin, making me look at him. "Tell me."

I let out a sigh. "I *used* to do it. I haven't cut in three years, ever since . . ." I stop myself, not wanting to admit anything. I have not told anyone—only Mum. Ever since that horrible day, I have not spoken about it until, well, now.

"Grace, you can tell me," he says.

I shake my head, the tears forming in my eyes. "I can, but I won't."

He narrows his eyes at me. "You don't trust me?"

"I do. It's just . . . the memories. I hate them," I say.

He lets out a sigh and places a small kiss on my wrist.

My eyes watch as the kiss lingers on the scar.

"I'm here for you," he murmurs.

I run a hand through my hair and let out a sigh.

"Fine. Three years ago, I began talking to this guy, and since he went to my school, I spent every day with him—until one night, he changed. He turned into some drug addict, and that scared me because he would want to kiss me and . . . t-touch me. I tried to avoid him, but one day at school, he came up to me and . . . put his hands . . . everywhere on my body. I felt so disgusted, and no matter how many showers I took, how many times I cried myself to sleep, I just couldn't be at peace. I was so stressed, and that's when I did it. I cut myself the night I saw him again . . .

when he touched me again," I say, as a few tears fall. I wipe them away and look up at the sky.

"I tried to stop him, and I tried to stay away, but everywhere I went, he followed me. Everyone at school thought I was a slut. I didn't like him touching me. I hated it so much, but no one listened, no matter how I tried to explain. The only person who actually listened to me and believed me was my mum," I say, and I bite my lip, looking into Luke's blue eyes.

"This must've been the time when I left school for a few months," Luke mutters.

I nod. I can still remember how upset some of the girls were when they found out he would be leaving for a few months. Something about a vacation—I'm not too sure.

I breathe out a sigh, continuing my story. "The last time he touched me was on the last day of school, and I remember him saying, 'I will see you again,' before he left." I grip my wrist as I say those words.

"Then from that day on, everything got worse—the bullying, stuff at home, everything. But you probably didn't hear about it because it had calmed down before you came back. Anyway, that's why I kept doing it—to release my anger through every cut. Pathetic excuse, I know."

Luke pulls me into a hug. "Gracie, I didn't know you went through all of this," he says.

I let out a chuckle. "I'm good at hiding it, I guess."

He frowns, obviously not liking the words that came out of my mouth.

I wave him off and kiss him on the cheek. "I'm fine, Luke. I'm fine."

"No, you're not. These—" He runs his finger along my scars. "These show you are not fine."

I run a hand through my hair. "Can we please move on from this topic? I don't like talking about this," I say.

He nods and lies down on the grass.

I lie beside him, my eyes watching as the clouds slowly drift to the right in a gentle motion, making my heartbeat calm down a little.

"Luke, I want to ask you something," I say.

He nods. "Go ahead."

I breathe in sharply before closing my eyes tightly.

Tell him, Grace, my brain urges, and I let out a sigh.

Here goes nothing.

"Uh, the other night, I heard your phone go off . . ." I say, my heart racing. I wipe my hands on my jeans and continue. "Do you actually like me, or is there . . . is there something in it for you?" I ask, finally building up the courage.

He sits up, looking down at me. "What do you mean?"

I sit up too and rest my hands on my thighs.

Don't beat around the bush, Grace. I bite my lip nervously, run a hand through my hair, and swallow the lump in my throat.

"Is this all a dare?" I ask quickly, my eyes immediately closing—I do not want to look at him right now.

"Gracie, look at me," he orders.

I open my eyes slowly and stare into his blue eyes.

He grabs the side of my face and pulls me closer, our noses almost touching. "I like you."

I shake my head and pull away from him. "Stop avoiding the question. Please, just tell me what is going on?" I ask.

He runs a hand through his hair. "Please don't get mad, and don't run either."

I nod slowly.

He holds out his pinkie, and I let out a sigh.

"I promise not to get mad or run," I say.

He nods, placing his hand by his side. He sighs and runs his hand through his hair once more before speaking. "At first, it was a dare to start talking to you because my friends thought that you were easy. After we talked for a few days, my friends dared me to make you like me, then break your heart—since you're the only girl left in the whole school who I have not at least talked to. But I did not want to do it—"

"What's in it for you?" I cut him off, tears stinging in my eyes.

He lets out a sigh and looks down. "Five hundred dollars."

My eyes widen.

Before I can say anything, he continues, "But it's for my father, Grace. I needed the money for my dad . . . for his surgery. I don't want him to die just like—" He stops himself.

My tears begin to fall when I realise what he was going to say.

He was going to bring up Mum's death.

I stand up and begin to run. I don't know where I'm running to, but my mind is screaming for me to run.

Thoughts rush through my head, but I shake them away, my tears still falling as I push myself to run farther. I ignore everyone's stares and just keep running.

I knew something was wrong from the start, but I was just too stupid to accept it.

CHAPTER NINETEEN
I'm So Stupid

I should be crying my eyes out after Luke's confirmation about the dare, but I'm not. I'm just sitting on the grass, staring at the sky. And whenever I'm in this mood, I usually talk to Mum, but she is not here anymore, and it still hurts to know that I practically have no one—not Mum, not Luke, no one.

When Luke told me his story about the "dare" and everything, I did not know what to think. I mean, once a player, always a player, right? He would do anything to get money and to live by his reputation through me, since I was the only girl left in the entire school whom he had not even talked to.

I guess that makes me one of his girls, right?

Being in love is a terrible thing. As much as you want to know that everything will be okay in the end, it always turns out badly, no matter how hard you try to keep it perfect. It's probably because the world wants us to be sad and alone—but maybe it's because the world wants to teach us a lesson. You know, like forgive and forget? But my situation is not even like that.

I can't forget Luke. As much as I want to, I can't. These past months that we have been spending together—it's like I'm used to seeing his face and hearing his laugh. It's like he has been here all my life, although in reality, he has only been here for a few months, and that's what makes everything complicated.

It's easier to fall for someone, but trying to get over them is probably the hardest thing ever. Well, competing for *the world's hardest game—whatever that is*—is probably harder, but that's not my point.

In the movies, they act like it's so easy to move on from someone you once loved, but—oh no—everything has to be harder in movies. I guess that's why they make movies like that: to teach us that life isn't a movie.

I guess that was what I was thinking when I first talked to Luke that day in the hallway. I thought that everything would turn out amazing and we would be together in the end. But, like I said before, even though you put your hardest into the relationship, it still ends badly, and that's what I hate about life.

"Can I just be happy for two seconds?" I scream out in frustration, and I run my hands through my hair. My eyes are probably red. I had cried as I ran to the cemetery to talk to Mum, but as soon as I turned up here, I have not cried at all.

I look at Mum's gravestone and let out a shaky sigh. "I made the wrong decision, didn't I?" I ask, looking at her name. I run my finger over it, and some dust collecting on my fingertip. I let out a chuckle and roll my eyes.

"I'm so stupid," I say, letting out a sigh. I cross my legs and play with the flower between my fingers, twirling it.

"Why did you have to leave me, Mum? You had to go at the worst time," I say.

Suddenly, a hand taps my shoulder. My heart races as thoughts of Luke standing behind me run through my head, but when I turn around, I look at the brunette.

"E-Eve?" I stutter, my eyebrows furrowing as she smiles down at me.

She takes a seat on the grass next to me and lets out a sigh.

"I knew I would find you here," Eve says.

I shrug. "Okay."

"Don't you want to know why I'm here?"

"Actually, I want to know how you know about this place . . ." I mutter, confused as to how she found me.

"Your father gave me directions," she says.

The look on her face practically says that she does not want to talk about my dad—the guy who lied to her about the death of his wife.

"Oh . . . okay." I shrug again. "Anyway, I have a lot on my mind right now, so just go ahead and spill it," I say.

Eve nods. "Okay, well, I just want to say sorry again. My baby sister was in the same position as you, you know? My parents didn't show any love at all, and when my mum cheated on my dad, my baby sister was broken. I mean, we were all broken, but my sister depended on my parents so much," she explains.

I turn to her, finding myself listening to what she has to say. "What happened to your dad?" I ask.

She smiles weakly before wiping a tear away from her eye. "He . . . hung himself," she admits, but the smile is still on her face. As I study her face, I can see that she is holding it all in— her emotions.

"I-I'm sorry," I say.

She waves me off. "It's okay. I'm just not used to the fact that he . . . he is not here, you know?"

I nod, a small smile on my face. "I understand."

She places her hands in her lap as she glances at Mum's gravestone.

"You know, I thought you knew everything. I thought my dad had told you," I say.

She rolls her eyes. "That's what I thought too, but all your father told me was that your mum passed away ten years ago and that he had a daughter who is living with him. If I had known that your father was cheating on your mum with me, I would've run for the hills, you know? I just hate people who think that cheating is okay . . . like it has no impact on the other person whatsoever," she explains.

I nod. "I know."

As silence settles between us, a question appears in my mind, and I turn to her.

"Wait, so where are you staying now?" I ask.

She shrugs. "My mother hates me since I slapped her for cheating on my dad. And my sister . . . I don't even know where she is. I guess I'll have to check into a hotel for a couple of days until I find somewhere—"

"You don't have to do that."

"Yes, I do. I don't want you to think that I am trying to take your mum's place while I am at your house. It will be uncomfortable for me," she says.

I shake my head. "I know you're not going to take my mum's place. Look, just stay for a few more days and sort things out with my dad if you want to. I mean, it's your life, so you can do whatever, but . . . uh, yeah, I'm just saying."

"Why are you saying all of this?" Eve asks.

I send her a small smile. "Because I don't want to see another woman leave because of my dad. And it's not your fault. You're just a victim too."

CHAPTER TWENTY
You Haven't Eaten All Day

It's been a week since I talked to Luke, and let me just say, avoiding him has been so hard, especially at school. I bump into him multiple times after lunch, but every time he wants to talk or say anything, I run away. Some people would call me a coward, but I would say that I'm only protecting my heart from getting hurt again.

You see, when you are in love, you become very vulnerable and let your walls down because you are certain you will not get hurt. That's what I thought—until Luke hurt me that day.

When you are in love with someone, it becomes really hard to stay away from that person because all you want to do is be with him and hear him say that it will be okay. But nothing like that has happened, and that's what is breaking me.

I want to hear his voice—I won't lie. But every time I try to let my walls down again, they just won't fall. It's like my mind is telling me to stay away from him, but my heart is telling me to stop doubting and just be with him. But I can't. It's not that I don't want to—it's just that I can't. I'm more fragile than ever, and if something goes wrong, I don't know where I'd be.

Luke has sent me a few messages this week, saying that he is sorry and stuff like that, but I cannot bring myself to reply. I mean, should I even bother wasting my time like that again? I wish this whole thing had never started. I wish he had wanted to talk to me simply because he wanted to. Take now, for example—

he wants to talk to me because he wants to, not because he was forced to, not because of some bet.

Sometimes, I wish none of this had ever happened—that I had never met Luke, and that my life was the same as before he helped me that day in the hall. Even though my life before Luke and I started talking was bad, I would still choose it. I'd rather get beaten up in the hallway than feel miserable.

The pain is just too much, and it's wreaking havoc inside me. It makes me feel like I can never put my heart into someone's hands, because it will always get thrown back to me, crushed and broken.

I guess this is what Mum warned me about. I thought I was ready. Well, I was not—and that's what put me in this situation. Mum warned me because she knew I would be this stupid. She knew I'd let my guard down so easily. Mum warned me, and I did not listen.

Suddenly, there's a knock on my door. I sit up, cross my legs, and place my hands on my thighs.

"Come in," I say, and the door opens, revealing a smiling Eve, holding a bowl of pasta.

I know what she is doing, but before I can tell her I'm not hungry, she interrupts.

"Don't pull that 'I'm not hungry' crap, because I know you're starving. You haven't eaten all day."

She hands me the bowl of pasta and takes a seat beside me.

Yes, Eve and I have become friends. I guess I can call her a friend now that she is helping me and all. Ever since we talked at the graveyard, we have started to become closer and tell each other things. I told her everything about Luke, and she has been helping me since "I am slowly breaking," according to her.

"Have you talked to Luke lately?" she asks.

I shove a spoonful of pasta in my mouth and shake my head. She lets out a sigh.

"Well, I guess that explains why he is at the door asking for you," she says.

Wait, what?

I swallow my pasta, and my eyes go wide. "He . . . is here?" I ask and she nods.

"Do you want me to tell him that you're not coming down?" she asks.

I nod slowly. "Yeah. I'm just not . . . ready to talk to him yet," I explain.

"I get it." She stands up and begins to walk out of my room.

I try to calm my heart by focusing on my food, eating the pasta slowly.

I'm not ready, Luke.

*   *   *

The weekend passed quickly, and now it's Monday, which means I have to try my hardest to keep my eyes open and not bump into a certain someone at school.

Yes, I'm talking about Luke.

The thought of seeing him again makes me want to move away, because every time I see him, my heart races and my head begins to spin. My body even shakes when I think about him—and believe me, I think about him a lot.

Eve says I'm "whipped," but come on, everyone knows that's just a stupid term. What "whipped" means is that you are so crazily in love. And that's what it is—I am crazily in love with Luke. And as much as I just want to hug him and forget about the "dare" thing, I cannot, and that kills me.

A knock interrupts my thoughts, and I let out a sigh.

"Yes?" I ask, opening the shower curtain so I can hear the voice.

"You're going to be late if you keep thinking about life, Grace," Eve chuckles.

I roll my eyes. "Two more minutes," I say. "Eve!"

Footsteps return to the bathroom door. "Yes?"

"Can you give me a ride to school? I don't feel like walking," I ask.

She lets out a laugh. "Sure, but you have to be ready in five minutes if you want me to drive you."

I turn off the shower.

Time starts now.

*   *   *

"Well, have a nice day, I guess," Eve says as she stops in front of the school.

I nod. "You too," I reply.

She smiles. "Do you want me to pick you up?"

I shake my head. "It's okay, I'll be fine. I'll walk home," I say, unbuckling my seat belt.

She nods and holds up her fist.

I smile and bump her fist with mine before getting out of the car.

As I begin to walk inside the building, the smile falls off my face. I let out a sigh, noticing Nicole by my locker. I walk up to her and frown.

"I thought I told you to leave me alone," I say.

"Yes, but this is important. Go to the cafeteria," she says.

I roll my eyes. "How do I know this isn't a trick?" I ask, raising my eyebrow slightly.

She shakes her head and places a hand on my shoulder, taking me by surprise. "Grace, this isn't a joke. I swear," she assures me.

I let out a sigh and agree to walk with her to the cafeteria, ignoring the confused looks from everyone staring at us. I know exactly what they are thinking, but instead of asking, Nicole's glare makes them look away instantly.

As we reach the cafeteria doors, I push them open—and the moment I see what's going on, I want to run to it, scream, or start a riot.

"Get your hands off my fucking boyfriend."

CHAPTER TWENTY-ONE
She Got What She Deserved

I never thought I would admit this, but when I saw the stranger latching onto Luke's arm a few seconds ago, I was jealous. Heck, I still am, and I guess that's why I'm glaring into the girl's eyes, my fists clenched by my sides.

"Well, well, who is this?" the girl asks, looking at Luke.

Luke has his eyes on me, and I know exactly why.

First off, he's never heard me swear because I explained to him that I think swearing is a bad habit and just plain rude. Second, he is surprised that I'm jealous. I was never jealous.

I know, Luke, I'm surprised too.

"My name's Grace," I tell the girl, confidence appearing back in my system. The last time I found myself being all confident was when I yelled at Dad and slapped him, but ever since then, I have been like a turtle—hiding away from everyone because I've been too scared.

Now, the confidence is rising in my body, and I would be lying if I said I did not like it because, inside, I love it.

The girl rolls her eyes and smirks at me. "So you're the little bitch."

I swallow the lump in my throat and grab her arm, pulling her out of the seat. She yanks her arm away from me and lets out a laugh.

"Something funny?" I narrow my eyes at her.

She shakes her head. "Nah. I'm just amused."

Before I can say anything, Luke speaks behind me. "Amy—"

"Shut up, Luke," Amy says.

I narrow my eyes at her again. "Don't tell him to shut up, okay?"

She snorts. "Yeah, okay." She rolls her eyes.

All of a sudden, someone in the crowd shouts out, "Bitch fight!" making me roll my eyes too.

Amy smirks and raises her hands in the air.

"Let's give the crowd what they want," she says.

Before I can even react, she throws her fist into my face, making me fall to the ground.

I let out a cough and get up, clenching my fists as I walk toward her. "Let me explain something first—"

Before I can continue, she throws another punch at my face.

I feel something run down my lips. I touch it and see blood. I hate blood, and the fact that Amy made me bleed makes me so angry. It reminds me of the time when Dad first hit Mum. There was so much blood.

I run up to Amy and tackle her, slamming her head against the marble floor. I pound my fist into her face, making sure she bleeds—just to make it even—but Amy does not want that.

She wants to make things interesting.

How? Oh, she decides to head-butt me. I let out a groan and lose my focus. She quickly takes the opportunity to roll me over, straddle me, grab my hair, and slam my head against the floor. Before I black out, Luke pulls Amy away from me.

The last thing I hear before I pass out is the words that slip out of Amy's mouth:

"She got what she deserved."

*   *   *

I blink a couple of times before rubbing my eyes and stretching out my legs. I open my eyes and look around the familiar room in front of me—the nurse's office.

I notice the principal sitting in the chair next to the nurse as they talk—obviously about the fight. When they see me, the principal stands up.

"Grace . . . ," our principal starts, and I let out a sigh, rubbing my forehead.

Damn, it hurts so much.

"How are you feeling?"

I shrug. "It's just my head."

He shakes his head. "Can you remember what happened in the cafeteria before you passed out?"

I nod.

He takes the seat next to the bed I'm sitting on.

"I know you always refuse to take statements about all the violence that comes your way, but I really need you to write one down, since this doesn't involve Nicole for once."

I let out a sigh. "I really don't want to," I mumble.

He nods. "I know what you're thinking, but the most important statement is the one coming from the victim, and since Amy has already written her statement—along with Nicole and Luke—I know your side of the story."

I let out a sigh. "Fine, I'll do it," I say.

He smiles, resting a hand on my shoulder. "Thank you. Meet me in my office once you're done here," he tells me and walks out of the clinic.

I let out another sigh.

The nurse, whom I call Mandy, walks over to me with a small smile.

"Are you feeling dizzy at all?" she asks.

I shake my head. "No," I reply, looking down at my fingers.

She takes the seat next to me and crosses her legs. "How are things going at home?"

I shrug. "Okay, I guess."

She nods, raises her hand, and feels my forehead.

"I advise you to keep your stress levels down, since your head is very sore. Also, your knuckles are bruised, so don't hit anything if you want them to heal quicker," she says. "Try and have a good day, okay?" she adds.

I stand up, nod, and smile at her. "I'll try to. Goodbye, Mandy."

"Bye, Grace."

*   *   *

After I finish writing my statement about the fight, I place the pen beside the paper and lean back in my chair, letting out a sigh as I watch the principal type a few things on his computer.

When he sees that I am finished, he grabs the paper and reads it. He lets out a sigh and runs a hand through his hair. "Wow, it's Amy's first day, and she is already starting trouble," he grumbles before going back to his computer.

Oh no, she is not starting here.

"Okay, Grace, would you like to be sent home for the day?" the principal asks.

"No, I'll be fine," I insist. It is the same answer that comes out of my mouth every time he asks me that question.

He narrows his eyes at me. "Can I ask a question?"

I nod.

"Does your answer have to do with your life at home? Is that why you never want to leave?"

I shake my head.

Yes, yes, it is.

"No," I say.

He sighs. "Okay, well, just let me write you a note explaining why you haven't been in class, then you can go."

I nod and watch him write my name and an explanation on the white slip. He hands it to me, and I thank him, walking out of the office.

As I begin to make my way to class, an idea appears in my head as I look down at the slip. I make a left, walking straight to the field.

I do not have to go to class straightaway if I have this.

Thank goodness.

*　　　*　　　*

As I lean against the tree, I close my eyes, the song *Ghost* by Halsey playing in my ears. My fingers tap my knee to the beat, and I let out a sigh.

"Gracie?" someone says from behind me, and I turn around to see Luke standing there with a small frown.

Just like that, my heart races, and my breathing becomes heavy as I look into his blue eyes. This time, I do not find myself running because I realise that if I run again, I might lose him for good. I do not want that.

"H-hi," I stutter.

He slowly walks over to me as he watches my reaction, like he is trying to be cautious. I nod, and he sits beside me, letting out a small sigh.

I take my earphones out of my ears and place them on my lap.

"Uh, I'm sorry," I begin.

Luke looks at me, his eyes staring into my green ones. "No, it's my fault. First of all, I said that I wouldn't break your heart, and when I told you everything that day, your face told me that you were so broken, and I didn't know what to do. I'm so sorry, Grace. I really like you, and I just want you to hear me out—"

"Luke, calm down." I smile.

He runs a hand down his face. "Sorry."

"Well, you can explain everything now," I say.

He breathes in deeply before letting out a sigh as he looks at the football team running laps around the field.

"Well, first, I'm going to explain what happened earlier," Luke begins, and I sigh, knowing that Amy is going to be mentioned.

"Please—"

"No, you need to hear this. Amy was sitting near me because today is her first day, and apparently, she wanted to fix a few things that had happened in the past. Then Nicole walked in, and we were the first two people she saw. I had a feeling she would go and look for you, so I wanted to drop the conversation and just walk away. But after a few minutes of her not accepting what I was saying, I heard someone say that you were coming with Nicole. When Amy saw my face and realised that I obviously wanted to leave, she made things look really bad."

I feel my blood boil at the thought of Luke and Amy having a past. Does he mean they used to date or something?

"I'm sorry you had to see that, Gracie. Honestly, I truly am."

As I think of accepting his apology, I remember when he just stood there while Amy and I were fighting.

"What about the fight? You . . . you didn't even do anything. You just stood there watching." I can feel my blood boiling again.

He sighs, looking at the ground. "I know I should've done something. But it wasn't my fault. Some guy was holding me back, if you didn't see it. He wouldn't let me go, and when I realised that I couldn't get out of his grip, I gave up. I should've done more, and I'm sorry. Ugh, just thinking of that makes me want to find that guy and break his fingers—"

A quiet laugh escapes my lips, cutting him off.

"I'm just glad you told me the truth." I smile.

He returns it immediately, grabbing my hand.

"Now . . . for the second part of my confession," Luke says, making my eyebrows furrow. "Two years ago, my dad was in a car crash and suffered brain damage, a broken leg, and a burned arm."

I nod. He does not look at me at all, but I know why. I can tell that he is still hurting and does not want to break down in front of me.

"The doctors said that he would be in critical condition for a while, but if he did what they told him to do, he could at least live a normal life and not be stuck in a hospital bed forever. One night, though, my mum began to feel a lot of pain in her stomach; she was pregnant at the time, which was why it was so important to get her checked out. When my dad heard about it, he wanted to leave the hospital right away and check on my mum. But it only put him in a worse situation when he got out of bed."

"My mum lost the baby that night, and when my dad heard about it, he went insane. Now, my dad is really sick, and he needs one thousand dollars for the surgery that could either save him or kill him. My mum is going to pay half since that's all she has at the moment, and I'm going to pay the other half—if I actually get the money from my friends."

He turns his head to look at me. "But the feelings I have for you don't have anything to do with the dare. I really like you."

"Why didn't you tell me this at the start?" I ask.

Luke shakes his head. "I was too focused on my dad to remember. The day I took you to the town's football field was when I knew that I should tell you, and that's why I did. I know the explanation is a little late, but if you can, please forgive me."

I let out a sigh. After everything, I don't know what to say. Luke only got himself into this because he wanted to save his dad—or at least give him a chance. I can't be mad at him because of this . . . I just can't.

"Fine," I say, a small smile on my lips.

He grins, placing a hand on my cheek. He brings his face closer to mine, and before his lips touch mine, he stops. "But I need you to help me."

"With?" I ask, moving away from him so I can see his face.

He holds my hand in his and sighs. "I need you to meet my friends, but you don't have to say anything—I'll do the talking."

I let out a sigh.

"Please, Gracie, I really need this money."

If Luke at least gets a chance to save his dad, I can't let the opportunity slide. I couldn't help Mum, but at least Luke gets to try and save his dad, and I guess that's what matters.

"Okay."

He smiles and brings my face close to his, my eyes slipping shut. His hands run down my thighs, making me feel—I do not even know how to explain it, but the moan that escapes my mouth obviously tells me that I like it.

Luke pulls away and smirks. "Now, that was different."

I hide my face in his chest, my cheeks heating up. Well, I guess that's one way to make a girl blush. I might as well be a walking tomato, since I blush way too much.

"Oh, you two look cute," someone says behind us. I turn around to see none other than Amy.

"Please get lost," I say.

She rolls her eyes. "Little Miss Goody-Two-Shoes over here."

Luke groans. "Go away, Amy. You're not wanted here."

"Not yet," Amy says with a wink before walking away.

I frown at Luke.

He pecks my lips and smiles at me. "Don't worry about her."

Something tells me I'm going to be running into Amy a lot now.

Great.

CHAPTER TWENTY-TWO
Just One More Kiss

I grab onto Luke's hand as we begin to walk out of the school building. Before we walk down the stairs, though, Luke grabs my waist and pushes me against the railing, his lips touching mine.

When he pulls away, I let out a chuckle. "What was that for?" I ask.

He twirls a strand of my hair around his finger. "Your lips are addicting. I couldn't help it," he grins.

I find myself blushing at his words. I grab his hand and drag him down the stairs as we walk towards his car.

When we are both inside, Luke starts the car and reverses out of the parking lot, driving towards my house.

"How is your jaw?" I ask, glancing at his face to see a light circle where the bruise is.

"Oh, you know, just painful," he says. "How is your head?"

I grin at him. "Oh, you know, just painful." I chuckle.

He rolls his eyes. "Enough with the jokes. I want to know how you're feeling."

He stops at a red light.

I shrug. "Nah, I'm okay, I guess."

"That's all you had to say," he says.

After a few seconds of silence, I begin to talk. "So, when are we going to see these friends of yours?" I ask.

He begins to drive when the light turns green. "Tomorrow after school."

I can't help but begin to think about his friends. Are they scary? Are they dangerous? Why haven't I seen them in school before?

My thoughts are cut short when I feel the car stop again. I look over at Luke, about to thank him for giving me a ride home, but his lips touch mine, making me forget about everything for a few seconds.

When we pull away, I lean my forehead against his, our breaths mixing. I close my eyes and try to regain my breath, but a knock on the window makes me jump and open my eyes.

Eve stands at the window, a small smile on her face. She motions for us to roll down the window.

Luke does as he is told.

"Hey, Eve," I say. A blush creeps onto my cheeks as I realise that I've just been caught kissing the guy I was ignoring only yesterday.

Eve smiles and looks over at Luke. "I would say that I am disappointed in you for making Grace feel like crap, but when I saw the heated scene, I'll let that slide. I am happy for both of you. Have you made up?" she asks.

Luke nods. "Yeah, she forgave me," he says, smiling at me.

I look away, trying to hide my smile.

Eve taps my shoulder, and I look at her.

"I want you to meet someone, so when you're ready to come in . . . ," Eve trails off.

I nod.

Eve chuckles and walks back into the house to give us some privacy.

"You two seem civil," Luke notices.

"Well, I never hated Eve. But after our talk and finding out the truth, I just thought it is not fair to continue hating her. I just . . . well, I didn't give her a chance to explain in the first place," I say.

"I agree. 'Alright, I don't want to be the reason your guest gets impatient, so I'll leave you to it," he says.

I press my lips to his, my eyes slipping shut as I let myself get lost in the kiss.

Luke pulls away and grins at me, tapping my nose. "See you tomorrow, Gracie."

I chuckle. "Just one more kiss," I say, quickly pressing my lips to his before pulling away. I open the car door, and before I get out, I peck his cheek.

"Please don't hurt me again," I say.

He smiles at me before pressing his lips to mine for two seconds. He pulls away and rests his hand on my thigh. "I promise I won't."

He holds out his pinkie.

Smiling, I connect my pinkie with his. He smiles, and I get out of his car. I shut the door and send him a wave before making my way to my door.

"Goodbye, Gracie," Luke says.

I roll my eyes and smile at him as he begins to drive off. I chuckle to myself and hold the door handle to my house, thinking about everything that has happened today.

Wow, I never thought I would be back with Luke again, and I never thought I would be in my first fight today. Yep, today has been weird. Let's just hope that whoever is behind that door is not going to make my day any weirder.

I push the door open, and before I can even process what is happening, my eyes widen, and my heart drop as a girl stares at me with a small grin on her face. Her red hair sits on her shoulders, and her piercing green eyes stare into mine, a hint of mischief in them as she looks me over.

No, no, please do not tell me—

Eve smiles and walks over to me, her arm slinging around my shoulder. "Grace, I would like to introduce you to my daughter," she says.

My hands begin to shake.

"Nice to see you again, Grace." Eve's daughter smirks as she holds out her hand.

I just look at it, not wanting to be anywhere near this person.

"Hello, Amy."

CHAPTER TWENTY-THREE
Go Run Away to Luke

Eve looks down at me in confusion, her eyebrows furrowing.

I glance over at Amy to see her grin still on her face, which makes my heart race with fear.

Why the hell does this have to happen to me?

"Do you two know each other?" Eve asks.

I look down at the floor after Amy sends me a quick glare, silently telling me to shut my mouth.

"I bumped into her today," Amy says. She walks over to me and wraps her arm around my shoulder, making me go stiff.

Tell her, Grace, my brain says, but I shake my head.

I don't want to mess with Amy again. Besides, Luke told me not to worry about her. But it's sort of hard when she is your father's girlfriend's daughter!

Eve frowns and motions for me to follow her into the kitchen. Amy quickly grabs my hand and narrows her eyes at me.

"Tell her one thing about today, and you'll be sorry," she says.

I nod before rushing off to the kitchen, where I find Eve sitting in a chair. She points to the seat next to her.

"Is there something you want to tell me? You looked a little uncomfortable when you saw Amy, and I don't want her to start trouble with you," she says, frowning.

I gulp, shaking my head. "N-no, everything's fine. I was just . . . surprised because I didn't know you had a daughter," I say, forcing a smile.

But Eve's frown does not fade, which makes me worry.

"Grace, please don't lie. If something happened today, you can tell me," she presses.

I shake my head again. "Everything's fine, Eve."

She sighs and stands up. "Okay, well, if she is giving you a hard time, just tell me, and I'll send her back to live with her dad."

My eyes widen. "Wait, is she staying here?"

Eve nods. "Only for a while. Your dad is okay with it, but by the looks of it, you aren't."

I shake my head, waving her off. "Nah, I'm okay," I chuckle.

She smiles. "Good. Well, I have to go to the mall to grab a few things for dinner. Your father should be home soon, so you won't be alone with Amy for too long."

I nod slowly, trying to hide the fear and dread inside me.

"That's fine," I say. When Eve leaves the kitchen, I grip the table in anger.

Why couldn't I tell her?

God, I'm so screwed right now.

*   *   *

"So, you and Luke, huh?" Amy asks.

I nod, trying to keep my eyes on the television.

It has been an hour since Eve left for the mall, and honestly, I just feel like running away if she does not come back in maybe . . . three minutes? Actually, make it two, because I really feel like I am going to explode any second now—all Amy has been talking about is stuff that does not even concern her.

"How serious is this relationship?" she asks.

I let out a heavy sigh, trying to focus my attention on Sheldon on the TV screen as he explains his gibberish to Penny.

"Very," I say, tapping my finger on my leg as I chew on my lip nervously.

Do not lose it, Grace.

"Have you two taken it to the next—"

"Oh, god, is that my phone? Oh yeah, it is. I'll be right back." I jump from the couch and run up the stairs to my room. I grab my phone and dial Luke in case Amy comes up and sees that no one really called me. I do not want to give her the impression that I am trying to get away from her.

"Hello, Grac—"

"Luke, help me," I say.

Luke lets out a laugh. "You want me to come and rescue you, Gracie?" he chuckles.

"Yes, please. I need to get out of this house," I say, chewing on the inside of my cheek while he continues to laugh on the other end.

"I'm on my way."

I let out a sigh and thank him before hanging up the phone. I walk down the stairs, let out another sigh, and rub my hands on my thighs.

When Amy notices me walking down the stairs, she smirks. "Am I really that bad?" she asks.

I push away the urge to shout yes in her face. "No, I just . . . uh—"

"Go run away to Luke. You will be seeing me later, though, because we are going to have a nice chat." She grins.

I rush outside without saying anything.

I close the door behind me and run my hands through my hair. I need Amy out of my house before I go insane. And I know exactly what to do.

*　　*　　*

"Wait, she is staying with you? For how long?" Luke asks.

I shrug. "Yeah, but I don't know how long. That is why I need you to help me."

He grins, placing his hands on my thighs. "I never took you for the 'revenge' type of girl."

I kick him away with my foot and push myself off the roof of the car.

"I don't think of it as revenge, Luke. I just think of it as saving myself, because honestly, I have a feeling that Amy is trying to ruin my life, even though I only met her today," I explain.

"That's Amy for you," he says.

I frown. "What's with you both? Do you two have some history or something?"

"Yeah, we were together for about a month until I broke up with her," he explains.

I raise my eyebrow at him. "Why?"

"Because she moved to Germany with her dad, and I didn't do long-distance relationships, so I broke up with her. It wouldn't really work out anyway. We kept arguing."

I narrow my eyes at him. "Is that why she said you don't do relationships? Because you broke up with her?"

"Yeah, I guess."

He grabs my hand and leads me into the school building. "Now, let's get started with your revenge," he grins.

I roll my eyes. "It is not revenge."

He shrugs. "Whatever makes you sleep at night, Gracie."

CHAPTER TWENTY-FOUR
I'm Going to be Moving to Mars

After staying at the school for two hours, working on my little plan to get rid of Amy, Luke and I finally finished without getting caught by any of the teachers, who were in the building for some faculty program.

Luke took me home after hanging out for a bit, and let me just say—I have never felt so mischievous in my entire life. The only other time I did something so, well, evil was when I scared my cousin by putting a fake snake around her sleeping form. And let me just point out something: I have never seen my cousin jump so high from her bed.

Anyway, now I am lying on my bed, looking at the ceiling, with the thought of none other than Amy. I have been asking myself why she chose to appear in my life now. Maybe because life hates me, or maybe because I am just unlucky—but either way, I could not be more curious.

I am also curious about Amy's life. Luke had mentioned that she liked to ruin people's lives for fun, which made me a little worried. I do not even know what Amy is capable of. Well, tomorrow is the day that she will be exposed to the whole school.

Okay, I think I am regretting my plan now.

A knock on my door makes me turn to see Dad standing there, a small smile on his lips. I frown at him and sit up, trying to figure out what he wants.

"Uh, what do you want?"

"I just wanted to check up on you."

"Well, you don't need to, because I'm perfectly fine," I tell him.

He nods and walks into my room. "Grace, I know I have been a terrible person to you and your mum, but I just want you to know that I'm still your dad, and I do love you."

I scoff, rolling my eyes. "You may be my dad, but let's get one thing straight—I'm not obliged to call you that. You have to earn that right," I say.

Before my father can say anything, I roll my eyes again and lie down on my bed, looking away.

"Close the door on your way out," I say.

After a few seconds, he lets out a sigh before the door closes. I growl and close my eyes, trying to forget everything and just get some sleep.

After all, I do have a big day tomorrow.

*   *   *

As I walk through the school gates with Luke by my side, I cannot help but think about my little plan. I mean, is it wrong of me to do something like this? What if it goes wrong? Well, we all know the answer to that—I am going to be moving to Mars. Yeah, Amy will never find me there.

I shake my head and breathe out a sigh, trying not to think about it too much. I notice Amy standing with a few people at her locker, which is a few steps away from mine.

Wow, she has made some friends already.

Amy turns her head and looks at me, studying me with a small grin on her face.

I just ignore her—and my racing heart. I stop at my locker and open it, grabbing the books that I left yesterday.

When I'm done, Luke sends me a smile.

I frown at him. "Why are you looking at me like that?" I ask, furrowing my eyebrows.

"I'm just trying to figure out why you look so beautiful right now," he says.

I roll my eyes with a chuckle. "Stop being cheesy and focus. Now, the plan should begin any second—"

"What the fuck?" Amy says a little too loudly, making people turn to her curiously.

I watch carefully as she pulls out the small white paper with the words "I know what you did" on it. I know because I wrote the words myself.

Guys, before you start thinking this is a horror movie or a scene from *I Know What You Did Last Summer,* think again—because this is just the first step in plan to send Amy back to her dad in Germany.

I know, I am actually very selfish and not thinking of Eve right now, but I'm sure she will not mind. Once Amy's gone, I can tell her everything her daughter did.

Yes, I have everything planned out. I just hope it plays out like I imagined.

Amy slowly turns her head to me and rips the paper, her eyes still on mine. My heart races as the people around her begin to stare at me too.

Before I can do anything, Luke grabs my hand and starts pulling me away from the situation.

As we walk past Amy, I see the slight grin on her lips, and from that moment, I know she has something up her sleeve.

*   *   *

I begin to eat my lunch slowly, just watching as Amy walks into the cafeteria with two other girls by her side. I do not recognise the two girls, but I push the thought to the back of my mind as she sits at the table next to the football team, which is on the other side of the cafeteria.

"Hey, it's okay," Luke whispers in my ear, his hand resting on my thigh.

I do not say anything because my eyes are too focused on Amy, who is grinning at the people surrounding her table. I look away after a few seconds and run a hand through my hair.

"I feel like we should do the next part of the plan now," I mumble.

Luke nods and grabs his phone. He goes to his contacts and dials a number, calling the one person who can send Amy back to her father in Germany.

"Hello? Yeah, everything is ready." Luke nods slowly, listening to the person on the other line. "Okay, I'll see you soon. Thanks. Bye."

He hangs up the phone, and I look up at him in worry. He smiles and kisses my cheek, grabbing my hand and pulling me out of the cafeteria.

"Everything is going according to plan, Gracie, so don't worry," he assures me.

I nod, looking back to see that Amy is no longer at her table, which makes me extra worried.

I hope this works—because if not, I'm done.

CHAPTER TWENTY-FIVE
How Dare You Waste a Gummy Bear!

I watch as Luke talks to Eddie, who is helping us carry out our plan. He is wearing a small grin on his face, his arms crossed over his chest, clearly listening to what Luke is saying. I lean against the wall, trying to be patient, but with every second that passes, it is like we are inching closer to danger.

When Eddie nods, I know their conversation is coming to an end. Luke shakes his hand and turns around, walking towards me, but my eyes are on Eddie.

Luke had mentioned that Amy's brother, Eddie, was in town the day I told him about her staying at my house. And since Eddie did not really like Eve or Amy, he decided to help us—he liked the idea of getting back at Amy for whatever she did to him.

"You okay?" Luke asks, his hands resting on my sides.

I snap out of my thoughts, nodding slowly.

He smiles as I wrap my arms around his neck, pressing my lips to his gently. I pull away after a few seconds and smile at him.

"Thank you for helping me with this, Luke."

He kisses my forehead. "It's all good. I just don't like you worrying too much. It's going to go just fine," he assures me.

I nod in agreement, trying to push away my thoughts.

He grabs my hand and swings it a little, a small smirk on his lips. "What do you say we ditch school and just chill at my house?" he suggests.

I smile, nodding happily. "I'd love to."

*   *   *

"Oh, we are not starting this again," Luke grumbles as I throw a piece of popcorn at his nose.

I let out a laugh and face the television, shoving some popcorn into my mouth. All of a sudden, I feel something hit my cheek. I look beside me to see a gummy bear staring up at me. I turn to Luke and glare at him.

"How dare you waste a gummy bear?!"

"How dare you waste popcorn?!" he throws back.

I roll my eyes, pick up the gummy bear, and throw it back at him.

I squeal when he begins to tickle me. Before I can protest further, the bowl of popcorn falls to the ground as I try to move away from him.

Luke stops in shock and turns to me, waiting for an explanation.

I roll my eyes and point at him. "You made me do it."

He lets out a laugh. "Yeah, because I dared you to drop popcorn on my floor."

I shake my head and brush the popcorn off me.

"I have a wonderful idea."

I shake my head. "All your ideas suck."

He raises an eyebrow at me. "So if I said that you were my idea—"

I cut him off with a squeal when I realise what he is going to say. I jump off the couch and cross my arms over my chest. "You are disgusting," I point out.

Luke shakes his head. "Nah, I'm amazing."

I roll my eyes, grab the plastic bowl, and throw it at him, earning a groan.

"Why did you do that for?"

I point a finger at him, narrowing my eyes. "You're dirty-minded."

He smirks. "But you understood it, so what does that make you?" He stands up.

I drop my arms from my chest and shake my head at him. "You can't put this back on me."

Luke lets out a laugh and crosses his arms over his chest. "Oh, but I did."

Before I can throw the remote from the coffee table at him, his phone goes off.

He grabs his phone. I walk over to him and stand by his side, looking at his phone to see a message from Eddie:

> *Everything is ready to go. Do you want me to make an appearance tomorrow?*

As Luke begins to type his reply to Amy's brother, I start thinking about the whole plan.

When I wrote the note to Amy, I realised that I did not have a plan B or plan C to follow it through. The note has nothing to do with the actual plan—it is just a distraction to confuse her. Hopefully, it is doing what I intended, and the plan will proceed perfectly.

Now, thanks to Luke's brilliant mind, the main plan is to get Amy's brother, Eddie, involved. From what I've heard, Amy thinks Eddie is dead since she has not heard from him since he left Germany. It has been years since they last talked. Before Eddie left, he and Amy were not on good terms. Amy did not want him to leave, but Eddie had no choice—he had gotten himself into a dangerous situation. He had to leave Germany, leaving Amy and their dad behind.

Anyway, the plan now is for Eddie to show up at the school. As Luke explained, Amy will be shocked and will reasonably demand an explanation from Eddie. Eddie will then tell Amy that he had to leave because of his gang. And now that he's back, he and Amy have to go back to Germany because he believes their father is in danger—which I personally think is somewhat true, given Eddie's real gang connection.

In fact, he actually told Luke that the people he was dangerously involved with had contacted him a few days ago, demanding that he return to Germany or they would go after his father—for real.

The only fake part is Amy's involvement in all this. She does not need to go back with him. But Eddie will lie to Amy and tell her that the only way for the people to leave their dad alone is for both of them to go back to Germany. I do not know how they will justify this to make it sound convincing, but Luke and Eddie discussed it further without me. I did not bother to listen and just left it all to Luke. I trust him that much.

And if this does not work, I have one more thing up my sleeve—and even though it will be risky, I would have to do it if I want Amy gone. I would have to tell Eve about Amy's threats and what she did to me at school.

Luke keeps convincing me that I will not have to do that because plan A will work, but a part of me tells me it will fail, and I will need a plan B.

I know that plan A is a bit of a stretch just to get rid of Amy. I mean, I could just go ahead and tell Eve what she did. But I don't know—I just don't have the courage to go through all the confrontations and the drama. I think I've had enough of that. If plan A succeeds, Amy will just leave without me having to speak to her or Eve.

And now, I just hope luck is on my side for once, because I do not want to find myself slowly breaking, just like when Mum—

"Gracie," Luke says, pulling me out of my thoughts.

I shake my head and frown at him. "I'm fine."

He frowns, holding my hand in his.

I look down at our hands, then back up at him to see his eyebrows furrow.

"Then why are you crying?"

I raise my hand to my face, and that's when I realise that I am indeed crying. I wipe away the tears and bite my lip.

Why am I crying? Is it because I was thinking about Mum?

"I . . . don't know," I say.

Luke sighs, pulling my body close to his, his arms wrapping around my small frame.

"Don't cry, Grace. I'm here," he says quietly.

I close my eyes, letting the last tear fall.

"Ow!" I scream, clutching my knee in pain.

Mum comes running up to me, a small frown on her face as she picks me up from the concrete and helps me stand.

"What happened?" Mum asks.

I point down at the ground, the tears beginning to fall from my eyes.

She sighs and pulls me into a hug, her arms wrapping around me tightly.

"Don't cry, Grace. I'm here," she whispers as she pecks my forehead.

I bite my lip, clutching onto her as tightly as I can.

"I love you, Mum."

Without thinking, my mouth opens to say the words I never thought would escape my lips at this moment.

"I love you, Luke."

CHAPTER TWENTY-SIX
Just Put Me Out of My Misery

Mum always used to tell me that love is something uncontrollable. You cannot control the feelings that are either telling you to let someone in or keep them out because, in the end, you will always end up letting that person in—and that is something you cannot prevent.

Mum also used to say that you might think falling seems like a good thing, but no matter how much you try to keep things perfect, there will always be difficult times—moments that can either break or strengthen a relationship.

In my situation, I don't know if this will cause Luke and me to fall—because the whole thing was unexpected. I never planned on confessing my love for him the way I just did. But to be honest, I didn't even know how to tell Luke how I feel about him. And even if I had an idea, I knew it would not go as planned, because—let's be realistic here—nothing ever goes exactly as planned, even when you really want it to. Unless you're really, really lucky, of course.

Anyway, so when those three words slipped out of my mouth, I did not know what to do. I still do not know what to do, and I guess that is why I am standing in front of Luke—with my eyes still wide and my heart beating rapidly.

"Uh . . . ," I say quietly, nervousness clear in my tone as I slowly step back. My hands begin to sweat, and my legs begin to shake. When I bump into the wall, I cannot do anything but slide down to the floor, my body going weak.

Luke stares at me as if he is still trying to take everything in, but despite the little strength I have left, I still cannot find the words to explain my confession, so I just look down at my feet.

"Gracie," Luke says, stepping forward.

I hold up my hand, stopping him from coming any closer as the tears begin to form.

No, stay strong, Grace. You can't do this to yourself.

I look up, the first tear falling. "I-I . . ." I stop and tug at my hair in frustration, trying to say something that will not embarrass me further. I mean, I have already embarrassed myself by telling him that *I love him*, even though he probably does not even love me back.

God, I am so freaking stupid!

"Grace, I—"

"Don't say anything . . . please," I mumble, slowly standing up and leaning against the wall. His eyes begin to show worry as he watches the tears fall, one after another.

I walk towards the door and hold my breath, trying to calm myself down. I grip the door handle with my shaky hand and rest my forehead against the door, breathing out a long sigh.

I feel a hand on my shoulder, and before I can turn around to tell Luke to step away from me, he chooses to speak.

"Gracie, listen to me, okay? Just listen," he says calmly.

I slowly turn around to face him.

"I know this might not be what you're expecting me to say . . . ," he starts.

I gulp.

"And I know this might hurt you a little bit, but listen. In books and even in movies, when one person confesses their love, the other person usually reciprocates by saying the same thing, and they both live happily ever after—end of story. But this isn't a book or a movie, Gracie."

I feel my heart snap at his words.

Wow, talk about letting me down gently.

"Just put me out of my misery," I whisper.

He looks down at me with a small frown. "Wait, I'm not finished."

I close my eyes, breathing sharply before releasing it.

"What I am trying to say is that people like us . . . we don't, uh, have that complete assurance of a happy ending because our lives aren't controlled by someone—unlike the characters in books. We are human beings, and Gracie, we might be two different people in two completely different worlds inside our heads, but with a little hope, we can at least try to make this work . . . Wait, did that make sense?" Luke says.

My eyes snap open in confusion.

"Huh?" I ask, and he smiles, resting his hand on my cheek.

"It's going to be tough, and we both need to work together to have our own happy ending. I am madly in love with you. What I'm trying to say is . . . I am madly in love with your beautiful smile, your dark purple hair, your captivating green eyes—everything. I am in love with you, Gracie, and you only," he says.

His words shock me.

"Huh?" I say again.

He lets out a chuckle. He runs a hand through my hair and kisses my nose.

"I. Love. You," he says slowly.

My eyes widen in disbelief. He just told me we don't have the same opportunity as characters in books or movies, and now he's telling me that he loves me?

Can he be any more confusing?

Before I can say huh again, Luke presses his lips to mine, and I cannot help but kiss him back. As our feelings pour into the kiss, I finally understand what he was saying just a minute ago.

I'm a romantic when it comes to these sorts of things. So when he said, "This might hurt you a little," he did not mean physically—he meant mentally, since his way of telling me he loves me is completely different from what I had in mind.

Luke breaks the kiss and smiles at me, grabbing my hand and pulling me to the couch. When I let out a yawn, he chuckles and sits down, patting his lap.

"Tired?"

I nod, sitting on his lap with my legs on either side of him. I wrap my arms around his neck, resting my head in the crook of his shoulder, while he wraps his arms around my waist.

"Just to let you know, I wasn't joking when I said, 'I love you.'"

"I know," I say with a smile.

He rubs my back, and I close my eyes at the feeling. I cannot help but let my mind wander as I relax against him.

When I woke up this morning, I was worried about the plan. When I got to school, I was scared Amy would find out. But when Luke and I came here because I was stressed, I never imagined the day would turn out like this—me blurting out my love for him and him telling me he loves me too.

I guess anything can happen when you're not expecting it, and I never thought I would be saying this, but I think everything is finally falling into place.

I just hope it stays like this for as long as possible.

But first, I need Amy out of the picture before my life begins to fall apart—again.

CHAPTER TWENTY-SEVEN
I Didn't Do That!

"Oh, look at that," a familiar voice says with a chuckle.

But I don't move from my spot on Luke's lap. Instead, I continue to lie against his chest, my head resting in the crook of his neck.

At the sound of footsteps approaching, I cannot help but let out a sigh, knowing I have to open my eyes to see what this person wants.

A hand taps my shoulder, and I slowly open my eyes, turning to see—Bree!

I squeal in fright and completely jump off Luke, falling to the ground with a thud. I groan loudly.

"What the hell?" Luke groans.

I get up slowly, rubbing my head in pain as Bree laughs in amusement. I sit next to Luke on the couch, resting my head on his shoulder and running my hands down my face.

"Did you really have to do that?" I ask her.

She chuckles and nods, setting her black handbag on the coffee table.

We both stare at her in confusion and annoyance as she wipes away the tears in the corners of her eyes. When she's done laughing, she crosses her arms over her chest and raises an eyebrow at us. "Why aren't you two at school yet?"

I look over at Luke and see him frown at his mum. "Because we were sleeping until you woke us both up."

Bree shakes her head, a small grin on her face. "Technically, your girlfriend woke you up."

Luke sends a playful glare at his mum. "Don't blame this on her, okay? Listen, we're both tired, so can we have five more minutes of sleep?"

His mum rolls her eyes and shakes her head again. "No, because you're already going to be late."

Luke and I both groan in annoyance.

"Please?" Luke begs.

His mum continues to shake her head.

He sighs heavily and runs a hand down his face. "I said please, though," he mutters under his breath.

Bree grabs her handbag and points at the front door. "I don't remember saying, 'Go back to sleep,' so hurry up and get to school before you both get in trouble for being late," she demands in a serious tone, then makes her way to the kitchen.

I stand up and sigh. "Come on. We have to call Eddie about today anyway," I say, remembering that we still have to start the important part of the plan today.

Luke sighs before standing up. "Fine."

*   *   *

"All you have to do is make your way down the hallway when you hear the first bell ring, okay?" Luke says to Eddie.

"Yep, got it." Eddie nods, pulling the cigarette away from his lips and dropping it on the ground.

Luke turns around and walks towards me. He sends me a smile which immediately makes my stomach flip and my heart flutter—I still have not gotten used to it yet. I don't think I ever will, actually, but who says that's a bad thing?

"You okay?" he asks.

I nod, grabbing his hand as we begin to walk into school.

He stops at my locker, and I suck in a deep breath to try and calm down as thoughts start to race through my head.

As we begin to talk and try to act like we aren't up to anything suspicious, I notice Amy walking down the hallway, her eyes scanning the area like she is searching for something.

Maybe even someone.

Oh God, please do not let it be me.

Before I can say a word to Luke about Amy—who seems slightly confused and angry—she suddenly shoves him to the ground.

I gasp when Luke groans as he hits the floor. I look over at Amy and see her narrowing her eyes at me, making me feel a little scared for my life.

She knows . . .

She knows about the whole plan . . .

I'm definitely screwed now!

"Explain," Amy growls, holding up her phone and practically shoving it in my face.

I move back against the locker to see the phone a little more clearly.

I look at the screen, a little confused. "Uh, someone is calling you," I say.

She groans and quickly taps something on her phone before shoving it back in my face.

I look at the photo on the screen, and my eyes widen in horror. It's a Facebook post of her naked photo with the caption that says *Slut*. No wonder she's extremely pissed at me—the person who posted the photo was *me*. Or at least that's what it says on the screen.

I did not do that!

"Amy—" Before I can continue, she shoves her phone back in her pocket and wraps her hand around my neck, choking me.

I gasp for air in desperation.

"Can't . . . breathe . . ." I mutter, my head beginning to spin.

Amy raises an eyebrow at me as she presses harder against my throat.

"Oh, really?" she asks, but I cannot say anything as I feel my body weaken with every second that passes.

All of a sudden, Luke pulls her away from me and pushes her against the lockers as I fall to the ground, letting air finally fill my lungs.

"Don't you dare lay a hand on Grace again!" Luke growls in anger, but I can't seem to focus since my head is still spinning and my vision is growing blurry.

All of a sudden, my body goes numb almost instantly—then I pass out.

CHAPTER TWENTY-EIGHT
Your Mum Would Be So Proud of You Right Now

I rub my head and open my eyes, taking in my surroundings. I notice Luke anxiously looking around the room while Mandy, the school nurse, writes a few things down on her notepad.

When I look at Luke, I see the fear in his eyes. The eyes that always held so much happiness are now clouded with sadness and fright, and I can't help but feel guilty for causing him to feel this way.

His hands rest on his knees as his legs bounce against the marble floor, his gaze fixed on the ground. I clear my throat, prompting both him and Mandy to look up at me in surprise.

"Oh my God, you're awake!" Luke says, jumping from his seat and wrapping me in a hug.

I smile and hug him back, savoring the feeling of his closeness.

He pulls away after a few seconds and sits next to me on the uncomfortable bed.

"How are you feeling?" he asks.

Before I can answer, Mandy chuckles and walks over to me, a clipboard in hand.

"I should be the one asking her that," she says, smiling at him.

Luke playfully rolls his eyes. He grabs my hand, making me smile slightly.

Mandy turns her attention to me and lifts my chin slightly before stepping back to look me over.

"How are you feeling, Grace?" she asks.

I shrug. "I'm okay, I guess. Like every other time," I say with a chuckle.

She shakes her head, the smile still on her lips. "You always seem to end up here. I want to know why."

I shrug again, looking down at my hand, which is holding Luke's. "I don't know. My life honestly sucks."

She sighs and sits in the chair in front of me. Clicking her pen, she bites her lip in thought. I have a feeling I know what she's about to say.

"Everything okay at home?" she asks.

I let out a sigh, knowing I cannot keep lying to her. I think of her as a second mother anyway, so what is the point of lying if I trust her?

"No," I say firmly before continuing. "I just want to leave this place, go hide away for the rest of my life, finally have some peace, and stay away from the danger that keeps following me around like a lost puppy."

She frowns and looks over at Luke, sending him a sad smile.

"Can Grace and I be alone for a minute?"

Luke nods, letting go of my hand. He quickly pecks my lips before leaving, and when the door closes, Mandy lets out a sigh.

"Grace, do you know why I chose to be a nurse?"

I shake my head, placing my hands on my thighs as I look at her, sitting with her right leg crossed over the other.

"The reason I chose to be a nurse is because, when I was younger, my parents fought a lot. They were very physical with each other, throwing whatever they had in their hands. Somebody had to tend to their bruises and cuts," she begins.

I frown, not liking this side of her.

She is always bright and happy, but now . . . it's like her walls are down, and she is showing me the real her—the one who has been through so much, yet no one ever noticed.

"You see, Grace, my parents weren't always civil. Moments when they lay on the couch, cuddled up next to each other while watching *Wheel of Fortune,* were very rare. And I liked those rare moments. The other moments—the bad ones—still haunt my mind to this day," Mandy says, tears forming in her eyes.

I bite my lip as I feel my heart clench at her story.

"The memory of my parents dying is the most painful one in here." She points to her head, a tear slipping from her eye as she smiles weakly.

"Do you want to know how my parents died, Grace?" she asks.

I find myself unable to speak.

"A car crash killed them. They were both angry at each other, and when they went out to get away, their cars ended up crashing into each other a few hours later," Mandy says, more tears rushing down her cheeks.

"I . . . I'm sorry, Mandy. I didn't know you . . . went through all of that."

She shakes her head, wiping away her tears with her free hand. "It's not your fault, Grace. Not even mine. I guess what I'm trying to say is that everyone lives with bad memories, and even though you want to escape yours by running, you must know that it doesn't always work."

She stands and walks over to me, pulling up her sleeves to reveal scars that make me wince.

She pulls her sleeves down and sends me a small smile. "Life's hard, Grace, but do you know why I'm still here, doing what I do now?"

Once again, I cannot answer her, so she continues.

"It's because I like to help people. I don't like to see people in pain because that tears me apart in so many ways. You see, people like me have stories too, and they might be mind-scarring, but like I said before, everyone has their own stories—good or bad. We still have them."

She walks back to her seat and sits down, letting out a sigh.

"I guess I'm telling you this because I know you're strong. You've been through so much over the years, and every time you come in here, you seem to block out your true emotions because you're afraid to say what's real."

I nod slowly.

She grabs her clipboard and clicks her pen, the small smile still on her lips.

"So, what I want you to learn is to never give up, no matter how hard things may seem right now—because eventually, the problems will fade, and you'll be able to say, 'I'm fine,' without lying to anyone. You'll actually mean it. You won't be afraid to scream it out."

Mandy's words settle in, and I smile, nodding again. I jump off the bed and pull her into a hug, taking her by surprise.

"Thank you, Mandy. Thank you so much."

She chuckles, hugging me back. "No problem, Grace. Just know that I'm always here for you, okay?" she says, pulling away.

Before I leave, Mandy grabs my arm, stopping me.

"Your mum would be so proud of you right now, you know?"

Suddenly, I feel a tug in my heart. The "your mum" circles in my head.

I smile and nod. "I know." I turn and leave the room.

Luke looks up at me and frowns. "Everything okay in there?"

I nod, taking his hand in mine. "Yep. Now, please tell me the plan still worked, because that would honestly make my day."

He scratches the back of his neck awkwardly. "Uh, not exactly."

CHAPTER TWENTY-NINE
What Do We Do Now?

I look up at Luke, a small frown forming on my lips as his words register.

"What do you mean, 'not exactly'?"

He sighs and tugs on my hand, clearly wanting to take me somewhere more private—people are still roaming the halls, obviously skipping class.

What happened to the plan while I blacked out? Does this mean I have to tell Eve about Amy now? Oh dear Lord, I will not be able to do that.

"Okay," Luke says, pulling me out of my thoughts.

I look around and realize we are now sitting in his car.

Wow, that was quick.

"When you passed out, the bell rang, and just as planned, Eddie walked in. But before Amy could see him, the principal dragged her to his office."

I groan, running a hand down my face. I knew something would go wrong.

"Well, where's Eddie now?" I ask.

Luke runs a hand through his hair, a sigh escaping his lips.

"He said that he has to go to Germany immediately because the people who are coming after his father have already gotten him."

My eyes widen in shock.

"What?"

"I know. I tried to get him to stay until he finds Amy, but he wouldn't have it. He is probably on the plane to Germany right now."

I let out a sigh. "What do we do now?"

Luke shrugs. "The only option we have is to go talk to Eve."

I shake my head, my hands covering my face. "I don't want to do that."

"You have to. It's the only way."

I lean into the chair, dropping my hands onto my lap as I close my eyes.

Luke runs his hand up and down my shoulder, trying to calm me.

"When do you want to do it?" he asks.

I let out a sigh and open my eyes, looking out the window at the school. I lick my lips and swallow the lump in my throat.

"Now."

He frowns. "Wait, what?"

I turn to him and send him a reassuring smile. "If I want Amy gone, this is the only way, like you said."

Before Luke can say anything, I buckle my seat belt and lean back in my seat.

"Let's do this."

*   *   *

The car stops in front of my house, and I let out a sigh as I unbuckle my seat belt. I open the car door and breathe in the cool air.

I look up at the house and chew on my bottom lip. I make my way to the pathway leading to the stairs. I notice that Eve's car is in the driveway, but my father's truck is not. I look back at Luke to see him leaning against his car, watching me. As we drove here, I told him to stay in the car, but now . . . but now, I don't even know if I will be able to do this without him.

Shut up, Grace. Stop changing your decisions and stick with the plan, my brain pushes, and I nod.

I cannot back out now.

I breathe in sharply, raise my hand into a fist, and knock loud enough for Eve to hear me. I would open the door myself, but I don't have my key.

A few seconds pass before the sound of footsteps approaching, and I breathe out a shaky sigh as the front door swings open, revealing a tired Eve.

"Grace? Why aren't you at school?" she asks, furrowing her eyebrows. She looks at Luke in the car and frowns, then looks back at me.

I let out a sigh and run my hands through my hair. "I need to talk to you."

Eve nods, stepping out of the way so I can walk in. I head towards the kitchen and sit in my usual chair, looking at her as she takes Mum's seat.

I push away thoughts of Mum. I cannot get distracted. I have to tell Eve about her daughter, Amy.

"I should've told you sooner," I begin.

Eve watches me carefully, trying to find any hint of emotion on my face.

I stare at her freshly painted nails, which are a bright red.

"The day you introduced me to Amy . . . I said that everything was fine between us, but it wasn't, and it still isn't. When Amy said that she bumped into me, she didn't exactly mean that," I say.

Eve narrows her eyes at me. "Go on."

I bite my lip, playing with my fingers as my heart begins to race. Amy's words ring in my head, as if my body is telling me not to continue.

"Tell her one thing about today, and you'll be sorry."

I gulp, shaking away the negative thoughts. I look up at Eve, hoping she will believe me.

"Amy and I fought. Like, actually fought. She told me not to tell you, or I'd be sorry. I didn't want to tell you because I don't even know what Amy is capable of. I guess that's why I haven't been myself around her—because she scares me," I say quickly.

Her eyes widen.

Before she can say anything, someone claps from the kitchen door, and we both look up to see Amy smirking.

"You actually did it!"

*　　*　　*

"When you arrived, I told you not to start any trouble with Grace because she's had a tough life, but what did you do? You pull this on me!" Eve shouts at Amy.

I gulp, not liking the tone Eve is using. It has been two hours since I told Eve everything, and now she's been yelling at Amy. I'm a little surprised the neighbors have not come over yet to complain.

"I warned you not to start any trouble. But what did you do? You started a fight on your first day at that school. Did you just suddenly decide to bring hell to everyone's lives? But for what reason? I honestly can't handle your attitude anymore!" Eve screams even louder.

Suddenly, I feel someone wrap an arm around my waist, pulling me closer. I look over my shoulder to see Luke frowning at me.

"Don't worry about them. Everything will fall into place, and Amy will go back to Germany," Luke assures me.

I let out a sigh, leaning against his chest. "How do you know that?" Fear, curiosity, and panic are evident in my tone.

He runs his hand through my purple hair, making me feel a little calmer. "I talked to Eve before heading up here and explained how you felt about Amy staying here."

I turn around and frown at him. "Why?"

"Because I don't like seeing you so stressed."

I cannot help but smile at him. I grab his hand and press it against mine, finding it somewhat funny how my hand is so much smaller than his.

"I'm so lucky to have you," he tells me.

I cannot help but blush at his words. I look up at him and stare into his blue eyes.

Before I know it, he presses his lips to mine, and I smile against his lips, closing my eyes and savoring the kiss.

The yelling from downstairs seems to grow quieter as I find myself lost in the kiss. All that matters to me right now is capturing this moment, storing it in my mind as if I'm afraid Luke and I will not be together tomorrow. But I know that will not happen. I may not be lucky, but the world can't really be that cruel. I know the universe wants me to be somewhat happy, and I should not lose the person who means so much to me.

Luke Peterson.

But what if the world hates me and wants me to be miserable? Then it can try its hardest to tear Luke and me apart, but I'm not letting go of Luke without a fair fight.

And that is a promise.

CHAPTER THIRTY
He Would See Me Again

I rub my eyes and let out a sigh, stretching my legs. The sound of my bones cracking makes me shiver in disgust as I pull my legs closer to my body. I snuggle closer to Luke's body, and he groans.

"What's the time?" he asks quietly.

I shrug, allowing him to pull me closer.

"I don't know. Just sleep," I mumble, pushing my hair away from my face.

He lets out a sigh.

I open my eyes to see him staring at me, taking me by surprise. I let out a laugh before untangling myself from his arms wrapped around me.

I get out of bed and walk over to my window, pulling the blinds aside to let the sunlight in. He groans, and I roll my eyes before walking to my phone to check the time.

"It's nine o'clock, Luke."

He throws a pillow over his head, groaning again. "Goddamn," he says between his groans.

I pick up a pillow from my bed and throw it at him. "Shut up, will you?"

Before he can reply with another groan, his phone goes off.

"Who is it?" he asks.

I walk over and look at the name on the screen.

Daniel.

The memory of checking Luke's phone makes me nervous. I look at the message, and when I finish reading it, I feel a sudden wave of relief.

If you have no plans, come over to my house so we can talk about the money. Bring Grace, too.

"It's Daniel," I tell him, and throw his phone on the bed.

He grabs it and looks at the message before letting out a sigh, ripping the sheets off him to reveal his half-naked body.

I bite my lip and look away, feeling my cheeks heat up.

He chuckles, his arms wrapping around my waist as his body presses against my back.

"Calm down, you just slept in the same bed with me."

"I-I know."

He kisses my head and lets go of me to grab his clothes from the floor. When he finishes putting on his clothes, he pecks my lips and heads towards my bedroom door.

"I'll be back in an hour, okay? So be ready by then."

I nod. As soon as he leaves, I head to the bathroom for a nice warm shower to wake me up.

I wonder what happened to Amy last night.

*   *   *

I gulp and pinch my arm, looking into the mirror at the girl who seems a little happier than she has been over the past two months.

Since Luke always says he likes to see my face without my hair covering parts of my forehead, I decide to clip the strands back. The small freckles along the bridge of my nose stand out, giving me a somewhat innocent look.

I decide to leave my piercings out today, but make a mental note to put them back in later so the holes won't close up. My bright green eyes, which I inherited from Dad, pop out nicely, but I can't help but think of him as I look into my own reflection.

It really sucks to have the same eyes as the man who does not truly care about me at all. I mean, he has shown that he cares sometimes, but if he completely cared the way Mum did, would he have waited before bringing Eve home? Would he have thought about my feelings in all of this if he cared?

Obviously not.

I shake the thoughts from my head and look myself over, actually liking the outfit I've picked today. I'm not usually the type of person who carefully selects outfits that go well together, but ever since I've been with Luke, my outlook on life has changed.

I'm wearing white ripped skinny jeans that make my legs look a bit nicer—shape-wise—and a black sweater that covers the shirt underneath, which says Totally in white. I finish the look with purple Vans to match my hair.

At the sound of beeping outside, I grab my phone and walk to the window to see Luke waiting for me. I leave my room and walk down the stairs.

But before I walk out the door, a small, dark red suitcase resting against the wall catches my eye. My mind wanders—does it belong to Amy?

Is she leaving? Where is she? Actually, where is everyone? It's Saturday, so my father should be home with Eve.

Maybe they're all at the mall shopping.

Oh well . . . I'll figure it out later.

I walk out the door with my phone clutched tightly in my hand as I quickly make my way towards Luke's car. When I enter, his eyes widen at me. I blush and turn away.

"I had a feeling I'd get that reaction from you," I mumble.

He holds my face, and I look at him . His smile makes my heart race in an instant.

Why do you do this to me, Luke?

"It isn't a bad reaction, Gracie. You are absolutely—" he takes one more look at me and grins "—breathtaking."

I smile at him. "Thanks." My cheeks heat up even more.

He presses his lips to mine gently, then pulls away after a few seconds and starts the car.

"Now, let's just hope my friends don't start gawking at what's rightfully mine."

*　　　*　　　*

After a few minutes of driving to Luke's friends' place, I start feeling a little nervous. It is probably because we just turned into a dark, eerie area that looks like something out of a horror movie—or maybe it is because I am afraid to meet Luke's friends.

What are his friends like? I have not seen them around school, so they must be older—or maybe they just do not attend classes or go to the cafeteria for lunch? Who knows? All I want to do is walk in and get out as fast as possible, because this area is literally sending chills up my spine.

The car stops, and I look at the house in front of us. It is small, yes, but the exterior looks somewhat decent, with a black gate in front. The front lawn is spotless, unlike all the other yards that are disgustingly dirty.

I turn to Luke to see him staring at me, as if waiting for my approval to get out. I give him a nod, and he nods back before getting out of the car. I let out a sigh and do the same, closing the door behind me. He walks over and gives me a reassuring smile.

"Just remember . . . I'll do all the talking," he says.

I nod, feeling a little calmer.

He grabs my hand, leading me up to the house. He runs a hand through his hair before knocking loudly on the door.

"Go and get the door!" someone shouts from inside. Another person groans, and a few seconds later, the door swings open.

All of a sudden, my blood goes cold, and the memories begin to flood back into my mind, making my eyes widen in horror.

Oh no.

"Hey, buddy," the familiar person says, making my legs shake as his voice rings in my head. The guy looks over at me, and his eyes widen slowly in realisation, but he quickly shakes his head to calm himself down.

Luke pulls my hand and frowns at me when he sees that I am not moving. "Gracie, you okay?"

Luke's words register in my head, but I don't say anything yet—I'm too focused on the guy standing in front of me.

I gulp and shake my head slowly, pinching my hand.

"I-I'm okay," I say, following behind him.

Luke begins to walk into the house.

As I pass the guy, he stares into my green eyes, and I stare into his grey eyes.

"I will see you again," Randy says with a small smirk before walking away from me, leaving me confused but disgusted.

He was right.

He would see me again.

CHAPTER THIRTY-ONE
I Can't Tell Him

I look at the four boys who are sitting on the couch, staring at Luke and me as we take a seat on the couch opposite them. I cannot help but look over at Randy to see him looking anywhere but at me.

I cannot believe he is freaking here!

I shake my head slowly and look at the other three boys. The one next to Randy has black hair that covers one of his eyes, and on his cheek is a deep scar that runs from the bottom of his eye to his jaw. Luke introduced me to him before we sat down, and I think his name is Jackson.

The guy next to Jackson is Daniel, the one who keeps messaging Luke about the payment. He has brown hair and bright blue eyes, and from what I can see, he has a necklace with a turtle on it. Actually, I think I've seen him at school before, during the assembly. The teacher had him sit next to me, and from what I can remember, he got caught trying to give me drugs, and that was the last day I ever saw him.

The last guy, who is sitting on the edge of the couch, is James. He has bright blond hair and hazel eyes, which seem to be staring deeply into mine.

Weird.

Before we all sat down, I had to ask how Luke knew all of these people. I mean, it must have been a coincidence that he is friends with the guy who assaulted me years ago. So, when I asked him, he had basically explained that he and Daniel had known each other a few years ago.

Daniel was known for throwing parties, and when Luke befriended him, he basically became friends with the other three. But according to Luke, he was never that close with James. He always wanted to drag Luke into his drug-dealing business, offering him tons of money. But Luke always said no.

"So . . . the money," Luke begins, and all eyes turn to him, burning into his blue eyes.

Daniel nods slowly and leans into the couch, a small grin on his face.

"Yes, Luke, you will get the money, but . . . I want something from Grace first."

Before I can even react, Luke jumps up in anger and shock.

"What the hell? You said that if I brought her here with me, I would get the money!" Luke shouts in rage.

I grab his hand and pull him back down on the couch.

"Yes, I did, but if you really want the money, you will give me what I want," Daniel says.

I feel my heart race when his eyes connect with mine.

"Can I have a conversation with you?" he asks, and my eyes go wide.

Luke's grip on my hand tightens, but I try not to show any pain as I look at the four boys.

"I-I . . ." I look over to Luke to see his jaw clenching in anger. I rub my thumb over his hand to try to calm him down, but he only frowns at me.

"We can just go," I say to him with a glare. "But Luke, you need the money for your dad, so just calm down. I'll just see what Daniel has to say, then he will give you the money, and we will go," I say.

He looks at Daniel before looking back at me.

"Are you sure?" he asks slowly.

I nod, a small smile appearing on my lips. He squeezes my hand and sighs before turning back to the four boys.

"Five minutes," Luke says.

Daniel nods, standing up from the couch. He tilts his head towards the kitchen, and I stand up, walking over to him.

When I enter the kitchen, Daniel closes the door behind him and leans against the counters, his elbows resting behind him.

I stand in front of him, leaning against the row of counters behind me, crossing my arms over my chest.

"What do you want?" I ask.

He points back into the room. "You and Randy need to sort your shit out. You see, my brother hasn't been himself ever since everything went down with you and him, which is why I told Luke to go for you. Yes, Luke will get the money for his father, but the reason I wanted you to come here is to have a talk with my brother and get him back to his old self. Do you think you can do that?"

I gulp.

The images of Randy touching me appear in my mind. My hands begin to shake, and I look around the room before looking back at Daniel.

"I-it's not that simple," I say.

Daniel nods, pulls a cigarette from his pocket, and holds it between his fingers.

"I know, but you just need to push everything away for a few minutes. I know it will be awkward, but I promise you, his fucked-up days are behind him. He can't sleep at night, he doesn't go outside, and he hardly eats because of what happened between you and him. He feels so guilty, and he just wants to apologize. I need you to let him, Grace."

I gulp, squeezing my hands together. I glance back at the door that leads to the living room and bite my lip.

"O-okay," I mumble, looking back at him, and he smiles.

"Good girl."

My jaw clenches at the sudden memory that appears in my mind.

"Stop trying to resist me. Just . . . there you go," Randy says, his hands going from my rib cage down to my jeans.

"Good girl."

I shake my head slowly and watch as Daniel goes into the living room to get Randy. I breathe in through my nose and out through my mouth, trying to calm myself down, but it does not work. I pinch my arm, holding in the tears that want to fall.

Be strong, Grace. You can do this, my brain says, and I nod slowly, looking down at my shoes.

The kitchen door swings open, and my breathing becomes heavy as I look over my shoulder to see Randy walk in with his head down. Daniel follows and closes the door behind him, walking back over to his original spot.

"Okay, let's begin, shall we?" he says, lighting his cigarette with an orange lighter.

I gulp and look over at Randy. He is standing behind his brother, his head still down.

"Grace . . . ," Randy begins.

His voice immediately sends chills down my spine.

I push the thoughts away and focus on him as he looks up at me, his grey eyes staring into my green ones.

"I'm so sorry. For everything. I know I can't take back those days that probably have been haunting you for a while, but it's killing me too. I ruined our friendship, and I ruined you," he says, his lips quivering as he continues to talk.

"I-I . . . I heard about your mum," he says, taking me by surprise. He takes a step closer to me, and I freeze up. He lets out a sigh and scratches the back of his neck.

"Please?" he asks.

I stay silent. I don't know why he is saying please, but I have a feeling that he wants something from me.

He takes another step forward, but this time, I don't move, and I don't tell him to stay away. He takes this as an opportunity to continue to walk towards me, and when he is directly in front of me, he engulfs me in a gentle hug.

"I'm sorry, Grace."

I nod slowly, deciding whether or not to hug him back. I look at Daniel, and he nods slowly. I breathe in sharply before wrapping my arms around the person who has caused me so much pain.

"Y-you know I can't just forgive you," I say quietly to Randy.

He nods and pulls away from me, staring into my green eyes.

"I know. I just want to say my apologies. I don't want you to forgive me because I've done so much to you, and I can't go back and change that, so don't worry," he says with a small frown.

I nod. I look at Daniel and see him grinning at his brother.

"That wasn't so hard, was it?" he asks, ruffling Randy's hair.

Randy shoves his hands away. "Shut up," he mutters.

I look between the two of them, and I cannot help but smile a little. Daniel really does care for his brother. Hopefully, I've done what needs to be done for Daniel and for Luke.

"Can we head back in?" I ask, and Daniel nods. I turn around, and when I walk through the door, Luke jumps up and grabs my hand, pulling me behind him.

"You okay?" he asks, watching as Randy and Daniel walk out of the kitchen a few seconds later.

I nod and pull him over to the couch, my hand still holding on to his.

Jackson hands a stack of cash to Daniel, who walks over to us and hands the money to Luke.

"Thank you," Luke says.

Daniel nods. "All good. Now, you can get out of this shithole and go back to making babies or whatever it is you two do."

My face goes red almost immediately. Luke rolls his eyes as we head to the door and towards his car.

When we get in the car, he looks over at me with a small frown. "What did Daniel want you for?"

I bite the inside of my cheek.

Does Luke know that Randy is the person who touched me three years ago?

Suddenly, the images of what he would do if I told him rush through my mind, and I shake my head.

I cannot tell him. At least not now anyway.

"Nothing important."

He nods slowly, his eyes still on me as if he knows that there is more to the two words that just came out of my mouth.

"Okay," he says before starting the car.

As I look out the window, I cannot help but finally feel somewhat calmer as Randy's words ring in my head.

"I'm sorry, Grace."

I lean into my seat and let out a sigh. After everything that I have been through, who knew that those three words would make me feel more at ease?

Now, I just have to deal with Amy, and hopefully, it won't be as difficult as I think it will be.

CHAPTER THIRTY-TWO
You Think I Did It?

The car stops in front of my house, and I let out a sigh when I notice that Dad's car is parked in the driveway, but Eve's car is not.

I unbuckle my seatbelt and run my hands down my thighs, back and forth, as my thoughts begin to circle in my head.

"Are you okay?" Luke asks.

I turn to him and shrug. "I don't know anymore," I mumble.

Luke frowns at me, grabbing my hand and holding it in his. "Do you want to come to mine?" he asks.

I shake my head. "I'll be fine."

He gives me a stern look and lifts my chin with his other hand.

I look into his blue eyes and watch as a small frown appears on his face.

"Smile, Grace," he demands.

I roll my eyes. "Not this again—"

"Smile," he repeats.

I let out a sigh and do as I am told.

He nods and places a gentle kiss on my lips, letting it linger for a few seconds before pulling away.

"Text me if you need to get out of the house, okay?" he says.

I nod, opening the car door and getting out.

As I walk up to the house, Luke lets out a loud whistle, making my cheeks heat up. I quickly run up to the door and turn around to send him a wave. He smiles before driving away. I grab my key out of my pocket and push it into the knob.

I push the door open, and the small smile slips from my face as my mouth falls open in shock. The living room is completely destroyed, broken glass scattered everywhere.

My eyes widen at the scene. Dad lies on the floor, eyes shut, a bottle of beer clutched in his hand.

I run to him and fall to my knees, grabbing his arm and checking his pulse. My heart stops when I don't feel anything. I touch his neck, hoping to feel something. When I don't, I jump up and pull my phone from my pocket, dialing triple zero.

As I give the lady all the details, I check on Dad—he's still not moving. The lady tells me that the ambulance is on its way, and I quickly hang up to call Eve.

After dialing her number three times with no answer, I gulp and glance around the living room. A million questions flood my mind.

What happened?

*   *   *

Usually, I wouldn't care about Dad or whatever mess he has gotten himself into. I would push him away and not give a single damn, but now, it's like my feelings for him have changed.

I mean, he has done some stupid and hurtful things to me and Mum, but he is still my father. He is a part of me, and I cannot help but feel bad for not caring. It has only been two months since I lost Mum, and if I lose Dad, I do not know where I will end up.

I'm the type of person to forgive and forget, but with the things that Dad has done in the past, it is sort of hard. I try to keep my anger towards him, I really do, but it's like the hatred is slowly crumbling away as I realise that he is the only parent I have left.

"Grace . . . ," someone say. I look up to see Eve frowning at me as I sit on the porch, staring at the two ambulance vans and the three cop cars in front of the house. I notice her hair is slightly messy, and her hands are shaking a little.

"Hey."

She takes a seat next to me, looking at the scene in front of her.

"What happened?"

I shrug, biting my nails. "I don't know. I thought you might know the answer to that," I say, looking over at her.

Her eyes widen in shock and disbelief. She points at herself and furrows her eyebrows.

"You think I did it?"

I shrug again. "Maybe."

She frowns at me, giving me a sad look. I look away from her and continue biting my nails as I watch the police officers.

"Grace, I didn't do it. I was at the airport the whole time. I didn't even know your dad was home when I left," she explains.

I look up at her, my eyebrow raised. "The airport?"

"I dropped Amy off. I told you I didn't want her starting trouble with you, but she did—so she's dealing with the consequences." She shrugs, and I nod slowly, hiding the happiness and relief bubbling inside.

After a few attempts to send Amy back to Germany, she is finally gone. I do not have to deal with her ever again. Thank goodness!

"Anyway, I didn't do it, Grace. As much as I hate what he has caused you and your mum, I would never put your dad in this situation, or *you* for that matter. You might despise your father, but inside, I know you care," she says.

I gulp when I notice a police officer coming and walking towards us.

The police officer crouches down in front of me and sends me a small smile.

"Hello, Grace," the officer says, and I nod slowly. He pulls out his notepad and clicks the pen in his hand.

"Are you ready to answer a few questions now?" the officer asks, and I nod. He takes a seat on the ground and looks at me, the smile slowly disappearing from his face. "What time did you walk inside and see your dad on the floor?"

I bite my lip thoughtfully. "Around four. I cannot remember the exact time."

He nods, writing the information down on the notepad. "Has your father ever acted out of control and ended up throwing things?"

"No."

"Is your father abusive?"

"No."

"Who do you think did this?" the officer asks.

I look down at the ground in thought. I mean, I did think that Eve had something to do with it, but her alibi sounds convincing, and the suitcases I saw before I left the house make sense with what she said. So, maybe it wasn't really her.

Who was it then?

"I-I . . . don't know," I mumble, looking away from the officer and down at the ground.

The officer holds my chin and gives me a small smile.

"Don't worry, Grace. We'll find out who did it." He smiles before looking over at Eve. He stands up straight, the smile is replaced with seriousness.

"Do you mind answering a few questions?" the officer asks, and Eve nods.

As he begins, I stand up and make my way inside the house, ignoring the detectives' protests.

I head upstairs to my room and find it has also been turned upside down. Letting out a sigh, I begin to pick up the pieces of glass from the floor and place them into the bin. Suddenly, my eyes land on a familiar photo frame. I walk over and pick it up, and my eyes begin to well with tears.

The frame is okay, but the glass that shields the photo is shattered. The photo of Mum is crumpled a little. I take it out of the frame and walk over to my table to try to smooth it out. I look at Mum's smile and blink a few times, fighting back tears as I attempt to fix the photo.

Suddenly, someone taps my shoulder. I turn around, swing my arm, and punch the person in the face. Instantly, the person falls to the ground, and I gasp when I see who it is.

"R-Randy!" I shriek, crouching down and holding his face in my hands. "I-I'm so sorry, Randy—"

He cuts me off, placing a finger on my lips to shut me up. I frown at him.

I'm so glad I did not hit him hard.

"I guess I deserved that," he says, sitting up.

I continue to stare at him with a frown. "What are you doing here?"

He points his thumb over his shoulder. "Your house is on the news, so I decided to make my way over here and see what was happening. Apparently your dad is going to the hospital."

I raise my eyebrow at him. "It's on the news?"

"Yep. Didn't you see the news van outside?"

I shake my head, and I stand up. I offer him a hand, but he refuses. Before we can say anything more, the same officer I just spoke to walks in. I quickly turn around and grab the photo of Mum, clutching it to my chest.

"Grace, we need you to come under protective custody until we get this place cleaned up. Are you okay with that?" the officer asks, and I nod. He looks between Randy and me before walking out of the room.

"Do you know who did this?" Randy asks.

I shake my head, walking out of my room. He follows me down the stairs and outside the house.

"Well, I hope you find out soon."

I nod and watch as he leaves. I frown in confusion as I look at his retreating figure.

Why do I have a feeling that he didn't just come here to see what was happening? What is Randy hiding?

"Come on, Grace. We have to go," Eve says, appearing by my side.

I nod slowly, and as we begin walking towards the cops' cars, my eyes widen at the sudden thought that appears in my mind.

What if it was Randy who did this?

CHAPTER THIRTY-THREE
I Like To Draw On My Arms

After going into protective custody and hanging out with the extremely nice police officer who kept me company the whole time, I decided to finally go and visit Dad after a sleepless night of thinking.

William, the police officer, asked me if I wanted a ride, but I refused his offer and told him that I would be getting a ride from a friend of mine. Well, the *friend* is my boyfriend, but he didn't need to know that.

Right now, I am sitting in the uncomfortable chairs they provide in each hospital room. I look over at Dad on the bed, not moving at all. His skin is pale. Then the monitor beeps, distracting me.

The door creaks open. I look over my shoulder to see Luke standing there with two cups in his hands. I stand up from my seat and walk over to him, taking the cup.

"Thanks," I mumble.

He sends me a small smile before making his way to the seats. I take my seat next to him and enjoy the warmth of the cup as it warms my cold hands.

"Grace," he calls quietly.

I turn to him, staring into his blue eyes in curiosity. "Yeah?"

"If I tell you something, will you promise not to be mad at me?"

I bite my lip. The last time I had promised him something, I broke it.

Can I keep this promise even if it is extremely bad?

I sip the coffee, looking away for a second. I turn back to him and nod slowly. "Okay."

He nods and places his cup on the small table beside him. He runs a hand through his hair, glancing over at my father before looking back at me.

"I had something to do with what happened to your dad and your house," he says a little too quickly, but I still catch every word.

And as soon as the words register in my head, my hands begin to shake. I place my cup on the table and fold my hands together to try to stop them from shaking.

"Wh-what do you mean?"

Luke lets out a heavy sigh, but before he can explain, his phone goes off. He pulls it out of his pocket, glances at it for a second, then stands up.

"I-I have to go," he says.

I stand up, my eyes starting to well up. "N-no, Luke, you have to tell me."

But he quickly walks over to the door. "I will . . . just not now. I'll text you later, okay?" he says and leaves.

I fall back into my seat as I try to control the thoughts running through my mind.

And my thoughts are instantly cut off when the monitor beeps uncontrollably. My eyes shoot over to Dad, and before I can do anything, doctors come rushing in, quickly ushering me out of the room. Shortly after, I see them pushing Dad's bed out of the room and into another room.

Suddenly, I feel the first tear fall from my eyes. The doctor looks down at me and clicks his fingers in front of my face to grab my attention. I look up at him to see the small smile on his face.

"Everything is going to be okay," the doctor says.

I look down the hallway. I cannot help but remember the day that Mum died.

That's exactly what you thought, but look at what happened, my brain reminds me. I sob, letting the rest of the tears fall.

I may hate Dad for everything he has done, but like I said before, he is my father, and if I lose him too . . . I'm going to be so broken. He is the only parent I have left, and even though he hardly acts like a dad towards me, it does not mean that I do not care at all.

Suddenly, the words that came out of Luke's mouth earlier ring in my head, and my hands begin to shake more.

"I had something to do with what happened to your dad and your house."

I really hope he is joking . . .

*   *   *

I walk into my house, my cheeks puffy and my eyes bloodshot from crying in the hospital. Eve walks in behind me, closes the door, and makes her way into the kitchen.

"Grace," she calls.

I stop in my tracks and turn around to look at her. She points into the kitchen, and I follow her as she begins to make her way into Mum's favourite room in the house.

Mum always loved to cook.

"Do you want something to eat?" she asks.

I take a seat at the table, pushing my dark purple hair away from my face, and shake my head when she raises her eyebrow at me.

"No, thank you," I mumble.

She sighs, walking over to the table and sitting at the opposite seat from mine. She crosses her arms over the table and sends me a small frown.

"You know we are going to get through this, right?"

I let out a sigh.

It has been two hours since Eve and I received the news that Dad had died from poisoning. I don't know what it was, but that was what the doctors told us—well, what they could only tell us, since that was basically everything they had found out in the short time they had left.

To be honest, after two hours of crying, it feels like my body is refusing to cry some more. Every time I want to release the pain in tears, it won't do it, and that makes me so angry.

"I know," I mumble, chewing on my bottom lip.

The silence hits us, and I find myself drawing small circles on the table with my index finger. Eve watches me, and a small smile appears on her face.

"Do you like to draw, Grace?" she asks.

I look up at her, my body freezing as her words sink into my head.

I like to draw on my arms . . .

"Not really," I say.

She nods slowly, standing up and walking out of the kitchen. I watch the kitchen door close and wait for her to come back.

If she comes back.

As I predicted, she comes back into the kitchen with a sketchbook in her hands. She walks over to me and places the sketchbook on the table.

When she opens it, I notice that the first drawing is of a man who I suspect is her dad. I look up at her in curiosity.

She smiles and points at the man. "This is my dad."

I nod, looking at the drawing. It looks like something from Pablo Picasso because it is just so good.

"You are really good at drawing," I say.

She continues to flip a few pages that have roses, portraits, and other things. She turns to a blank page and pulls out a pencil from her pocket.

"Let's see what you've got." Eve smiles, handing the pencil to me.

I grab it, holding it tightly in my hands. I bite my lip, thinking of something to draw, then it hits me.

I breathe out a sigh and begin to draw, trying to keep the image in my head. I know it's weird to draw this when Eve is here, but this is what I want back.

My parents.

CHAPTER THIRTY-FOUR
Did Luke Tell You Yet?

It is three o'clock in the morning, and for the past hour I have been staying up, waiting for a message to appear on my phone from a certain person. I have texted him a few times, but still no answer. He might be asleep, but it still hurts because he said he would message me later, but he has not.

I need an explanation.

Now.

I throw the sheets off my body and let out a sigh, slowly climbing out of bed. I know Eve is sleeping after a rough two hours of drinking three bottles of alcohol because of her boyfriend's death. Dad's death.

After Eve and I drew for an hour, the feelings began to kick in, and that was when she decided to consume all the alcohol in the house. She stayed up for two hours just sitting in the kitchen, staring at the wall, and I could not help but feel sorry for Eve.

I am not the type of person who feels sorry for others—most people do not like being pitied—but I could not help it. I took all the alcohol away from Eve and held her in my arms for about half an hour as she cried on my shoulder. It did not feel awkward when she held on to me like her life depended on it. She had listened to my loud sobbing before, so why should I not help her now?

I walk out of my room and down the hallway towards the spare room, which now belongs to her. She did not want to sleep in the same room she used to share with Dad—where Mum used to sleep too. She said it was not healthy for her to be in there, and I could not blame her.

I push the door open to see Eve snuggled into the sheets. I nod to myself, mentally patting myself on the back for successfully helping her. I close the door and make my way to the bathroom to clean myself up, because I am pretty sure I look worse than the Grudge and a drag queen put together.

I flick the light on and look at myself in the mirror. A small frown spreads across my face when I realise I was right.

Wow, the good things about being me.

I pat down my knotty purple hair and rub the sleep from my eyes, then wash my hands. I grab the towel, wet it with warm water, and press it to my face. Afterwards, I look at the piercings on the sink and sigh.

Mum always loved seeing me with my piercings on because it showed everyone I was different.

The only reason I hardly wear them anymore is because they remind me so much of Mum and the smile she wore when she saw me walk out of the shop with my piercings on.

I clench my jaw and grab the piercings, squeezing them tightly in my hand. I cannot keep myself out of this depressing state if everything in this damn house reminds me of my parents.

I throw them into the bin and look back into the mirror, trying to blink away the tears. I shake my head, shaking the thoughts away, and turn around to walk out of the bathroom and into my room.

The green light flashing on my phone makes my eyes widen in surprise, and I run to it, hoping that it is a message from Luke. I switch the screen on, and my face falls when I see that it is a message from an unknown number.

> *Hey Grace, it's Randy. I need you to come and meet me at the police station, ASAP . . . if you're awake. If you see this in the morning, come anyway. I'll probably be here all night.*

After reading the message twice, I get up and immediately run to my wardrobe to take off my pajamas.

This better be important.

*　　*　　*

I run into the police station, go inside, and look around the room. I notice Randy sitting on the bench with his head down, and I rush over to him, tapping his shoulder to catch his attention.

"Grace?" Randy says, a little surprised.

I flash him a smile. "Hey."

He pats the seat next to him, and the smile that was once on his face fades into a small frown.

"Did Luke tell you yet?"

I frown. "If it's about being involved in my dad's death, then yes," I reply wearily.

He sighs, nodding. "Did he explain it to you?"

I shake my head, watching as his frown deepens.

"That's why I am still awake. He told me he would message me, but he hasn't, and I need to know what he was talking about," I say.

He sighs again, running a hand through his hair.

"Don't tell Luke that I told you, but I'll explain everything to you."

"Thank you," I mumble.

Randy looks around before looking back at me.

"Okay, a few days before you came over, Luke explained to us about how he didn't like your dad for everything he did to you and your mum. He didn't make any threats towards your dad until James asked what he wanted us to do. Luke replied with 'I just want him in pain since he has caused Grace so much pain,' and that's when something coincidental happened."

I hold my hands together, stopping them from shaking.

This usually happens when I am either scared or nervous, but right now I think they are shaking with anger.

"Go on," I mumble.

"Your dad called a guy and asked if he could get a tattoo. That guy was James's boss. James offered to do the tattoo. Since your dad was drinking and couldn't drive, James went to your house instead. When he arrived, he did what he was told—he did the tattoo. But what no one knew was that he had mixed poison into the black ink. James then trashed the house and placed a beer bottle in your dad's hand to make it look like he had passed out from drinking, but that wasn't the case. The poison in the ink made him pass out—but of course, no one knew that except James," he explains.

No words escape my mouth as I continue to listen in disbelief.

"That is why Luke thinks that it was his fault that your dad is dead. But technically, it was James who did it. Luke never told James to poison your dad. Do not hate him, Grace. Luke just wanted your dad to go through the same pain that he put you and your mum through. He wanted to teach him a lesson. That's all."

I bite my lip. "How do you know this?"

Randy points behind him. "James is in there."

"Can I ask you a question, Randy?"

"Anything."

Nothing comes out of my mouth at first, but I find my voice after a few seconds. "Do you know what the tattoo was?"

"Yes, Grace, I know what the tattoo was."

I stare at him, waiting for him to speak.

"It was your name. On his ribs."

CHAPTER THIRTY-FIVE
I Want the Cotton Candy!

"Good morning, Eve," I say, placing a plate of bacon and eggs on the table. I grab the glass of water and two tablets and hand them to Eve, who holds her head in pain.

"Thank you," she mumbles as she takes the tablets.

I turn back to the stove, making sure that my food isn't burning. I scrape the eggs onto my own plate, pick up the bacon with the tongs, and set it on my plate too.

After placing the plate on the table, I walk back to grab my orange juice, take my seat opposite Eve, and begin to eat, even though I am not really hungry.

As we both eat our breakfast, I glance up at her to see her staring at something behind me. I raise an eyebrow at her and set my fork on my plate.

"Everything okay?" I ask.

She looks at me, shakes her head, and continues to eat.

"Yeah, it's just my brain playing with my eyes."

I nod and take a sip of my orange juice. When we both finish, I grab the plates and place them in the sink, doing the same with the glasses.

I turn back to her with a small smile on my face.

"Eve," I call.

She looks up and stares at me, waiting for me to speak.

"Why don't we go out and do something today?" I ask.

She sighs. "And here I thought you would leave me alone in the damn house again."

I chuckle, pushing my chair in.

She stands up, and I guide her up the stairs.

"Go get ready," I say.

She walks to the bathroom. Before she closes the door, she sends me a small smile, and I return it, watching as the door closes.

I turn around and walk over to the couch, grabbing my phone from where it lies on the pillow. I notice the green light and switch it on, looking at the name I had been hoping to see last night and early this morning. It is Luke:

Want to hang out today? I'll explain everything.

A small sting hits my chest, and I bite my lip as the memory of what Randy told me at the police station about my father surfaces.

No need.

I switch my phone off and stand up, swallowing the lump in my throat. Today is going to be just Eve and me because we both need to get out of this house. Eve was right when she said that she thought I was going to leave her in the house; I cannot leave her again by herself.

We both need to focus on something other than the loss of my father. Maybe what I have in mind will help us forget the pain, even if it's only for a short while.

*   *   *

"I want the cotton candy!" a little girl yells as she runs past us and towards her dad. I quickly look away, ignoring the pain in my heart, and continue to walk to the ticket box.

With the money Mum gave me, I have more than enough for Eve and me to try all the rides twice. I am just hoping that Eve can turn her frown upside down and at least try to distract herself while we are here.

When I get the tickets, we step away from the line and look around the large space, trying to find a good ride to start our time at the fair. I glance at Eve and notice that she is looking at a ride, with a small smile forming on her face.

There we go.

"This one," she says, walking towards the line, and I smile.

The line is pretty long, but that does not seem to bother her—she keeps smiling all the way until we reach the ride.

That's when her smile turns into a full grin.

"Have you been on this ride before?" I ask Eve, and she nods.

"The most fun I've had in years. It is truly the best ride ever," she says.

A voice from the large speakers tells us that the bars will now come down, so we have to hold our hands up. As the bar comes down, I make sure it is secure before leaning back in the slightly uncomfortable seat. I let my feet dangle as the seat begins to move upward, and before I know it, it swings back and forth, making my heart race from the adrenaline.

"Are you ready?" the voice in the speakers yells.

The riders—including Eve and me—shout, "Hell yeah!" into the air as the ride begins to swing higher. I find myself hanging upside down in the air.

A scream escapes my lungs, and Eve laughs as it begins to flip and do all sorts of wild, random things that make us scream, laugh, swear, and cry.

Eve really did choose the best first ride.

*   *   *

"Okay, if you were trying to make me feel better, you succeeded," Eve says, taking a bite of her pizza slice.

I smile and do the same.

"I'm glad," I say.

She looks at the waves crashing against the water, making their way towards us.

Doing the same, I savor the relaxed feeling washing over me.

"You know, when I first met you, I thought you would hate me forever," she says.

"Exactly what I thought, too. It's not every day your dad brings home a girl not even two months after his wife passed away."

"Yeah," she says, taking the last bite of her pizza. "What was your mum like? I mean, you do not have to talk about her. I am just curious."

I shrug. "It's fine," I say as my eyes catch a small crab digging in the sand. I smile and look back at the sea.

"My mum was one of a kind. She always loved to draw, and whenever she was down, she would do exactly that. She was outgoing, caring, always so full of joy, and she never gave up on the people she loved."

She smiles. "She must have been some mother, huh?"

"She was perfect."

Eve stands up. I watch as she turns around to look for something. My eyes follow her gaze. She looks down at me and smiles. "Want some ice cream?"

I smile, jumping from my spot on the sand. I give Eve a grin and look at the ice cream parlour. "Last one there has to pay."

She grins, nodding. "You're on."

CHAPTER THIRTY-SIX
What Did You Just Say?

After spending the weekend with Eve, Monday arrives. To be honest, I could not care less about the stares I will be receiving from the students.

It is my life, and they cannot keep acting like they control it.

"Want me to pick you up? We can go shopping after school," Eve says, a small grin on her face.

I nod, returning the smile. I get out of the car and send her a wave before walking towards the school building.

As I predicted, everyone's eyes turn to me, just like when Mum died. The looks of sympathy flash through their eyes, but I pretend not to notice as I make my way towards my locker. I open it and place inside the books I will need later. I make sure not to glance at the people looking at my back, watching me. I close my locker and turn around to see Luke standing in front of me, his face furious.

"Come with me," Luke says, grabbing my hand and dragging me down the hall.

As I pass Nicole and her group of friends, she sends me a small smile, but I pretend I did not see it. Luke walks into a classroom, pulls me in, and slams the door behind him, making sure to lock it so no one can interrupt us.

I sit on the table, watching as he runs a hand through his hair.

"Why haven't you been answering my calls, Grace?" he asks, his blue eyes staring into my green ones.

I don't answer.

Oh, so now he wants to call me when I turn my phone off?

Luke raises his eyebrow, walks over to the table that I am sitting on, and slams his hand down, making me jump.

"Don't go mute on me."

His eyes narrow at me, and a flash of pain passes through them.

"I have my reasons," I choke out.

And he raises an eyebrow, looking up at the ceiling.

"Oh?" he says.

I nod slowly.

He steps away from me and crosses his arms across his chest. "Like to share?" he asks.

I frown, getting off the table.

"Should I tell you, or are you going to tell your friends? Who are they going to kill next, Luke? Eve? Me?" I ask, my heart racing in fear.

It is not like me to be so confident, and from what I have learned, it ends badly when I am confident.

Shut up, Grace, my brain reprimands, and I watch as Luke's eyes go cold.

What the hell is happening to him? He surely is not himself today, I can tell you that.

"What did you just say?" he asks, and I step back.

"Y-you heard me."

He shakes his head. "I'm afraid not." He moves closer to me.

I bump into the table and place my hands on it, trying to steady myself. He unfolds his hands and stares at me.

"Go on, Grace. Say it again."

I gulp, shaking my head.

He nods. "That's what I thought," he mutters.

Something in his tone triggers a reaction in me, and without thinking, my leg shoots up, kicking him where the sun does not shine. Before I can even say sorry, he drops to the ground in pain and groans.

Again, without thinking, I run to the door and unlock it with my shaking hands. I hurry to my first class, ignoring the person shouting my name—Nicole.

I enter the classroom and notice that I am early.

Mr. London looks up from his book and smiles at me. "Eager for class, are we?"

I nod, trying to hide the obvious fear.

He does not say anything as I walk to the back. I take a seat and rest my head on the desk, steadying my breathing.

What the hell just happened?

*   *   *

I walk into the cafeteria, trying not to look around to see if *he* is watching me, anger obvious in his eyes.

"Grace," someone calls from behind me, and I quickly duck, my head nearly hitting the table. I hold my arms above my head in an attempt to hide from the person, but the tap on the shoulder tells me that I have failed.

I raise my head to see Nicole looking down at me in confusion.

"Are you okay?" she asks, and before I can say anything, she taps her forehead and shakes her head. "Of course you're not. Why the hell would I ask you that?"

I just watch her, my own confusion appearing on my face.

She shakes her head again and looks back at me. Raising an eyebrow, she points at the seat beside me. I nod slowly. I'm not quite sure why Nicole wants to sit with me or why she wants to talk to me in the first place. Is it important? Is it about Luke and why he has been acting so strange?

"Grace," she starts. "First of all, I'm sorry for being such a bitch to you. It's just that you have such a better life than I—"

I stop her by holding my hand up.

"Both my parents are dead, Nicole," I say in a firm voice.

"Did you watch your aunty murder your uncle, then watch her shoot herself in front of you right after?" she asks.

My face falls, my heart stops at the news.

She nods and crosses her arms on the table. "Exactly. Now, as I was saying, I'm sorry. I know sorry doesn't cut it. It can't erase everything I have done—the name-calling and bullying—but I want to make it up to you." She holds out her hand.

"Friends?" she asks.

I look at her hand, trying to decide if I should do this or not. I mean, Nicole is right about what she just said. She cannot take away the pain she has caused me, but sometimes you have to move on from those things to become stronger.

"Why are you doing this now?" I ask, and she smiles at me.

"I'm trying to start fresh here. Now, what do you say? Friends?"

I look down at her hand, feeling my hand twitch in anticipation.

Do it, Grace. Think about it—you finally got someone to talk to other than Eve about boy troubles, school, and life! Exactly what you wanted, remember? You have to do this . . . my brain urges.

I let out a long sigh before raising my hand and shaking it with Nicole's.

"Friends."

CHAPTER THIRTY-SEVEN
Why Did You Cheat on Mum?

After spending two hours at the mall, shopping for new clothes with Eve, we finally decided to end the day and go home.

Eve is now making dinner while I am in my room, drawing a few random things in the sketchbook she bought me today.

I sketch the inside of the eye, making sure to put as much detail in it as possible to make it look real. Before I can start drawing the eyebrow, something bangs against my window, and I let out a sigh, placing my sketchbook on the bed.

Don't tell me it's Luke.

I stand up and walk over to my window, pulling it up. I look out, and a frown spreads across my face.

Luke.

He points towards his car parked out front.

I shake my head at him. "No, Luke."

He runs a hand down his face. "Come on, don't do this."

I shake my head again. "No, Luke, don't do this. I waited two days for a phone call from you so you could explain the events of my dad's death, but no—you didn't call. I found out from someone else, and you know what? That actually hurts. The fact that you had to run away for whatever you had to do, and you couldn't at least call me after you were finished, is stupid. You couldn't be busy for two days and not even bother to call me. It takes only a couple of seconds to go to your phone, click my name, and call me. But I guess you couldn't spare those seconds, could you?" I spit out.

Once again, I feel my heart race, and I pinch my arm, trying to calm myself down.

The light from the streetlight shows me the look on Luke's face, and from what I can tell, I know he is not happy with my words. Without another word, he turns around and walks to his car, not bothering to respond to what I just said.

I groan and close my window, trying not to slam it too hard because of the anger I feel.

Then there's a knock on the door. I turn around to see Eve with a small smile.

"Everything okay?"

"Perfect," I mutter.

Before she can walk in, though, the smell of the food stops her. She holds a finger up before running down the stairs and back to the kitchen.

I let out a sigh. I sit on my bed and grab the sketchbook, then lean against the headboard as I continue drawing.

Honestly, I need a reason to keep loving Luke, because if we keep this up, I feel like we might break apart soon.

*   *   *

A knock at my door makes me jump. My head turns to the door, and a smile appears on my face.

"Mum!" I squeal, jumping out of bed, running to Mum, and pulling her into a hug.

She laughs and hugs me back.

"Hello, sweetheart. How's it going?" Mum asks.

The smile I am wearing fades a little.

"You know about—"

"Your father? Yes," Mum quickly cuts in.

I nod, looking away from her—well, until she grabs my chin and makes me look at her.

"You know, he would like to talk to you."

I frown. "Why?"

Mum smiles, letting go of my chin. "Because he is your father, of course. You are his daughter."

"Mum—"

"Shush." She places her index finger on my lips.

I let out a sigh and let her talk.

"Just let him say what he has to, okay? I'll be right here watching, so there is nothing to worry about."

My eyes widen. "Is he here?"

Mum nods, crossing her arms over her chest.

"Of course. Why wouldn't he be?"

Before I can say a word, Dad steps into the room with a small smile on his face.

"Hello, Grace," Dad says.

I send him a small smile.

He walks towards me and holds out his arms, waiting for me to step into them.

Without thinking, the tears I have been trying to hold in fall down my cheeks as I run to Dad, letting him hold me in his arms.

"It's true," he says.

I look up at him, trying to control my sobs and tears.

"Wh-what's true?" I ask, confused.

He smiles and pulls away from me, lifting his shirt to reveal the tattoo Randy was talking about.

I look at my name in cursive writing on his skin.

"It's beautiful," I choke out, and Dad nods.

"It is, isn't it?" he says with a smile.

Mum steps in, looking at the tattoo herself. "He stole my idea." She looks over at me.

Dad laughs. "No, you're just jealous that it's that good." He grins.

Mum shakes her head. "Nope."

I stop, looking at my parents, who seem so happy in this moment.

"Wait," I say, catching both my parents' attention.

Dad puts his shirt down, and Mum stands beside him, still smiling.

"Why did you cheat on Mum?" I ask, looking at Dad.

He looks at Mum. She sighs, running a hand through her hair.

"Grace, he didn't cheat on me," Mum says, and my eyebrows furrow.

"What do you mean, he didn't cheat on you? He did!" I say, looking at my parents in confusion.

Does she not know? Wait—of course she does.

"Grace," Mum says, walking up to me. She places her hands on my shoulders and presses a kiss to my forehead.

"I'll explain everything soon," she says.

All of a sudden, without even saying goodbye, my parents disappear from my room.

I lift my body from my bed and look around. Ugh, these dreams are going to be the death of me.

Wait—why are my parents telling me this in my dreams? That shouldn't be happening, should it? Am I going crazy? Do I need help? Does anyone have the same problem as I do, or am I the only one?

"I'll explain everything soon."

Why does everyone keep telling me that? They cannot just expect me to be cool with that and not worry at all. I am a curious person, and Mum should know that!

Suddenly, I have an idea. I look out the window, noticing that it is still dark. Okay—so it should be early in the morning, which means I can go back to sleep and continue talking to my parents.

I lay down on my pillow, force my eyes shut, and wait. Unfortunately, after doing this for ten minutes, I know I am not going anywhere.

"Why do you do this to me?" I mutter, running both hands down my face. I let out a sigh and stare at the wall, not bothering to try falling asleep again.

Mum's words ring in my head, making me let out another frustrated sigh.

"Grace, he didn't cheat on me."

I guess all I can do is wait.

CHAPTER THIRTY-EIGHT
Why Are You Crying?

"Wow, you look like you haven't slept at all," Nicole comments, standing by my locker. I walk over, open it, and nod.

"That's because I haven't," I reply quietly, placing my books in the locker. I close it and turn to see Nicole with a small frown on her face.

"Are you okay?"

I wave her off.

"Everything will be better soon," I say as we walk to our first class. It feels weird talking normally with the person who used to bully me every day. Well, why would it feel normal anyway? Wait—could Nicole be up to something? Is that why she suddenly asked to be my friend again?

Ugh, I don't need a repeat of the past.

As I enter the classroom, a certain blond-haired boy catches my eye.

Luke.

He sits at the back of the class. His hood is over his head, and his eyes are fixed on his phone on the table. Usually, I wouldn't be worried—this is what he always does—but the look in his eyes makes my heart clench.

They do not look like the usual blue eyes I used to get lost in every day. They are dull, and I can see a small hint of pain in them. As I take my seat, I notice a trace of red around the blue, telling me he either hasn't been sleeping or he—.

No. He doesn't do drugs. I mean, he hardly even swears!

I slide my bag off my shoulder and take out my pen and book for today's lesson. As the class starts, I cannot help glancing at Luke, who is still on his phone, not paying attention to a word Mrs. Dargen is saying.

When his head shifts in my direction, I quickly look away and focus on our teacher, who is standing at the front of the class.

"Okay, so we will be going on a school trip soon—"

The class erupts into cheers, while a few, including me and Luke, stay in our seats, not saying a word.

"Settle down. Now, the trip will be in two weeks, so make sure you pay the money by the end of this week," Mrs. Dargen announces, handing out the notes for the trip.

I take a look at the note.

Nicole gasps. "To the ranch? Oh, hell yes!" she says.

I let out a small chuckle. I place the note in my bag, and once again, I find myself glancing over at Luke. When someone knocks at the door, I quickly look away.

Mrs. Dargen opens the door, and the school's counselor walks in.

"Can I borrow Luke for ten minutes?"

All eyes snap to Luke—except mine. Instead, I begin to wonder why the counselor wants to talk to him. Is he in trouble? I feel a small tug of pain in my heart as I watch Luke walk out the door.

I hope he is okay.

*   *   *

"So, the girls and I are going to the mall this afternoon to buy some new clothes for the school trip," Nicole says.

"Cool."

"Indeed. Do you want to come?" she asks.

I look up at her and frown.

"Why would you want me to join you and your friends—"

"Grace, you are my friend. I am asking you because I would like you to come with us."

I let out a sigh. "No thanks. I have stuff to do this afternoon."

She raises her eyebrow. "Like?"

I pinch my arm, trying to come up with something that is somewhat believable. Sadly, my mouth opens, but no words come out, making her grin.

"Okay, I'll pick you up at four."

I look away from her, take a chip into my mouth, and begin to get lost in my thoughts.

Ever since Luke went with the counselor, I have not stopped thinking about him—especially since he did not come back to class. The counselor did say ten minutes, so why would he be gone for an hour? Has he been having a rough day? Is it because of me? Oh god, it probably is.

Am I the reason Luke looks so depressed?

Ugh, I need to talk to him.

"I need to go to the bathroom," I say.

"Do what you need to do," she says.

I get out of my chair, and when I am about to walk into the bathroom, I look back at Nicole. She is on her phone, not paying attention to anyone around her. I turn away from the bathroom and head for the cafeteria doors.

When I walk out, I look around the empty hallways. "Where are you?" I ask quietly as I begin to walk around, hoping that Luke will be somewhere nearby. I walk up two flights of stairs, and as I get lost in my thoughts, I find myself at the top of the building where I was once close to ending my life.

A gasp escapes my lips when I see Luke sitting at the edge, his feet dangling off the building, singing quietly. I gasp again at the tears falling from his eyes.

"L-Luke?" I manage to say.

He lets out a sigh and quickly wipes his face with his hand.

I walk closer to him, waiting for him to push me away or say "stop," but he doesn't.

I take a seat next to him and look at him. "Why are you crying?"

He shakes his head. "No reason," he mumbles, looking ahead at the field.

I sigh and do the same, trying to push the past to the back of my mind. "I'm sorry."

He looks over at me. "For?"

"For hurting you. I mean, you obviously had your reasons why you couldn't tell me straight away about my dad. It made me angry, and I didn't think of it from your point of view. I even pushed you away that night, when you were at my house. I said some mean things that probably made you angry at me, and when I saw you today—"

Luke taps a finger on my lips, cutting me off.

"Stop talking and breathe," he says calmly, taking his finger away from my lips, and I do as I am told.

I run a hand through my purple hair and sigh. "I'm sorry."

He shrugs. "Don't worry about it."

I look down at his hand resting on his leg. I reach for it and hold it.

He sends me a weird look, but I ignore it, sending him a small smile.

"I'm here for you now, just like when you were there for me. So, if you need to get anything off your chest, you can—"

"My dad died."

CHAPTER THIRTY-NINE
I Don't Want to Live

After Luke told me that his dad had died, he decided to explain everything at his house. I told Nicole I could not make it because I had to attend something really important, and she simply understood and let me be. I did not have to tell her that I would be spending time with Luke to talk about everything because did she really have to know? Exactly.

So, right now, Luke and I are sitting on the couch in his living room, just lying in each other's arms. I don't want to pressure him. He can tell me whenever he feels comfortable. In the state he is in, I am not in any position to push him for answers, even if I am really curious.

"Okay," Luke starts, his hand still stroking my hair.

I close my eyes at the affection, relaxing in his arms as I wait for him to continue.

"Do you remember that day when we were in your dad's hospital room and I got a message? That was my mum," Luke begins.

"She sent me a message about my dad, and instantly my heart raced with fear and hope. She said the doctors had kicked her out because something was happening to him, and I started to panic. I had to leave right away to see what was going on. So, don't think I didn't want to explain—because I really did. I wanted to tell you, but everything just happened so fast. Since my dad was in a hospital in the next town, I knew I wouldn't be able to message you until later. I tried my best to hurry. I thought my dad would be fine—that it was just something minor, something the doctors could fix. But I was wrong." His voice breaking a little.

I grab his spare hand—the one resting on my stomach—and stroke it, calming him down a little.

"When I gave the doctors the money for my dad's surgery, everything went as planned. The surgery went well. All my mum and I had to do was wait for him to wake up, since the doctors said it would be a few hours before we could finally talk to him. So when my mum said something had gone wrong, I expected the worst. When I reached the hospital, I saw her sitting in a chair outside his room, her hands covering her face as she tried to stifle her cries. That's when I knew my dad hadn't made it."

I look up at him and notice the small tear running down his cheek. I use my other hand to wipe it away. He just lets out a sigh and looks at the television.

"I thought everything would be okay, Grace. I really did. Now my mum tries to stay at work as long as she can, just to stay away from this place, because it brings back a lot of memories. She is so broken. Now I understand how you feel about your parents' death. She has that look in her eyes—the one that says all she wants is to be with her husband. She doesn't say it, of course, but it's in the way she walks, the way her face changes when she steps into the house—the look in her eyes says it all." He shakes his head, closing his eyes.

"I saw my mum early in the morning with pills in her hand. She just kept staring at them, like she was deciding whether to leave me—and the world—just to be with Dad. It hurts so much to see her in such pain. You know, I'm not ready to lose my mum. Heck, I wasn't even ready to lose my dad," he says, his eyes filling with tears.

My heart clenches in pain.

Every word that comes out of his mouth makes me want to stay with him forever and never leave his side. I can hear the pain in his voice—how it cracks when he talks about his mum or dad. He does not deserve to lose his mum, too. No one deserves to lose anyone, but it just happens. Even if we're never okay with it, we have to learn to accept it—even when we do not want to.

"Luke, you won't lose your mum," I say, looking into his blue eyes.

He shakes his head and sighs. The next words out of his mouth break my heart in two.

"The empty look in my mum's eyes tells me I've already lost her."

*   *   *

I look down at Luke's sleeping form in bed, the blanket wrapped around his body. A soft smile spreads across my face as I crawl over to him and place a small, gentle kiss on his lips. Then I pull away, grab my phone, and walk out of his room, closing the door behind me.

As I make my way to the staircase, the sound of a closing door makes me stop and crouch against the wall. I look down into the living room and see Bree walking towards the couch. She drops her bag onto it, grabs a pillow, and throws it on the floor. Then she rests her head on the arm of the couch. The soft glow of the lamp reveals that her eyes are closed.

"I'm sorry, Luke," Bree mumbles, bringing her hands to her face.

She wipes away the tears trailing down her cheeks and lets out a sigh. "I'm sorry for disappointing you. I'm sorry for making you see me in this state. I just can't keep it all together— especially when I know that your dad, my husband, is gone. I just can't keep doing it." Her voice breaks slightly.

She sits up, wipes her face again, then stands and heads into the kitchen. A few pans clatter to the ground, and I quickly make my way downstairs and into the kitchen.

A gasp escapes my lips, and I freeze when she holds a gun to her head.

"I don't want to live," she mumbles.

But before she can do what might break Luke forever, I run to her and grab the gun just as she pulls the trigger. A sharp pain shoots through my shoulder, and my eyes widen as I fall to the ground.

"Grace, stay with me!" she cries, just before I black out from the pain.

CHAPTER FORTY
You Can't Handle the Truth

I feel my body come alive, and just as my eyes begin to open, familiar voices make them snap shut.

"You had a gun? Why the hell do you have a gun?" Luke says, the anger in his voice clear.

Then a sob, followed by a weary voice—definitely Bree's.

"I have it for emergencies," she says, her voice breaking.

"Oh, and risking your life is an emergency? Is that right, Mum?"

A sudden urge to stop them from arguing rises in me. I open my eyes and see Luke staring into his mum's—hurt and anger flashing in his.

I clear my throat loudly, hoping to get their attention. Just as I expect, they both turn and rush over to me. Luke wraps his arms around me, but I let out a sharp groan, wincing and gnashing my teeth as pain shoots through my shoulder. He immediately pulls back, frowning.

"Sorry," he mumbles.

"It's okay."

Bree steps in front of Luke and gives me a small frown. "I'm sorry I did this to you. It shouldn't have been you—it should've been—"

But before she can continue, Luke growls, cutting her off. She sends her son a sad look before turning back to me. "Are you okay?"

I glance down at my shoulder, which is wrapped in a bandage.

"I guess so. Just no hugs," I say, cracking a smile, which makes Bree chuckle.

A doctor and a police officer walk into the room, their eyes on me.

"You're awake," the doctor says. He walks over, grabs the clipboard at the end of my bed, and reads it before pulling out a pen and ticking something off.

"Grace," the doctor starts, "we've successfully removed the bullet from your shoulder, but just to make sure that you're okay, we need you to stay overnight. You know—to check your blood pressure, heart rate, all that stuff."

I nod, completely fine with staying one more night. I just hope it really is only one night. After everything I've dealt with in hospitals, I do not want to start having nightmares.

Oh, I'm so lucky I haven't been having nightmares.

"Now, I'll be back soon. In the meantime, Constable Wilkins wants to have a chat with you," the doctor says before leaving the room.

I look over at the officer, who gives me a small smile.

"I believe we've met before," Constable Wilkins says, and as I begin to think, a small smile spreads across my face. The police officer who took me into protective custody, I think. Oh, what's his name again?

"William," I say, finally remembering.

He nods, the smile still on his face. He looks me over and chuckles lightly.

"You seem to have one hell of a life, huh?" William says.

I nod, the smile still on my face.

Before I can say a word, Luke stands beside William and sends him a glare. "I'm getting a vibe that I don't like . . ."

I chuckle. "Luke—"

"Are you flirting with my girlfriend?" Luke asks.

William's eyes widen slightly. He laughs and shakes his head.

"I'm twenty-five, dude. I don't hit on people's girlfriends," William says, and Luke's features soften.

I shake my head at Luke and give William an apologetic look.

William just laughs it off.

"It's fine, it's fine. Everyone is jealous of me because, well, I'm hot," he says, and I burst out laughing.

William laughs with me, placing a hand on Luke's shoulder. "I'm joking, buddy. I'm no creep."

Luke nods. "Good."

William turns to me, rolls his eyes playfully, and sits on the edge of the bed, pulling out a notepad. "Now, what happened this time?"

*   *   *

After talking to William for an hour about what happened, how I am feeling, and other things, he finally decided to head off—not before talking to Bree of course.

William has arranged for Bree to meet a friend of his, a counselor, to talk about a few things, since she is feeling low and depressed. She did not want to at first, but after having a chat with Luke outside of my room, she seemed to look at it all from a different perspective, which is good for everyone, I guess.

I called Eve since no one had notified her that I am in the hospital. To say that Eve was relieved was an understatement. She did not even sleep at all last night because she was worried about where I was and what had happened to me.

Well, that's what I heard.

When I told her everything, she initially wanted to punch Bree in the face. But once I explained the situation, she finally understood. She said she would visit me later, when Luke leaves—but judging by how I feel right now, I do not think he is going anywhere.

"Luke, you know you don't have to do this. It's just my shoulder," I say, watching as he tucks the blanket around my body.

He shakes his head and lifts my neck, fixing my pillow. "I don't care. You shouldn't be here anyway if it weren't for my mum. So I'm helping you out here. I can't imagine the pain you're going through right now."

"My shoulder is numb. I can't feel a thing."

He shakes his head again. "I still don't care."

I shake my head at him and watch as he throws the rubbish from my lunch in the bin. When he sits on the edge of the bed, he lets out a sigh.

"I'm sorry again that this has happened."

I narrow my eyes at him. "What have I said about apologizing for this? It wasn't your fault—and it wasn't your mum's either. If someone is to blame, it's me."

He frowns. "No, it's not your fault. Don't talk like that."

"You can't handle the truth."

He narrows his eyes at me. "You did not just say that."

I grin. "Do you want me to say it again? I don't think you heard me."

Luke shakes his head. "You wouldn't say it even if you wanted to."

"And why is that?"

"Because if you say it, I'd have to do something very terrible to you," he says.

I scrunch my nose in disgust. "Eww, you creep."

He laughs, shaking his head. "No. That's not what I meant, Gracie. I didn't mean I'd touch you."

"Then what?" I ask.

He places a finger on his lips, telling me to be quiet.

"Don't say it—if you know what's good for you," he says with a grin.

I grin back, raising an eyebrow. "Are you testing me?"

He shrugs. "Maybe, maybe not."

I nod slowly. "Okay then." My grin turns into a teasing smile. "You can't handle the truth."

I wait for his reaction, but he only raises an eyebrow before leaning closer. His lips brush against mine, and just as I am about to press mine to his, he pulls back—grinning.

"No kisses for you," he whispers.

I frown at him. "You're honestly the meanest person ever."

"I know, I know." When he notices the glares I am sending him, he laughs. "You can't be mad at me forever."

I turn my head away, proving that I definitely can.

He frowns and grabs my hand. "Gracie, you can't do this to me."

"But you can do this to me?" I ask, looking over at him.

He grins, giving me a questioning look. "Do what?"

I roll my eyes. "I know what you're trying to do, you know."

He shakes his head. "Nah, I don't. Go on, tell me what you're talking about."

"Nope."

"Tell me."

"No, I'm fine."

"Grace . . ."

"You won't kiss me!" I suddenly burst out, and I feel my cheeks go hot.

He smiles and brings his face closer. "Now, why wouldn't I?"

I glare at him, trying to stop my heart from beating like crazy.

"Because you're a bitch," I mutter.

His eyes widen as he gasps. "Oh, you just swore!"

I roll my eyes. "So?"

He shakes his head in disapproval. "I'll make a deal with you, okay? Never swear again, and I'll kiss you."

I raise an eyebrow at him. "Really?"

He nods.

A small smile spreads across my lips, and before his lips reach mine, I place my hand in front of my mouth to stop him, making him groan. I throw him a grin and push him off the bed with my leg.

"Karma really does suck."

CHAPTER FORTY-ONE
Why Not Get Her the Full Package?

"You are now free to go, Grace," the smiling doctor says, taking the clipboard under his arm.

I smile at him just before he leaves the room. I get off the bed slowly, careful not to put too much pressure on my arm. I don't want to be back here anytime soon, so it is best to take my time and watch my step.

"I have a surprise for you when we get home," Eve says, walking beside me as we walk towards the elevator.

I look up at her and raise an eyebrow.

"A surprise? What kind of surprise?"

She shrugs. "Oh, just a little something I put together."

I nod, trying to block out the terrible elevator music. Honestly, I just want to hit the person who created elevator music.

When we get into the car, I lean my head back into the seat, enjoying the wonderful song *Scared to Be Lonely* by Martin Garrix and Dua Lipa coming through the speakers. A small smile spreads across my face.

> *It was great at the very start*
> *Hands on each other . . .*

I hum the tune of the song as the car starts to move. As the song continues, Eve sings along to the song, making my smile fall off my face.

Since when could Eve sing?

As the car stops, I open my eyes and look at the house that once was my happy place. Now, it's just like any other place to me.

You're getting mixed up in your thoughts again, Grace, my brain warns, and I sigh, knowing that I have to control myself.

I mean, I have Eve, right? I at least have someone to rely on, other than Luke.

I get out of the car, and when I walk up to the door, Eve chuckles slightly. I turn around, but she waves me off. I open the door, and all of a sudden, my aunty and Luke scream out the words that make me mentally laugh at myself for forgetting about today.

"Happy birthday, Grace!"

*   *   *

I walk into the kitchen, a small smile on my face as I let my thoughts take over. I can't believe Eve did all of this for me. Every detail, every single detail—is perfect. I know she put a lot of time and thought into this. The only thought that I really wish I could push away is the one that's telling me that I don't deserve this.

"Shut up," I mumble, grabbing a glass from the cupboard and pouring some water into it. I place the jug of water back on the counter and take a sip of the refreshing cold water.

"Decided to run away from the party, huh?" someone asks.

I turn around to see Aunty Carol smiling at me. She closes the door behind her and takes a seat on one of the stools. I grab another glass, pour in some water, and give it to her. Aunty Carol thanks me before drinking it, and I take a stool opposite her.

"How have you been?" Aunty Carol asks, and I shrug.

"Better than I expected," I say.

"You're a very strong girl, Grace. I always love that about you." She smiles, and I chuckle, nodding.

"So I've been told. Anyway, how are you? We haven't talked much ever since—"

"Ever since Rose's funeral," Aunty Carol cuts in.

I nod, taking a sip of my water.

"Yeah. Well, you don't need to worry about me. Oh, before I forget, I've been meaning to ask you this for a while now," Aunty Carol says.

I sit up, interested in what she has to say. "You and that boy . . ." She points behind her, and I smile.

"Luke," I say.

She nods. "Yeah, him. He is a keeper, so don't let go of him."

I chuckle.

"You two will have some beautiful children too," she adds.

I blush, shaking my head. "Really? Did you have to say that?" I ask, placing my hands on my cheeks.

Aunty Carol shrugs. "It's true—"

"Grace! Time to open your presents!" Eve calls.

I chuckle as I get out of my seat.

Aunty Carol follows me into the living room and sits next to me on the couch. Eve and Luke stand in front of the coffee table.

Eve smiles and places a fairly large present on the table, and claps her hands together. "Okay, this is from me."

I lean forward, slowly unwrapping the present. When I finish, my mouth opens in shock.

"Wow," I gasp, looking at the large brown case. I unlock the latches and open it, my eyes widening.

"This is . . . ," I trail off, not really finding the right words to say to describe how I feel about her gift.

She grins, looking between me and the case. "You have a gift, Grace. So, I thought, why not get you the full package? I hope you like it."

I smile, looking at the row of coloured pencils, crayons, lead pencils, and all sorts of drawing materials. I stand up and hug her for a few seconds before letting go.

"Thank you," I say, and she waves me off.

"Oh, it's fine. Now, time for the other presents," she says, stepping back.

I sit back on the couch, close the case, and put it to the side. Luke steps in front of her and holds out a small box.

"For you," he says with a smile, handing me the box.

I take it in my hands and unwrap it. In my hand is a blue box, which instantly makes my heart race. I open it, and just like before, my mouth drops.

"Now, before you squeal like a madman—"

I cut him off by jumping from the couch and wrapping my arms around him. When the pain in my shoulder comes to say hello, I wince but do not let go of him.

"This is beautiful," I tell him.

He smiles, placing a kiss on my forehead. "I'm glad you like it."

I take the ring into my hand, gasp at the small pink rose shimmering in the light, slide it onto my pinkie where it fits, and hug Luke again.

"Thank you," I mumble.

"No worries, Gracie," he says.

After a few more seconds of holding onto him, which is probably making things awkward for everyone, I finally sit down.

Aunty Carol smiles and hands me a box the same size as Luke's. I take it, open it, and tears fill my eyes.

"I know you have had a rough time with your dad, but I felt like this photo truly shows how proud he is of you. Also, I like the photo because it has all three of you in it—your mum, your dad, and you, when you were a baby," she says.

I look into her eyes and notice tears in them. I pull her into a hug and let one tear fall.

"You truly know how to bring me to tears," I whisper.

She smiles, placing a kiss on my cheek. "And you truly know how to make me smile."

I look at the silver necklace and the locket connected to it. The locket shows me a picture of my parents when I was a baby. Mum is holding me in her arms, and Dad is standing behind her, looking down at me like he was the happiest man in the world. I clutch the locket and wipe my eyes. After giving Aunty Carol one last smile, she grabs the necklace from my hand and places it around my neck. I close the locket and hold onto it, a smile still on my face.

"Thank you, guys. You all are truly something," I say.

They all smile before giving me a hug. I clutch onto the three main people in my life like my life depends on it, and let out a sigh.

My parents might not be here, but I know they are looking down on me, wishing me a happy birthday, even though I cannot hear them.

*   *   *

After saying goodbye to my aunty and Luke, I finally made my way upstairs with a smile on my face. I walk down the hallway towards the guest room to see if Eve is asleep. Just as I figured, she is already quietly snoring away. I close the door and walk down the hallway.

I look over at my parents' room for a moment. Suddenly, instead of going to my room, I find myself walking into theirs. I turn on the light and look around. Everything still looks the same, even though Eve had slept in here after Mum died, but when Dad died . . . I guess it was just too much.

I walk over to the bed and sit down, looking around. When my eyes land on the drawer, I notice a piece of paper under a plastic tin. I get up and walk over to the drawer. I grab the paper, and my eyes widen when my name's on it.

Did Eve write this?

I unfold the paper and feel my heart race when I read the words on the paper.

Dear Grace,

> *Oh, my beautiful daughter. I'm going to miss you so much, you know? I'm going to miss your smile,*

your laugh, that twinkle in your eyes when you are so happy or excited . . . everything about you is what I'm going to miss. What I'm going to miss most is telling you that I love you and hearing you say you love me back right after.

Now, before you start to blow up with questions, I'm going to explain everything. I knew about what your dad was doing at work. I'm actually okay with that. You know why? Because I told him that this wouldn't work—that the marriage wouldn't work. I know this would hurt you, and I know you would start hating your dad, but it's not his fault. We both knew this wouldn't go as planned, so we divorced. You don't know this, but we divorced ten years ago.

Shocker, I know. Grace, you have to understand that we only kept pretending because we didn't want you to be so upset. We aren't like any of the parents who stay together and grow old together. I told your dad that he can see whoever he wants because I knew I was going to die soon. No one escapes from cancer, and you might be thinking that it's your father's fault with the whole secondhand smoke thing, but it's my fault. I could've moved away, but I chose not to. Don't blame your father, Grace. Everyone dies; we just don't know when or how.

I know I'm being blunt about it all, but I'm just being realistic right now. I mean, you might have the perfect boy of your dreams, and you might be living your life and have everything all planned out, but trust me, it all doesn't go to plan. Nothing goes to plan.

I don't know when you will read this, but please just remember I still love you—and so does your dad. I hope you can forgive him if you do hate him, but remember, it's not him you should hate.

Actually, you shouldn't hate anyone. Hate is a strong word, so use it carefully, okay? Again, forgive your dad. Don't throw your time away and push him away, because if you need someone to blame, blame me. Just don't blame your dad for something he didn't do in the first place.

I love you, Grace. Stay strong, okay?

Kisses and hugs,

Mum

I drop the letter into the drawer and let my shaking hands fall to my side. My legs begin to tremble, and before I can reach for the wall, I collapse to the floor, sobbing.

Dad didn't cheat on Mum . . .

"I w-was wrong."

CHAPTER FORTY-TWO
This Is My Girlfriend, Grace

"Let's skip school today," Luke says.

I frown, picking up my bag off my bed. I put the phone on speaker and place it on top of the drawer as I clip a strand of my hair back.

"I don't want to. Do you know how many days I have skipped ever since I first talked to you?" I ask, patting my hair down.

He chuckles.

"It's only one day, Gracie."

"No, Luke."

He sighs. "Fine, but I hope you're ready, because I am already outside," he says.

My eyes widen as I walk over to my window and see his car parked in front of my house.

I shake my head in disapproval. "You need to stop showing up like this. It's creepy," I say, grabbing my phone and placing it to my ear.

"And you need to stop checking if I'm lying or not. It's really disappointing," he mocks.

I roll my eyes before hanging up. I walk out of my room and down the stairs. Eve is sitting on the couch with a piece of toast in her mouth, and I send her a wave when she notices me.

"Bye, Eve," I say with a smile, and she returns it.

"Try not to move your shoulder too much," she says.

I nod, opening the front door.

"I'll try," I say before walking out of the house and towards Luke's car. I get in and place my bag between my feet.

"Good morning, Gracie." Luke smiles, reaching over and pecking my lips.

I kiss him back for only a few seconds before pushing him away.

"Just because I didn't want to skip school today does not mean that I want to be late, so drive," I say with a grin.

He rolls his eyes playfully before starting the car.

*   *   *

"Okay, students," Mrs. James starts as we all take our seats. She stands in front of the class, a small smile on her face. "As you all know, the principal wanted to cancel the school dance—"

"Boo!" the class shouts.

Mrs. James raises a finger, silencing them. I let out a sigh, knowing that the boos will turn into yeahs after she finishes speaking.

The only reason I know this is because Nicole told me this morning that her father had threatened to get the school shut down if they didn't allow the school dance, which is next week, to proceed. She was determined to have the dance this year and would do anything to make it happen.

"Students, please listen, though. After a few . . . meetings that the teachers and the principal have had, we have finally decided to proceed with the school dance. But, of course, there are rules," Mrs. James says.

After the cheering stops, she grabs a marker and turns to write something on the board.

Rules for the School Dance:
NO alcohol
NO drugs
NO fights
NO guests from other schools

NO short shorts, crop tops, or anything that may be considered inappropriate

As the students groan at the rules, I smile to myself. I'm so glad the school dance will not be as terrible as last year.

Oh, what happened last year? Well, since the principal said there were no rules at all and told everyone to just have fun and be *responsible*, everyone took that as an opportunity to turn the school dance into a full-blown teenage party.

It was absolutely horrifying.

Now the principal has—thankfully—learned his lesson and made actual rules for the school dance. I mean, no one wants a repeat of last year, right?

Well, except for the stupid teenagers at this school.

"Now, these are the rules. If you don't want to follow them, don't even bother coming. The school dance is on Friday next week, so make sure to listen for any updates," Mrs. James says.

The students begin to gossip among themselves.

Oh, I hope that this year will be different from last year.

I am crossing my fingers.

*   *   *

After sitting in a classroom with Mrs. James, who is actually sleeping right now (she's always tired during class, but of course, the students use this to their advantage, that's why they don't tell on her), I finally hear the bell ring. I jump from my seat and make my way out of the classroom as fast as I can.

You might be wondering why I am so eager to get out of this place. Well, there is only one answer to that—Luke.

At lunch, he messaged me, telling me to hurry up when the bell rings and meet him at his car. He wants to take me somewhere. I have no idea why he is doing this now, but something tells me that I am going to like it either way.

I look around the parking lot, and my eyes land on his car right away. I jog over to him. As soon as he sees me, he jumps out of his convertible and holds his arms out for me to wrap mine around him.

"I see you got my message then," he says.

I look up at him and smile. "Of course I did. Now, why don't you stop talking and take me to this secret place?"

He raises an eyebrow at me. "Eager?"

I nod. "Always."

He lets me go and walks around the car to the driver's side as I climb in beside him and buckle my seatbelt. He starts the car, and I lean into the seat, enjoying the breeze touching my face.

I wonder where Luke is taking me . . .

*   *   *

"This place is beautiful! Oh, and look, there are horses here!" I squeal and run over to the fence where the brown horse is. I smile and stroke its ear, trying to keep myself calm.

Luke appears beside me and leans against the wooden fence.

"Ever ridden a horse, Gracie?" he asks.

I cannot help but laugh at how dirty that sounded coming out of his mouth.

Oh, dear Lord, what has Luke done to my mind?

"What's so funny?" he asks.

I shake my head, waving him off. "Don't worry."

He shakes his head a little, looking a bit confused. All of a sudden, someone whistles, followed by some clapping.

"Long time no see, Lukie boy," someone says.

Luke and I turn around to see a redhead holding two helmets in her hand. I look over at Luke and frown.

"If this is another one of your exes—"

"I'm actually his cousin, missy." The girl suddenly appears beside me.

I squeal and jump away from her and bump against Luke's chest. The girl smiles and holds the helmet out for me to take. Luke grabs my hand and steps beside me, taking the helmets from her hands.

"Thanks, Michelle. And yeah, it's been a long time," Luke says.

Michelle crosses her arms over her chest.

"So, who's the girl?" Michelle asks, looking over at me.

Luke rubs his thumb over my hand as if he knows that I am nervous.

God, he knows me too well.

"This is my girlfriend, Grace," he says, sending me a small smile.

I look at Michelle, who stares at me from head to toe. She walks over to Luke and pats him on the shoulder. "You should stick with this one before I take her."

My eyes widen in shock.

She bursts out laughing and crouches down to the floor, her hands on her knees.

Luke waves me off and rolls his eyes. "Michelle is just trying to scare you. She does this to everyone."

I look down at Michelle, who suddenly burst out laughing.

"Is she on drugs?" I whisper as I stare at Michelle, who is still laughing.

Luke stares at his cousin. "I have no idea."

*   *   *

I lean against the rock, looking down at the river in front of me. I lean forward and swirl my finger in the water, enjoying the sound of the peace in the countryside.

"I'm back," Luke says.

I turn around to see him on a horse with a guitar in his hand, while controlling the horse. He gets off the horse, ties the rope to a tree branch, and sits next to me, leaning against the rock.

"You went all the way back to get a guitar?" I ask.

Luke shrugs. "I always play the guitar when I'm here."

I look up at him, a small smile on my face.

"Play a song."

He frowns. "Now?"

"No, tomorrow." I roll my eyes. "Yes, now," I say with a chuckle.

He sighs, nodding.

I lean my head against his shoulder and close my eyes when he begins to strum. The familiar tune fills my ears, and I cannot help but smile when he begins to sing.

"You with the sad eyes, don't be discouraged. Oh, I realise it's hard to take courage. . ." He softly sings, playing the chords perfectly. As he continues, I cannot help but join in when he sings the chorus.

We both sing the words, I cannot help but let my mind wander back to the time my parents used to sing me this song when I was young. If I was sad or feeling down, they would always sing this song to help me calm down and relax.

As we sing the last bit, a small tear makes its way down my face as an image of my parents appears in my mind.

Forever and always.

CHAPTER FORTY-THREE
Please Don't Fall

I run through the forest, ignoring the sweat dripping down the side of my face. I turn around, following the sound of a certain voice that keeps calling my name from different directions, confusing me. I stop and close my eyes.

"Grace!" the person yells again.

I shake my head, collapsing to the ground and leaning against a large, thick oak tree.

"Grace!" the voice calls again.

I cover my ears with my hands, still shaking my head.

"Go away!" I scream, but the voice continues to call my name. I begin to breathe heavily as my heart races.

"Grace, it's okay," a gentle voice says.

I open my eyes to see Luke smiling down at me. He holds out his hand, and before I can grab it, I feel my body drop to the ground.

I scream and look down to see my parents fighting. Suddenly, I fall onto the kitchen floor and watch Dad throwing a bottle at Mum, a scream escaping her lips.

All at once, Luke appears in front of Dad and throws a punch. Eve runs in and pulls Dad away from Luke, whose face is as red as a tomato.

I gasp when I feel hands on my hips. I spin around and see Randy. I scream and shut my eyes, wishing I could disappear from it all.

Suddenly, I am standing on the ledge of the school roof, nearly all the students staring up at me with daring looks, as if they are challenging me. Tears rush down my face as I take a step forward—but before my body hits the ground, my eyes open.

These dreams are going to be the end of me, I swear. I suddenly sit up, panting heavily.

I look around to see that I am in my room, a sleeping Luke by my side. I let out a sigh as I stretch my arms above my head. I also stretch my legs until they crack, immediately stopping at the sound that makes me shiver in disgust. I rub my eyes before opening them, looking back at Luke, who has his face buried in the pillow.

I get out of bed and yawn again as I make my way out of my bedroom and into the bathroom. I look at myself in the mirror and cringe slightly. My hair is a mess, and my face is as pale as ever.

"Yuck," I mutter, grabbing my toothbrush.

I spread the toothpaste on my brush before running it under the tap for a second. I turn the tap off, then begin brushing my teeth while looking at myself in the mirror. After brushing my teeth for three minutes, I wash my toothbrush and rinse my mouth, wiping it with the towel after I'm finished.

"You're up early," someone says.

I turn to the side to see Eve standing in the doorway with a small smile.

I rub my eyes once more before nodding. "Yeah . . ." I trail off, and Eve lets out a sigh.

"Grace, can I ask you something?" Eve asks, grabbing my attention.

I look over at her, frowning slightly. "Yeah, go ahead."

She looks down and then looks at me, shaking her head. She waves me off and sighs. "Actually, never mind."

I nod slowly, a little confused. I push my curiosity away and nod again. "Okay," I say, walking out of the bathroom.

I look over my shoulder to see her walking back to her room with her hands on her stomach, like she is in pain or something.

What did she want to ask me?

I walk back into my room and glance at the time. My eyes are heavy from lack of sleep. I climb into bed and snuggle into

Luke's chest. When his arm pulls me closer, I smile and let myself drift off, finally feeling somewhat safe.

*   *   *

"So, what do you feel like doing today?" Luke asks, sitting on my bed as he dries his hair with the towel.

I bite my lip and turn around, not wanting to blush, but something tells me that I already am.

"I-I don't know," I mutter, feeling his warm body pressing against my back. I suck in a breath, remembering that he is only wearing a towel.

Please don't fall.

"You know, I thought you would be used to me by now," he says.

I can practically imagine the smirk on his lips. I turn around and press my back against the wall, trying not to feel shy or intimidated by him.

"I-I am," I stutter.

He raises an eyebrow at me, his blonde hair sticking to his forehead. He places his hands on my sides, caging me in. I look into his blue eyes, trying to push away the weird feelings that are in my stomach.

"No, you're not. You're as red as a tomato," he grins.

I shake my head. "You're seeing things," I tell him promptly.

He takes off his hand and places it on my cheek. "And you're burning," he adds.

I shake my head again. "I'm sick," I say, trying to hide the fact that he is right.

But I cannot let him know that he is right, because who knows where his ego might take him? It is already up in the clouds, obviously, so if he knows that he is right, it might just end up breaking through the atmosphere and landing on Jupiter.

"Really?" Luke asks.

I nod. Before he can say anything else, I quickly place my hands on his chest and push him away from me at the sound of a knock on the door.

God, one minute I'm comfortable with him, but now I'm acting as shy as ever. What is wrong with me?

I walk over to the door and swing it open to see William smiling at me. I look over my shoulder to see Luke glaring at William. I roll my eyes and point over to his clothes so he can get them on. He scoffs before grabbing his clothes and pushing past William to go to the bathroom.

"Wow, he still thinks that I am hitting on you, huh?" William laughs, and I nod.

He points into the room. I nod and allow him to walk in. He sits on the bed and pats the seat next to him. I take a seat next to him on my bed, watching as he takes his cap off his head, revealing his short brown hair.

"So, has Eve told you?" he asks.

I furrow my eyebrows. "Told me what?" I ask.

He lets out a sigh. "Okay . . . ," he starts. "She is at the hospital."

I gasp, covering my mouth.

Before I can say anything, William waves me off, obviously noticing my reaction. "Nothing bad happened."

I let out a sigh, nodding. "Well . . . why is she at the hospital, then?"

"She has an appointment with one of the doctors."

I nod for him to continue. He places his hand on my shoulder and sends me a warm smile that makes my heart race.

"She believes she might be pregnant, Grace."

CHAPTER FORTY-FOUR
I Miss Them

I feel my heart practically stop when the words finally register in my head after two long minutes. My blood runs cold, and I stand up, ignoring William's questioning looks.

Eve is pregnant . . . with Dad's child? Oh, who am I kidding? Of course, it is my father's baby.

Wait—what will Mum think about this?

No, that's not what I should be thinking.

The question I should be asking myself is: What do I think about this?

"Where are you going?" William asks as I walk to the door, grab my coat off the rack, and open the front door.

"For a walk," I say, not bothering to look back at him. I walk out the door and begin heading to the only place where I can actually let my thoughts take over my mind.

*   *   *

"And then he told me that Eve is pregnant with his child," I say, playing with my fingers as I look down at the ground. After a few minutes of silence, I let out a sigh, staring at my mother's gravestone.

"I don't know if I should be happy or not. I mean, is it bad to be happy about this sort of stuff?" I ask, looking at Mum's name.

I swallow the lump in my throat and let out a dry laugh.

"Wow, look at me. Talking to my dead mum, who only appears in my dreams. I guess someone needs to go to the mental house," I say.

Suddenly, a hand taps my shoulder, making me jump in fright. I look over to see Eve smiling at me.

"E-Eve . . ." I hold my chest upon seeing her.

She sits next to me and wraps her cardigan around her.

"You hate me, don't you?"

My eyes widen. I shake my head and frown at her.

"Hate you? Why would I hate you?"

She places her hand on her stomach and frowns. I look at her stomach for a brief two seconds before meeting her eyes.

"Hate is a strong word," I say.

"I know," she says, glancing over at Dad's gravestone next to Mum's. She smiles and runs her hand over the words "loving father," and I cannot help but look away.

I cannot cry.

"You know, I found that letter in your parents' room the other night," Eve says.

My eyes widen. "What did you do with it?"

"Well, first of all, I read it," she says. "I'm guessing that the news was a huge shock to you."

I nod, not saying a word. I would've done the same thing if I were in her position.

She pulls a piece of paper from her pocket. I gasp when I recognize the letter. She holds it out to me.

"I . . ." I look away, hesitating whether I should take it from her, and blink away the tears that are trying to escape my eyes.

She sighs and reaches for me to look at her.

"You can cry, Grace. It's okay to cry." As she says this, she takes my hand, opens it, and places the letter in it. I look down at it, and when I see my name on the front, I feel the first tear fall.

"I miss them," I choke out.

"I know you do. Look."

She points at the spot between my parents' graves and sticks her finger into the grass that is separating them. She holds her hand out, and I give her the letter, watching what she is doing. She rolls the letter up and places it in the hole in the ground. The letter sticks out, and before she can dig any further, I stop her.

"I like it this way," I say.

She smiles, nodding. She claps the dirt off her hands and stands up. She holds her hand out to me to help me stand. I take her hand, and as we begin to walk away, I look behind me and take one last look at my parents, a small smile forming on my face.

"Forever and always."

*   *   *

Dear Diary,

I haven't written for a while now, so here I am. The last time I wrote was when I nearly jumped off the school's building, and ever since that day, a lot of things have happened. But the three main things are: Luke and I are now dating, Nicole and I are friends again, and Eve is pregnant.

About the first one—it has been, I think, a month now since we started dating. I don't know, because I haven't been counting; I am just not the kind of person who counts. I find it weird. But anyway, there have been a lot of ups and downs—like when Luke's ex-girlfriend came back to get revenge, or whatever she wanted to do.

I read a message on Luke's phone that said something about a dare. The dare was about me, obviously. Basically, the bet was $500, and it was for him to start talking to me and eventually date me, which led to something serious. He agreed to do it to save his dad. Unfortunately, even after Luke received the money to help with the operation, his dad couldn't be saved, which tore Luke and his mum apart—to the point where Luke's mum wanted to die.

The second one . . . well, there isn't much to say about this. I guess it was just that loneliness (even though I still have Luke by my side) got to me and made me want a best friend again, even if it had to be the one who bullied me every day for the past six years or whatever. What ran through my mind that day, when she asked me to be her friend, was the saying "forgive and forget," which is why I accepted Nicole's friendship again.

The last one basically says it all. Eve is pregnant with Dad's child. Also, my dad just passed away. My life is so damn great, right? I don't know how this baby is going to live, but all I know is that this baby—whether a girl or a boy—is going to be my half-brother or sister, which makes me somewhat happy. I have never had a sibling, but the thought of having one makes me happy, because I never had that person who looks at me and is proud to call me his sister. All I know is that I have to try my hardest to prove to this child that I can be someone he can talk to, even though I didn't have that at all.

Until next time . . .

Grace Leigh Parkinson

CHAPTER FORTY-FIVE
Should I Get It?

A week passed by quickly, and now I find myself looking at the flyer on the wall on a Wednesday morning. My eyes scan the words on the purple flyer. I let out a sigh and rip it off the wall.

I hope they cancel that damn school dance.

"Hey! Now I have to print out another one!" a girl comments, walking past me. I don't bother to look at her. I throw the flyer in the bin and continue walking to class, hating every single stare coming my way.

Why the hell is everyone staring at me?

"If you have a problem with my girlfriend, speak up," a voice says behind me.

I turn around to see Luke. Immediately, I throw my arms around his neck in a hug.

He laughs, kisses my hair, and rubs my back.

"Hello, Gracie."

I lean back to look at my boyfriend. "I feel like I haven't seen you in forever!"

He laughs, scratching the back of his neck with his free hand. "That's because we haven't seen each other since William paid a visit. I thought you would be too busy with the baby thing, so . . . ," he trails off.

I roll my eyes. "You're a liar."

He shakes his head, placing a hand on his heart. "I lie not, Gracie. It's the truth." He smiles.

I roll my eyes playfully before grabbing his hand. Together, we walk to our first class. We enter the gymnasium and stand with the other students, waiting for Mr. Peters to arrive.

*   *   *

After running ten laps around the field and doing about fifty push-ups, I have officially turned to jelly. My legs are shaking, and my arms are so sore. I now know how the football team feels after training.

I let out a sigh and place my hands over my head, blocking out the sun. The grass beneath me tickles my legs, and I shake them, trying to get rid of the weird tingling sensation.

"Tired?" someone asks.

I move one hand away and look at one of Nicole's friends, grinning at me. I frown and sit up, placing a hand over my face to cover it from the sun as I look up at the stranger. Suddenly, the memory hits me like a bus. I gasp and immediately stand up, stepping away from the girl.

"Please," I choke out, placing my hands in front of me. "Just . . . leave me alone. I don't want any trouble," I say quickly before running away from the girl.

I ignore the pain in my legs and continue running up the hill and into the school building. I brush off the strange looks coming from the students as I head to the girls' bathroom, open one of the stalls, and close the door behind me.

I sit on the toilet and sigh, running my hand over my hair. I close my eyes and take in a deep breath, trying to block out the memories of what happened last year.

After a few seconds, the door opens and a familiar voice calls my name. "Grace, are you in here?" It is Nicole's voice.

I stay quiet, just wanting to be left alone. I wait for Nicole to leave, but instead, I keep hearing the clicking of her heels against the tiled floor as she walks around the bathroom. The door to the first stall slams against the wall, and I instantly know she is going to find me.

"Grace . . ."

Closing my eyes, I calculate the amount of time it should take her to get to my stall, counting down as she pushes every door open.

When I know that she's finally reaching the stall where I'm in, I let out a sigh and open my eyes. I wait for Nicole to open the door or say something. I frown in confusion when nothing happens. A few seconds later, a paper slides under the door. I look at it, my eyebrows furrowing.

Should I get it?

"Just pick it up, Grace," Nicole says.

I immediately grab the piece of paper and unfold it. I squint my eyes at her scribbled writing, trying to recognise the words.

Come out and we will talk, okay? - Nicole

I let out a sigh and clear my throat, standing up. I open the door and see her smiling at me.

"Thank you," she says.

I nod at her, walking out of the stall. I look at myself in the mirror and turn on the tap, washing my face with warm water. As I do this, Nicole begins to talk.

"I saw Ember approach you a while back, Grace. You looked pretty disturbed by her presence, and I'm thinking it was because of what happened last year. Am I right?" she asks.

I pause and let my hands rest under the warm running water for a moment. Then I turn off the tap and grab a paper towel, drying my face and my hands before turning to her.

"Don't speak of that day. I . . . I don't want to remember it at all."

She sighs, nodding. "I know but—"

"Nicole, I said no," I cut her off sternly. Before she can say anything else, I turn on my heel, toss the paper towel into the bin, and walk out of the bathroom.

I ignore her voice calling my name and head back to the gymnasium, where Luke is.

I don't want to remember . . .

*   *   *

"Why do we have to go back to Daniel's?" I ask Luke as he turns a corner, entering Daniel's street.

We stop in front of the house, and Luke cuts the engine and turns to face me.

"We just have to." He gets out of the car.

I let out a sigh and follow him, standing beside him as he looks at Daniel's house.

We walk to the porch. Luke knocks on the door loudly, and after a few seconds, it opens, revealing a tired-looking Daniel.

"Hey guys," Daniel greets, stepping to the side so we can enter. We walk towards the couch and sit. Luke glances over at Randy and Jackson, who are huddled near the television, talking about something that looks pretty serious.

"They are talking about the business," Daniel informs Luke.

Luke nods, leaning back into the couch.

Daniel does the same and rubs his eyes, a frown etched across his face. "So . . . why are you here?" he asks.

Luke glances over at me and lets out a sigh, leaning closer to my ear.

"Can you go to the kitchen? I . . . I have to talk to Daniel about something private," he whispers.

I stand up and make my way to the kitchen, closing the door behind me. I walk to the table, sit on a stool, grab the water jug, and pour myself a cup.

But before the cup touches my lips, a hand snatches it from my grip. I turn around and see Randy frowning at me.

"Tequila," he says, and puts the cup down on the table.

I frown. "What?"

"Tequila. What you were about to drink was tequila. You know . . . alcohol . . . ," he trails off.

I gape at him, finally understanding. I nod and cross my arms over my chest, feeling quite cold.

"Could you maybe get me a glass of water, please? I am a little tired from school today," I say with a chuckle.

He nods, walks to the cabinet, takes out a glass, fills it with water, and hands it to me.

I thank him, taking a sip.

"So . . . ," I begin. "What's this business you boys are in?" I ask, a little interested.

Randy scratches the back of his neck awkwardly. "I sort of can't tell you that."

"Oh . . ."

Randy lets out a short sigh. "I mean, it's not like I don't want to tell you, it's just that I can't," he clears up.

I wave him off, nodding.

"I understand. It's fine."

He nods. "Okay."

All of a sudden, an awkward silence fills the air, making me feel very uncomfortable. I think he begins to feel it too because he starts looking around the kitchen, tapping his foot nervously.

"Grace . . . ," he says, breaking the silence.

I look up at him, taking a sip of my water.

He sighs and takes a seat next to me. "I'm sorry again for doing all that stuff to you."

I swallow the water and let out a sigh. "Randy, you've already apologized—"

"I know, but I feel like saying it again. The pain I put you through and the nightmares . . . I feel like a horrible person. I promise, though, that I will never do that again—"

"Never do what again?" a familiar voice asks.

We both turn around to see Luke standing in the doorway with a concerned look on his face.

I gulp, remembering that I have not told him about my past with Randy.

He looks between the two of us.

I shake my head, waving him off. "Don't worry about it. It's nothing." I assure him.

He shakes his head. "No, tell me," he insists.

I gulp and glance over at Randy, who is looking down at his shoes, ashamed.

I don't think I'm going to get out of this one . . .

CHAPTER FORTY-SIX
I Didn't Mean to Scare You

I glance between the two boys and gulp once again, not wanting to tell Luke that the boy who assaulted me is the one standing next to me. I mean, how am I supposed to tell him that? *Oh yeah, so, remember when I told you I started cutting my arms because of the boy who touched me? Well, that boy is, like, right next to me!*

"Talk, Grace," Luke says, his tone serious.

I rub my arm and let out a sigh, glancing once more over at Randy.

I can do this. I mean, what harm can it do?

Luke will probably break a few of Randy's bones, but at least he will still be alive, right?

Just calm down and speak, my brain says.

I look up at Luke and open my mouth, ready to say the words that might start a brawl between the two of them. But just as I am about to speak, Randy cuts me off.

"I touched Grace . . . ages ago. When we were young. I was stupid and—"

Before he can continue, Luke lunges towards him.

He grabs the nearest thing and clutches it in his hand.

I gasp. A knife!

"How dare you do that to Grace?! You have no idea what pain you put her through, and you think 'sorry' is just going to make her feel happy as freaking Larry? You should be dead!" Luke screams, pressing the knife to Randy's throat.

I let out a scream.

I want to move and stop Luke. I want them to just calm down, but not a single bone in my body can move. It's like my feet are glued to the ground, and my mouth just hangs open as I watch the two of them.

Watch.

All I can do is watch.

Daniel and Jackson storm into the kitchen and immediately pull Luke off Randy. Jackson snatches the knife from Luke's hand, gripping it tightly. Daniel shoots them both a warning glare before releasing Luke.

Luke leans against the wall, clenching his fists.

I have never seen this side of Luke before. If I am being honest, he is scaring me.

I sink to the floor, my body going numb. I lean against the wall and let my eyes shut as the voices are drowned out by the ringing in my head. All I hear is a blur of voices, and I feel the boys' hands shaking my arms and shoulders in an attempt to wake me from the nightmare.

But I guess I can never escape something called reality.

* * *

Someone taps my shoulder, and I stop walking, freezing in my spot. I slowly turn around to see my parents standing side by side, with smiles on their faces. I smile and pull both of them into a hug.

"Why do I feel like I haven't seen you in ages?" I ask.

Mum chuckles as I pull away. "Because we were busy with a few things," she says.

I furrow my eyebrows, looking between her and Dad. He notices my confusion, and a smile appears on his face as he raises his arm, revealing a new tattoo.

I step forward to take a closer look, my eyes scanning it. When I finally realise what it is, tears begin to fill my eyes.

It is a small, detailed tattoo of him, Mum, and me. I still remember the place where that photo was taken, and I can't help but smile. It was my tenth birthday. Mum and Dad always knew I wanted to go to the beach, and on my birthday, we drove for three hours to see the water, the sand, and the sun. The scene is burned into my memory. Just as the sun was setting, Dad asked a man to take a picture of the three of us. We all instantly loved it when we saw it.

I look up at Dad and smile, pulling him into a hug. "I love it."

He chuckles. "I knew you would."

I pull away and glance at both of them, the smile still on my face.

"Grace, we have to go, okay?" Mum says.

I nod slowly, knowing she would say that eventually. I pull them into one last hug—then let my body come alive, waking up.

I get up from the mattress and look around, not recognising the room at all. I frown and rip the sheet off me, then step off the bed. I walk over to the door and open it, looking at the empty hallway. I step out of the room and head down the hall. To my left is a flight of stairs, and I let out a sigh when I realise that I am still at Daniel's place.

I walk down the stairs and glance around, hoping to find Luke. I enter the kitchen and see him sitting at the table with Daniel beside him. I smile and knock on the wall, grabbing their attention. Both boys turn around, smiles spreading across their faces. I walk over to Luke and pull him into a hug.

"Hey, are you feeling okay?" he asks.

I nod, stepping away. I look up at Daniel and wave. "Hi."

He nods. "Afternoon."

I frown. "Afternoon? What's the time?"

He glances at his watch. "Six o'clock," he says.

I let out a sigh, running a hand through my hair. "Oh, okay. Where is everyone else?"

Daniel points towards the living room. I nod, then look back at Luke, who is frowning at me.

"I'll leave you two alone," Daniel says.

I nod, watching as he leaves the kitchen.

Luke pulls me into another hug.

"I'm so sorry, Gracie. I didn't mean to scare you. I . . . I was just so angry with Randy, you know? I really didn't mean to scare you. I swear."

I nod, hugging him back. "I know. Just don't ever scare me like that again."

"I won't," he says, a smile spreading across his face.

CHAPTER FORTY-SEVEN
Do You Know the Gender of the Baby?

I sit on the couch and place the bowl of popcorn beside me, grabbing the blanket and throwing it over my body. I get comfortable and place the bowl on my lap, watching as the movie Romeo and Juliet begins to play.

After hanging out with Luke for a few hours at his place, I finally decided to head home alone. Well, that was the plan—until he insisted on driving me home because he was afraid someone would hurt me. I did not complain, though, because that would mean spending more time with him. Now, it is ten o'clock and I have decided to watch a movie, as I cannot seem to fall asleep.

The door opens, and I look over to see Eve walk through it, a sigh escaping her lips. She looks over at me and sends me a small smile.

"Hey, Grace."

I wave at her after shoving a handful of popcorn into my mouth.

She walks over and looks at the television, a grin playing on her lips. "Romeo and Juliet, huh?"

I nod, looking back at the television. A chuckle escapes from her mouth. She appears in the reflection of the butterfly mirror beside the TV, places her handbag on the counter, and walks over to the couch to join me.

She sits beside me, and I share the blanket with her. She thanks me and places it over her legs. I set the popcorn between us and watch as the reporter on the screen begins to talk.

All of a sudden, the television goes black, and the lights turn off. I gasp and immediately jump up, feeling the popcorn run down my bare leg.

"What the hell is happening?" I ask. When I feel a hand on my shoulder, I let out a scream.

Eve laughs.

I look to my left, where a bright light comes from. Eve is shining the flashlight on her face.

"It's a blackout, Grace," she explains.

I let out a sigh of relief, standing up. "I knew that . . . ," I mumble.

She lets out another laugh. "Do you know where some candles are?" she asks while standing up, and I nod.

She hands me her phone, and I use the flashlight to guide me to the kitchen, where Mum hid the candles from me since I loved to keep them in my room at bedtime.

I pull open the cupboard door under the sink and grab the three cylinder glasses, placing them on the counter. I grab three candles and place them with the rest.

"Now, we just need to find a match or something," Eve says.

I nod, trying to remember where my father left the lighters. I walk towards the kitchen door and head upstairs. I walk into my parents' room and start searching the drawers.

Instead of finding a lighter, my eyes widen at the sight of a tape recorder.

Another explanation from my parents?

"What the . . . ," I gasp, grabbing the tape recorder and placing it in the pocket of my jumper. I look behind me to see Eve entering the room. I continue looking for the lighter.

I check one of the drawers and move the clothes aside to find a blue lighter. I let out a sigh and grab it, closing the drawer. I turn around and hand it to Eve, not wanting to be near the lighter, let alone be holding it.

"Good job, Grace. Now, let's go and light some candles."

*   *   *

"Do you know the gender of the baby?" I ask, glancing down at Eve's stomach. It is still flat, but I can tell that in a month or so, a little bump will begin to show.

She smiles and shakes her head. "No, not yet. It's still pretty early. We won't know till later."

"Well, when the time comes and the doctor asks if you want to know the gender of the baby, what will you say? Do you want to know or keep it a surprise?" I ask, curious about the whole thing.

Eve chuckles and shrugs. "I have no idea. One minute, I want to know if the baby is a boy or a girl, but a second later, I don't. I'm still deciding . . . ," she explains. "What about you? What do you think, Grace?"

"Huh?"

"What do you think I should do?"

I furrow my eyebrows.

"About the gender of the baby . . ," she adds when I still do not say anything.

I shrug. "No idea. I mean, you should do whatever you want, so I don't see why you're asking me. I'm not the one popping a baby out of . . . there," I say, looking away from her.

She grins at me.

After a few seconds, she stands up from the couch and holds her hand out to me. "Come on, I want to show you something."

I take her hand and stand. She takes one of the candles and holds it in her left hand as she guides us to the stairs.

After walking up the stairs, she walks down the hallway and into her room—the spare room. She places the candle on the table and sits on the bed, reaching under her pillow to grab something. I take a seat next to her and watch as she moves her hand under the pillow, clearly searching for something.

She pulls her hand out, and when she shows me the item, I furrow my eyebrows in confusion.

"This is a picture of me, my sister, and my parents," she says, pointing at the people in the picture.

I take it from her hands and study it, noticing how she looks a little . . . uneasy in the picture. Her mum's hand is on her shoulder, which is probably why she looks so uneasy. I mean, she did say that she did not like her mum because of what she did to her dad.

That sounds a little like my life . . .

I look at her sister and smile, noticing how close they seem. You would expect sisters to stand a normal distance apart, but in the picture, they look like they do not want any space between them at all. I glance at her sister's blonde hair and frown in confusion—Eve's parents do not have blonde hair, at least from what I can see.

"Eve," I say, and she looks at the picture. "Your sister . . . why does she have blonde hair when both of your parents have brown hair?"

She sighs. "You know how I said my mum cheated on my dad? Well, my dad isn't actually Ella's father, if you get what I'm saying."

I nod, my lips parting as I piece it all together. "So, where is Ella now?"

She lets out a sigh. "You'd think I would know, since we were so close, but ever since my dad died, it's like she didn't want to be around me. And it's been years since Ella ran away."

I frown. "What about your mum? Wouldn't she have some connection to her? Wouldn't she know?"

She shrugs. "I wouldn't know. Besides, I have no plans of talking to my mum. She is the one who broke my family apart anyway."

I nod. "Yeah, but don't you want to see your sister? I mean, she would be happy that you're having another child." I smile.

Eve lets out a sigh. "I do . . . it's just so complicated. I don't even know where to start looking for Ella. I don't know her dad, and I don't want to talk to my mum." She furrows her eyebrows and looks over at me. "Wait—"

She grabs the candle and turns to me, then smiles. "You could help me."

"Me?" I frown. "I don't even know how to help myself. How will I be able to help you?"

She chuckles. "I'll work out the details. Until then, clear your schedule for the weekend. We are going to go visit my hometown."

CHAPTER FORTY-EIGHT
Yes, A Sleepover!

I sit down on my bed and turn on my lamp, looking down at the tape recorder in front of me. The power is back on and has been for the past ten minutes.

Anyway, it has been an hour since Eve fell asleep in her room. I have tried going to bed, but every time I shut my eyes, my mind wanders back to the tape recorder. Well, aside from that, my mind is still pretty active, thinking about the dance and other small stuff. I still cannot help but feel that going to the dance is a bad idea.

Yes, I have decided that I am going to the dance. Actually, Luke forced me, saying I should not worry because nothing bad would happen. How sure is he? Oh, yeah, he told everyone who has a grudge against me or has had a bad past with me, warning them that if he catches—or even hears about—someone planning a revenge plot or a prank against me, he will ruin their life.

Oh, how funny he is.

I mean, he hardly even swears, and the only thing he calls people—whether he either does not like them or I don't—is "gorillas." What can he possibly do to ruin somebody's life? Call them something worse than a gorilla? Honestly, Luke is one strange but amazing boy.

Ugh—I'm getting off track here. What was I talking about? Oh, yeah—the tape recorder. Okay, so I have no idea what is on that tape recorder, and to be honest, I do not even want to know. It could be something good, but then again, when is anything ever good in my life? The letter . . . that was life-changing, not good. The baby . . . again, life-changing . . . not good. I'm still confused about the baby. I do not know if I want to be part of the baby's life.

Is it bad that I do not want a sibling? I mean, what if he or she hates me? What if he or she doesn't want me in the family? What if—

Oh, here I go again with the what-ifs. I wish I could just push all my problems away and never deal with them. Imagine if you could do that. I swear, I would be the happiest, most carefree person in the whole—

Oops, getting off track again. Anyway, the tape recorder . . . I do not know if I should listen to whatever is on it. What if it is something that will make me think too much? Like, what if my parents are not actually my parents or . . . what if I was a mistake—

Good thoughts, Grace. Good thoughts . . .

My brain cuts in, and I let out a sigh, glancing at the black tape recorder again. Maybe I should ask someone what to do.

Luke? Oh, I doubt he is still awake at this hour. Besides, if I message him now, he will probably ask me in the morning why I was still awake at this time. I could just say that it was the tape recorder—since it is exactly the reason I messaged him—but ugh . . . I really do not want to keep answering his questions.

Eve? No—she is asleep. I do not want to wake her up; she has a lot of stuff going through her head already. I do not want her to worry. But then again, before she fell asleep, she did say that if I needed anything, I should tell her. No—I cannot. She needs rest.

Wait—what about Nicole? I mean, we are friends again, aren't we? Friends are supposed to come to each other for help and advice, but . . . would she listen? What would she even say about it? I can already see it: Nicole is going to say "Listen to it," because she is honestly the nosiest person ever. Just because she would listen if it were her, that does not mean she has to tell me to listen.

I look at my phone in the drawer, and let out a frustrated sigh.

Should I?

Do it, Grace—my brain pushes—and I find myself reaching out to grab my phone. I type in my password and open my contacts, searching for Nicole's name on the screen.

What if she isn't awake? What if she is at a party? What if she—

"Breathe . . ." I mutter, inhaling through my nose and exhaling through my mouth. After a few seconds of thinking, I finally decide to click her name. The beeping begins, and I press the phone to my ear, hoping she will answer.

"Hello?" she asks.

I frown, a bit confused why she sounds so awake at this time. Maybe she is up thinking as well . . .

"Uh, hey, Nicole . . . it's Grace," I say.

Nicole sighs. "Thank goodness. I have been getting calls from different people all day, and when I saw a number on the screen, I was ready to yell."

I furrow my eyebrows. "Wouldn't your phone show my name?"

She chuckles. "I got a new phone. Anyway, what's up?"

I let out a sigh. "Uh, do you think you could come pick me up? I need you to . . . help me with something."

She gasps. "Really?"

I laugh. "Yeah."

"Yes—a sleepover! I'm coming now."

*   *   *

I sigh, brushing my hair out of my face once I finish packing my bag. I grab the piece of paper that I wrote on when Nicole ended the call and read it over, nodding in approval.

I leave my room and walk to Eve's. I push the door slowly, cringing at the soft creaking. Slowly, I step inside, thankful for the moonlight in the room so I don't trip over anything. I walk to her drawer and place the note next to her phone.

I'm pretty sure she will see it. Who would not wake up and immediately go for their phone?

I take one last look at Eve's sleeping form and let a small smile appear on my lips. I haven't known her for a long time, but from what we have recently been through, she has become very important to me. She has done so much for me. Some people might see her as a mum because she is over thirty, but to me, I see her like a sister. I do not know what I would have done without her.

I turn around and walk out, closing the door quietly behind me. As I pass the stairs, I notice a figure approaching the front door. Quickly, I walk to my bedroom, grab my bag off the bed, and sling it over my shoulder.

That must be Nicole.

I hurry down the stairs and swing open the door. All of a sudden, the figure grabs me, and before I can scream, someone hits me over the head with something hard, knocking me out immediately.

CHAPTER FORTY-NINE
Some Asshole Hit Me

Suddenly, I feel my body come alive, and I gasp, trying to look around, but since the room or wherever I am is pitch black, I can't see a thing. I try to think about the possible people who could have kidnapped me, but all of a sudden, my head begins to hurt, stopping me from thinking. When I try to reach for my throbbing head, I realise that my hands are strapped to something. I let out a cry.

Wow, Grace. You just had to get yourself into this mess . . . I say to myself, shaking my head. I bite my lip and try to hold the tears in. I have no idea where I am, and now I am strapped to a chair and my head is killing me.

"Pssst!" a voice says, and my head shoots up. I let out a groan at the sudden surge of pain. Once the pain subsides, after taking a few deep breaths, I furrow my eyebrows.

"Who was that?" I ask, trying to move my hands. All of a sudden, the light turns on, making my head hurt much more. I close my eyes, trying to take in the pain, but it does not work. I breathe in through my nose and out through my mouth before opening my eyes.

I look at the boy in front of me, who has a string in his mouth, near the light switch. I breathe out a sigh. He spits out the string and begins to shuffle his chair towards me.

"Grace . . ." he breathes out.

My eyes widen in shock. "How do you know my name?"

The boy stops moving when his knees touch mine. I look at his face and notice that his eyes are the same colour as mine—

an emerald green—and his hair is a little darker than mine, just like Mum's hair.

Could he be . . . related to me? No, that's impossible.

"I'm Bennet. You don't know me, Grace, but I know you," Bennet explains.

I frown. "Well, duh."

He smiles and looks at my face for a few seconds before smiling some more. "You really do look like *Mum*," he says.

My eyes widen in shock, and before I can say a word, the door swings open, and we both look over at the person who is standing in the doorway. Almost immediately, my eyes go dark with anger.

"James!" I shout.

James walks into the room, glancing between me and Bennet. He grabs the back of Bennet's chair and pulls him back to where his chair was before. I glance over at Bennet to see him glaring up at James.

"Nice to see you again, Grace," James greets, walking over to me. When he reaches me, he crouches down and grabs my chin, forcing me to look right into his eyes.

"Get your hands off me!" I shout, shaking my head.

He smiles and stands up, looking down at me. At a loud knock on the door, he sighs and runs a hand through his hair.

"I'll be back, you two. Then we shall start," he says, winking at us before leaving the room and closing the door behind him.

I glance back over at Bennet, and he frowns at me. "You two know each other?"

I nod. "Unfortunately," I mutter.

He leans back in his chair and looks around the room before letting out a sigh. "This James guy does not know anything about hygiene," he says, nodding his head towards the sink, where there is no soap.

I narrow my eyes at him but suddenly wince when my head begins to hurt.

"What happened to your head?" Bennet asks.

I grit my teeth. "Some asshole hit me."

He raises his eyebrow at me. "Who? James?"

I nod. "I'm not sure, but if I had to guess, I would have to say yes. Him."

He shakes his head, clenching his jaw. "From what I have already heard, I hate this James guy."

"Trust me, if I had the chance to never meet him, I would've taken it," I say.

Bennet nods.

As the silence gets the better of us, I watch as he looks out the window, his brown hair falling to the side of his face. I notice the small freckles running across the bridge of his nose.

Mum had freckles . . .

"Bennet . . . ," I say.

He looks over at me, his eyebrow raised. "Yes?"

Before I can ask him the question that has been running through my mind since I saw him, the door swings open, and there stands James with a smirk on his face.

"You would not believe who paid me a visit just now," he says.

Before I can even ask, a blond gets thrown into the room, a bandana around his mouth. I gasp when I realise who the blond is.

"Luke!" I scream, watching as his body hits the floor.

I look back at James to see him walk in with a chair. He grabs Luke from the ground and sits him in the chair. I clench my jaw as he grabs some rope to tie Luke's hands and feet to the chair. He turns to me and grabs a gun out of his back pocket, taking Bennet and me by surprise.

"Anyone moves dies," he says before walking out of the room again. I look over at Luke as tears start to form in my eyes.

"Luke, can you hear me?" I ask, looking at his closed eyes.

I gulp and bite my lip, calling his name again. When I do not get a response, I let out a cry, letting hot tears rush down my face.

"Ah, ah, don't cry! I won't allow that," Bennet says.

I look up at him, biting my lip. "Why won't you?"

He sends me a small smile. "Because your big brother doesn't like seeing his baby sister cry."

CHAPTER FIFTY
Chances Left, James

Brother? What the hell is my life turning into? A goddamn movie? Okay, director, why did you let Mum die? Why did you let Dad die? Why did you make Luke be an ass at the start? Why do I now have a brother? Why do you hate me so much?

This is unbelievable and unacceptable. Wouldn't Mum tell me if I have a brother or sister? What about Dad? Wait . . . maybe this guy is playing some sick joke.

Yeah, that is probably it.

"I don't believe you," I say, my tears stopping.

Bennet frowns and furrows his eyebrows. "What do you mean you don't believe me? I am your brother, Grace."

I shake my head. "I need proof."

He sighs. "Fine. Uh, ask me any question."

I nod, leaning back in my chair. I bite my lip and look around the room, thinking about a good question to ask my "brother."

"If you are my brother, when is my birthday?"

He frowns. "I don't—"

"You don't know? Oh, I knew it was too good to be true. You are a liar and an asshole. How dare you come out and say you're my—"

The door swings open, immediately shutting me up. I look over to see James walk in with a chair. He closes the door behind him and drops the chair in front of the three of us—

Bennet, Luke, and me. He grabs the gun, threatening us. He holds it over the chair, staring at us.

Wait, is Luke even alive?

Ah, ah, you can't talk that way about your boyfriend, my brain says, and I mentally let out a sigh.

He better be alive. Otherwise, I have to kill someone. I do not care if I go to jail. No one is taking another person I love away from me.

"What do you want, James?" I ask, breaking the silence.

James looks over at me and smirks. "Finally! The question I have been waiting for you to ask."

I just glare at him.

"You see, I'm going to jail for the murder of your not-so-precious dad," he explains.

I suck in a deep breath, trying not to explode.

"I will have a chance at bail, but only if three people don't testify against me. You know who those people are?" James asks, glancing between Bennet and me. I clench my jaw and nod, still trying to keep my cool.

He has three chances . . .

"It's you." James points at Bennet with his gun. "And you," he says, pointing at me, then at Luke. "And your fucked-up boyfriend."

Two chances left, James.

"Wait, he is your boyfriend?" Bennet asks, looking over at me.

Before I can answer him, James points the gun at Bennet.

"Questions at the end, thank you," James says, silencing us. "Anyway, I know you three are going to testify against me, unfortunately. I have a business to run, so that must not happen. I have brought you three here today to explain a few things." He clicks his fingers.

All of a sudden, a tall man walks into the room and walks over to Luke, untying the bandana from his mouth. When the guy sticks a needle into Luke's arm, all of a sudden, Luke jumps up and looks around.

"Where the hell am I?" Luke asks, and his eyes widen when he sees James, Bennet, and me. "Explanation, please."

"I'm doing exactly that now," James says.

Luke stands up and takes in what is happening, taking notice of our tied legs. He glares at James and clenches his fists. "Why are we tied up, James?"

James smiles and points the gun at him, shutting him up but prompting me to scream.

"Questions . . . at the end," James warns, getting fed up. When we all shut up, he turns to the man and nods. The man walks out of the room and closes the door behind him.

"So, as I was saying, I have brought you here to explain a few things. Firstly, I won't let you go until you can guarantee me you won't say a word to anyone about this. Not to the police, not to your parents, and not to your friends. No one must know."

We all nod.

"Now, when the trial comes up, I don't want any of you to be there. You cannot testify against me. You come, you die. If you even think about coming, you die. And Grace . . ." James turns to me. "Tell Eve that you two are going to end up like your dad."

I clench my jaw.

One last chance, you son of a bitch . . .

"I won't tell anyone," I say.

He smiles. "Good girl. So, any questions?"

When we stay silent, he stands up, walks over to me, and throws me a wink. "Stay gorgeous, Grace."

I gather all the saliva in my mouth and spit it at him, hitting him right on his nose. He clenches his jaw and wipes it away with his sleeve. He holds the gun to me and shoots a bullet at my leg. I scream, my eyes widen. He rolls his eyes and walks out the door after muttering, "Bitch."

Luke and Bennet immediately begin to shuffle their chairs over to me. I look down at the graze on my leg.

God, I am so lucky that he missed. Your chances are gone, James. When I'm free from these ropes, you are so going to pay.

CHAPTER FIFTY-ONE
How Did You Get My Number?

I breathe out a sigh and sit on the porch, placing my bag beside me. I grab my phone, turn it on, and cringe at the number of missed calls and messages from Nicole.

I click on the messages and scroll down to the start. As I read through more than fifty messages, my phone goes off. I frown, looking at the No Caller ID.

Don't answer it, my brain says. I let out a sigh and click the Decline button. Suddenly, my phone goes off again, and I furrow my eyebrows in confusion.

Who the hell is this?

I press Decline again and roll my eyes. I look up and watch as a few cars pass by almost silently. I glance over at my driveway to see Eve's car still not there. I look back at my phone and lick my dry lips.

It has been an hour since I left James's hideout. Okay, well, I did not really leave—James untied me, letting me go first and leaving Luke and Bennet behind. I was not going to leave Luke, but James refused to let him go with me; however, he assured me Luke would be fine. Of course, I did not believe him. I stayed and glared at him, but his *associates* came and threw me out. They threw me out—literally—and I painfully landed on the grass.

After gathering the strength left in me, I began my long walk home. I check the time; James told me he would not keep Luke longer than half an hour, or I would call the police. I honestly do not care anymore. Like I said, I am not letting that bastard take another person I love away from me. I do not even know what he could be doing to Luke now . . . hopefully nothing bad.

"There you are!" someone says.

I look up and see Nicole storming towards me, a frown etched on her face. My eyes widen at her presence; I was not expecting her.

Wait—has she been walking around looking for me?

"Uh, hi?" I say, a little frightened and confused.

She grabs my hand and pulls me to her, sending me a glare. I stand in front of her and watch as her frown slowly turns into a small smile. All of a sudden, she brings me into a hug.

"Oh my God, I'm glad you're okay," she says.

I freeze, completely shocked.

She lets go of me and looks me over. "Did he hurt you?"

I frown in confusion. "Huh?"

"My brother. Did he hurt you?"

I step back and gasp. "Y-your brother?"

She frowns; concern is clear on her face. She narrows her eyes at me and crosses her arms over her chest.

I sit down on the porch, scared that if I stand too long I might fall down. My chest begins to tighten, and Nicole crouches down in front of me.

"Grace . . . ," she says, lifting my face towards her. "I'm talking about James."

My heart clenches in shock. I stand up and walk over to the grass, crouching down.

"Are you okay? Holy shit, what the hell did he do to you?" she asks, rubbing my back.

I push her away. "Move. I'm going to—"

Without finishing my sentence, I throw up the food I had last night. I immediately lunge forward as my stomach tightens. When I am finished, Nicole grabs my hand and pulls me towards the house. We sit down on the porch. She rubs my back and frowns.

"Explain everything to me."

"You're not serious . . . ," Nicole says.

I nod, wiping tears from my eyes.

She shakes her head and stands, placing her hands on her hips.

I have just told *everything*. We are still outside, sitting on the porch, since Eve is still not home and I stupidly forgot my spare key.

Hopefully she reads my note . . .

"So, you're telling me that my brother killed your dad and now he's threatening to kill you if you testify against him next week?" Nicole asks.

I nod. "That's exactly what I just said."

She lets out a growl. "I swear I should've put him in jail when I had the chance."

I furrow my eyebrows in confusion. "Huh?"

"I just spotted James selling ecstasy pills at a party one night, and the police were there and caught him. But since James said earlier that if he gets caught, I have to bail him out—meaning . . . I have to make an excuse and admit to doing it instead of him. So, I took the blame, and I got questioned, thrown into a holding cell for a few hours until he bailed me out. I got out since I never had any previous record, and I tested negative. If I didn't help him out, they would have locked him up since he had a history of selling drugs."

I gasp. "What? Why would you do that?"

She sighs. "James threatened that if I didn't take the blame, he would tell my parents that I lost my virginity—but I haven't, I swear!" she says, waving her hands.

I nod. "Okay, well, not to point fingers, but a few students said that you were a . . . uh—"

"Slut? Whore? I know, I hear it all the time. They are just rumours spread by my ex who got pissed when I broke up with him. Well, he drank a lot at a party and, uh . . . he tried to sexually assault me."

My mouth drops. I nod. "Oh . . ."

"Anyway, back to the topic at hand . . . I can't believe he killed your—sorry, I should stop bringing it up," Nicole says, biting the inside of her cheek.

"Yeah . . ."

All of a sudden, my phone rings. I immediately grab it, hoping that it is Luke or Eve. I answer the phone—not even checking the caller ID—press it to my ear, and wait for the voice to speak, as though I've lost the energy to say hello unless it could be James or—

"Hello, Grace," the familiar voice speaks.

I furrow my eyebrows. "How did you get my number?"

He lets out a sigh. "I want to explain. Please . . . ," Bennet says.

I shake my head. "That's not happening. I need a good reason to—"

"Your birthday is the 18th of August, Mum's birthday is the 9th of December, and Dad's is the 1st of February," he says quickly.

I narrow my eyes at the small flower beginning to bend towards the ground.

"Who is that?" Nicole asks.

I frown. "Bennet. The guy I was telling you about."

Nicole's eyes widen. She rushes over and sits down next to me, motioning me to put it on speaker. I do what she says and clear my throat.

"You could've just looked that—"

"Ask me a question, then, Grace. Any question at all."

"Fine," I say, and I turn to Nicole.

She shrugs, and I bite my lip, thinking of what to ask Bennet. All of a sudden, the perfect question appears in my mind.

"What is my middle name?" I ask.

The reason I asked this is because no one—no one at all—knows my middle name. Not even Nicole or Luke. Only Mum and Dad knew. If Bennet gets this, he can explain what he needs to explain.

"It started with an L," he says.

My eyes widen.

"Is it . . . L-Leigh! It's Leigh!"

I look back at my phone. "You get one chance to explain everything. Meet me—wait, do you know where I live?"

Bennet chuckles nervously. "Is it creepy if I say yes?"

I roll my eyes. "Only if you don't have an explanation for that, too."

"Oh, I do," he says. "I will come over now."

CHAPTER FIFTY-TWO
Maybe We Are Just Meant to Be Friends?

I watch as Bennet walks towards the porch, his hands in his pockets and a hood over his head. I stand up, and he stops walking, standing directly in front of me.

"Hi," he says.

I nod, pointing down. "Sit. You need to explain everything before my mind literally explodes," I tell him.

He chuckles and sits down on the porch next to me, leaning against the wooden planks that make up the railing. My phone buzzes beside me, and I pick it up. Nicole says:

> *I'll take care of James for you. Don't worry about a thing :)*

I let out a sigh of relief and place the phone back beside me before looking back up at Bennet. I watch as he takes the hood off his head. I can't help but smile when his brown hair falls to the corner of his face. He looks a lot like Mum.

"Okay, so what do you want to know?" he asks.

I raise my eyebrow at him. "Aren't you supposed to be doing all the talking?"

"Yes, but I need to know what you want me to explain."

I force a small smile. "Right. Okay, why did James kidnap you? Do you two know each other?"

Bennet shakes his head. "No, we don't know anything about each other—well, that's what I know. I have no clue who he is or what he does for a living. He, on the other hand, probably knows a lot of stuff about me, which is how he found me and kidnapped me while I was in my hotel room. Why he kidnapped me, I have no idea."

I frown at him, not completely convinced. "Are you sure? I mean, you might've just forgot—"

"I'm sure, Grace. I know what I know." He smiles.

I let out a sigh, nodding. "Okay. Well, why are you around here? How did you know about me? Why haven't I heard about you before? Why—"

He laughs, cutting me off. "One question at a time."

I apologize. He waves me off before letting out a sigh.

"I'll answer your first question. I was around because I heard about Mum. My adoptive parents kept Mum's death a secret from me for a while, which is probably why I missed her funeral, yes?"

I nod, and a sad frown spreads across my face.

"Anyway, after my adoptive parents kept acting suss, I went through their latest emails and messages. That's how I found out about Mum. I also discovered that I had a sister. I looked up a few things about you. I realised you aren't over eighteen yet and thought you'd still live with Dad. Then I made a few inquiries and found Dad's personal information," he explains.

"My adoptive parents were on holiday, so I figured it was the best time to leave. I went to find you and Dad. When I got here, I decided to sneak in by climbing up the side of the house. When I nearly reached the window, though, a car pulled out. I saw a guy walk to the door with a toolbox in his hand. Out of instinct, I jumped down and ran, deciding to see Dad later when he was alone and not busy. Later that day, I came back and noticed an ambulance and some police. I had no idea what happened. But just when I was about to leave, I saw you sitting right here," Bennet says, pointing to the spot he is in.

"And you had a woman next to you and a police officer in front of you, probably asking questions. Before you could notice me, I ran back to my hotel room. I found out that the reason there was an ambulance was Dad."

I hold back the tears as my mind recalls that day. Now, I just want to cry.

I do not know what to say to him, since everything he's told me so far has checked out.

Maybe he is my brother after all.

"Wait . . . ," I say, finally finding my voice. "Mum and Dad would've told me about you. So why didn't they?"

Bennet shrugs. "I have no idea. I'm still confused as to why they put me up for adoption."

I look down at the grass, thinking.

Why did you hide this from me, Mum and Dad? Why did you hide my own brother from me?

I try to think of any reason, but nothing comes to mind.

I let out a sigh and run my hands down my face.

All of a sudden, something pops into my mind. I gasp and turn to the bag beside me—the tape recorder!

I rummage through my bag for the tape recorder and pull it out as soon as I find it.

"A tape recorder?" Bennet asks.

I nod. "I found this in our parents' bedroom. I haven't listened to it yet, but maybe this has the answers we are both dying to know."

When I look up to see Bennet's reaction, he is already grinning.

I furrow my eyebrows in confusion. "Why are you smiling?"

He chuckles. "You said you found it in *our* parents' bedroom."

"Yeah . . . so?"

"Think about it, Grace." He is still grinning.

When I realise what I have said, I cannot help but smile.

"Well, let's see if what's in this recorder answers our question. And perhaps after that I'll be able to call you my *brother*."

"Then let's find out."

I look down at the tape recorder and stare at the little play button.

Am I ready for this?

I gulp and press the button. I feel my chest tighten, and I cannot help but suck in a deep breath, scared of what I am going to hear.

What if nothing is in it that will answer our questions?

But out of nowhere, a lady's voice begins to speak.

"So, what do you think the main problem here is?" the lady asks.

I move closer to Bennet, holding the tape recorder in front of us.

"Maybe we are just meant to be friends?"

Unexpectedly, my finger presses the pause button out of shock.

That's Mum! That's Mum's voice!

I feel tears sting in my eyes. I can't help but bite my lip. It has been forever since I heard her voice!

"Press play, Grace," Bennet says softly.

I can't help but let the first tear fall. I press the play button and try to control my shaking hand.

"Or maybe you're hiding something . . . ," Dad says.

My heart squeezes at the sound of his familiar voice. My hand begins to shake more, but Bennet grabs my wrist softly, stopping it from shaking. I look over at him, and he smiles. I bite my lip and look back down at the recorder.

"What would I be hiding?" Mum asks, her tone full of confusion.

"A baby," Dad says.

Both Bennet and I gasp.

"Where is this baby?" another woman's voice asks.

Dad lets out a laugh. *"Oh, in Rose's stomach, of course."*

Mum sighs. *"Okay, it's true. I'm pregnant, but I'm only eighteen! I'm not ready to have a child at this age! I don't know what to do or how to do my job as a mother! On top of that, I'm scared as hell!"*

The other woman sighs. *"Okay, I think the problem—"*

"You don't have to be scared, Rose. I'm here for you. I will be with you every step of the way, even if we aren't ready for a serious relationship," Dad says.

Mum sighs. *"I know. Thank you."*

"So, as I was saying—" The tape recorder stops.

I gasp. "What the hell just happened?" I scream, slamming the recorder on my knee.

Unfortunately, the small screen goes blank, and my eyes widen as tears fall down my cheeks.

"No, no, no—"

Bennet grabs my hand and stops me from doing any more damage to the recorder. He looks down at me and gives me a weak smile.

"Grace, we both got what we wanted. We got our answers."

"No, you got your answers! I didn't get mine!" I protest.

He raises an eyebrow. "What did you want to know, Grace?"

"I wanted to know why they didn't tell me!"

Bennet sighs and pulls me into a hug. I begin sobbing, holding onto him as if my life depends on him.

"Maybe that's it, Grace . . . they couldn't tell you. They just . . . couldn't."

CHAPTER FIFTY-THREE
At the Police Station?

"Luke!" I squeal. I run past the kitchen towards my boyfriend, standing in the doorway with his arms wide open. I envelop him in a hug, and he chuckles, holding me tightly.

"Good morning, beautiful. Ready for school?" Luke asks.

"Yes, but I have to say goodbye to someone first."

I dash back inside to hug Bennet. He laughs and stumbles backward, sending us both tumbling off the couch and onto the floor.

Believe it or not, Eve got home at midnight—she'd had to go into the city for a hospital check-up because of the pain she had been feeling. When I introduced her to Bennet, Eve was initially in shock. She argued first, saying he was probably just a homeless guy off the street, but when I told her everything, she believed me and decided to let Bennet stay for the night. Eve went to bed since she was tired, while Bennet and I watched movies and laughed at the silliest things.

To say that I feel happy is a huge understatement.

It is like my broken heart is whole again. I may have lost both of my parents, but I still have one last person left I can call family—Bennet.

It is like that saying: "You lose one but gain one." That is exactly what is happening. The only difference is—I lost two, and that still hurts.

"Wait—is that the guy from yesterday?" Luke asks.

I nod. "Luke, meet Bennet . . . my brother."

His eyes widen; he stares between us before laughing. When Bennet and I exchange puzzled looks, he stops and points at us.

"Oh, you're not joking?"

I shake my head. "No, I'm not."

He stands up straight, clears his throat, and walks over to Bennet. Extending his hand for a handshake, he says, "Uh, nice to meet you . . . I guess?"

Bennet clears his throat, stands, shakes Luke's hand, and nods. "Take care of my sister, Luke."

Luke glances over at me. "Are you sure this isn't a prank?"

I chuckle, shaking my head again.

He looks back at Bennet. "I'm doing exactly that."

His tone is confident now, but his free hand is slightly shaking—I can tell he is still struggling with the idea of me having a brother.

"Good. Now, you two run along. You don't want to be late, do you?" Bennet says.

Luke grabs my hand and drags me outside. When we reach the car, he turns to me.

"Now . . . are you positive you two aren't playing a trick on me?"

I let out a laugh and slap his shoulder, shaking my head. "Just hurry up and start the car."

*   *   *

Once Luke and I enter the school building, the bell rings loudly through the halls, urging everyone to sprint to class in fear of being late. I look up at Luke, hoping for a quick goodbye so I won't be late. I have already missed several days of school—I can't miss any more.

He rolls his eyes playfully. "Go on—get to class, goody-two-shoes." He laughs.

I thank him and place a quick kiss on his cheek.

I sprint down the hall and let out a sigh of relief when the class has not started yet—students are still filing into the room.

I walk in and take my seat.

Once everyone is settled, Mr. Simonds begins writing today's agenda on the board. As I watch him, my phone buzzes in my pocket. I pull it out and read Nicole's text:

We need to talk now. Any chance of escaping Mr. Simonds?

I glance up at the teacher. He is still writing. I quickly type a reply:

I just entered the class. Where are you? Why aren't you here?

She replies immediately:

Because I just can't. I'll explain if you come to the girls' bathroom near the main entrance.

I sigh in frustration and raise my hand, hoping he will permit me to go. "Sir?"

Mr. Simonds stops writing and turns to me.

I gulp when the class turns to me.

"Yes, Grace?"

"Uh, may I go visit the nurse? I don't feel well."

He frowns. "Do you realise how many days you've been absent? This won't look good on your end-of-year report."

"I know. Can I just . . . please?" I beg.

Mr. Simonds sighs, walks to his desk, and grabs a yellow note, scribbling something on it.

I stand up, sling my bag over my shoulder, and walk over to take the note.

"Thank you, sir," I say before turning on my heel.

I quickly exit the classroom, read the note, and mutter, "Thank goodness . . ."

I make my way to the bathroom, where Nicole asked me to meet her.

This better be good.

*   *   *

I find Nicole in the girls' bathroom, one hand resting on the sink, her head hanging low. I frown and walk towards her.

"Nicole? Is everything okay?" I ask, my voice quiet and gentle.

She breathes out a sigh and lifts her head. "Do I look okay?"

I look at her and gasp in shock at the purple bruise around her eye. "Wh-what happened to you?"

Shaking her head, she turns back to the mirror. "My stupid dad. I knew he wouldn't understand or believe a word I had to say about James. He thinks I am lying. When I told him yesterday, he hit me. My dad thinks so highly of that idiot, and I guess he doesn't even give two shits about me." Anger rings in her voice.

I can't believe her dad hits his own daughter.

"Did you tell your mum?"

She shakes her head. "I didn't even bother. If my dad doesn't, of course my mum wouldn't. I just can't believe he went so far as to hit me."

I let out a sigh, reach out my arms, and pull her into a hug. She rests her head on my shoulder.

"It's no use. James is still free to ruin people's lives," she murmurs.

I shake my head, pulling her back. "No, he won't be. We just need proof . . . and I know exactly what to do."

*   *   *

"Wait, so where are you again? At the police station?" Luke asks over the phone.

"Yeah."

He sighs. "If I ask why, will you tell me or make me wait?"

I chuckle. "Sorry, Luke. I will call you later and explain everything, okay? Don't worry about me."

"That's a little hard, since you're my girlfriend and all."

I roll my eyes. "Just don't worry. I have to go."

"Wait—" he says loudly before I can hang up.

I pause and press the phone back to my ear. "Yes, Luke?" My eyebrows furrow.

After a moment, he says, "I love you."

I cannot help but smile. My heart tightens, and butterflies flutter in my stomach.

"I love you, too," I reply and hang up. I slip my phone back into my pocket.

Nicole furrows her brows at me. "Honestly, you two make me sick," she says.

I roll my eyes, and before I can reply, the police officer I have been waiting for steps out of his office.

"William," I greet him with a smile.

"Good afternoon, Grace. Now, what's keeping you out of school on a Thursday, huh?" he asks.

I let out a chuckle. "Numerous things—but right now, I need your help for Nicole and me."

He looks over at Nicole.

Nicole gives him a small smile.

William nods. "So—what can I help you two with?"

CHAPTER FIFTY-FOUR
Look in Your Bedroom

"Grace, you know I can't arrest him without any proof. A lot of people have come into this station telling us stuff about him. Without any proof, we can't do a thing. I mean, I am not saying that I don't believe you—it's just, I need proof to do something," William explains.

Nicole and I share a look, frowns etched on our faces.

"William, please. You had James in here before—when he murdered my father—so why isn't he in jail?" I ask.

William sighs. "Again, we had no proof. Three guys around your age came in here doing the same thing you are doing now. We brought James in for questioning, and when we had no evidence, we let him go."

I let out a frustrated sigh. "You police officers make so many people angry, you know that?"

"Sadly, yes—but we are just doing our jobs. We don't make the rules; we just enforce them. That's all."

Nicole taps my shoulder. I look over, and she waves me closer. I excuse myself from William and join her.

"You know how we need proof?" Nicole whispers, and I nod. "This should be enough proof." She points to her bruised eye. "I'll say it was James. I'll make up a story, and hopefully that will be enough to get William to arrest him, and pin him for the murder of your dad, the kidnapping, and everything else he has done."

My eyes widen.

"But what if they find out it was your dad who hit you?" I ask, pointing to her eye.

She shakes her head. "The only way they'd know that is to ask him, and I know my dad won't confess. He'd have to say no if he doesn't want to go to court for a child abuse charge."

I cannot believe it. I think her idea might actually work. I may know the truth, but William does not. The story is believable enough, but I just have to hope that Nicole will be able to cover any loopholes that any police officer may notice.

"Are you sure?" I ask.

She nods. "Positive."

I sigh, then stride back to William. Nicole slips in beside me, and I give her a look, hoping that she gets the message. She nods and turns to him.

"I have the proof you need," Nicole says.

William's eyes widen in surprise. He turns around and motions for us to follow. I notice that we are going to the interrogation room.

Fingers crossed this works . . .

*   *   *

"So," William says, "you're telling me that when you went to confront James about Grace's kidnapping—including Luke and Bennet—he punched you a few times, causing this bruise, and then ran off?"

Nicole nods. "Before that, I asked him if he'd killed Grace's dad, but he didn't even deny it or anything. Then I decided to confront him about the kidnapping."

William grabs a sheet of paper and slides the form across the table, handing it to her.

"I know you just told me what happened, but I need you to write a statement about it. Start at the very beginning until the part in which he ran away," William says, handing Nicole a pen.

She nods and starts writing her statement.

"Grace, can I have a word with you outside?" William asks.

I nod and stand.

He walks over to the door, and I glance back at Nicole, who slightly smiles and mouths, "You're welcome."

Before I can return it, William clears his throat.

I turn around and walk out of the room.

He closes the door and crosses his arms over his chest.

"Are you sure about everything? Absolutely positive that James is the one who murdered your father?" he asks.

I nod. "Trust me—James is definitely the person who killed my father. I'm sure of it."

"Okay. Once Nicole is done writing her statement, I'll go track him down."

I smile at him. "Thank you. You're a good cop."

He chuckles, flipping his imaginary long hair. "You don't have to tell me twice."

I let out a laugh. "No, I don't."

*   *   *

After Nicole finished her statement, we decided to head back to school. We probably had a few more hours left, but we decided that it was best not to miss any more days of school.

Honestly, if it were not for Nicole's smart idea, we would still be at square one, finding ways to put James behind bars. If her idea had failed—William not buying it—I would have been doomed.

I sit down in the cafeteria and place my tray of lasagna in front of me. Nicole takes her seat beside me, while Luke sits on the other side next to me. To be honest, it is a little weird to have both of them at the same table, but we will just have to get used to it.

Suddenly, a guy comes up and drops his hands on the table, looking down at Nicole. I look up at the guy, who looks a bit familiar.

"Nicole," the guy says to grab Nicole's attention. When he sees her bruise, his features soften. "Can we talk?"

Nicole narrows her eyes at him. I glance at Luke—he only shrugs, watching Nicole and the guy.

"You think that after everything you did to me, I would just let you come back into my life? Please, I'm better than that," Nicole says confidently.

The guy raises an eyebrow at her. "Who do you think you're talking to?"

All of a sudden, everything hits me: Nicole's ex-boyfriend! Wait—why would he want to talk to her now?

"A player who can't keep his dick in his pants, of course. Now, please leave." She glances at her phone on the table.

Derek rolls his eyes and walks out.

"Slut!" he shouts back.

Nicole stands and glares after him.

"I'm not the one sleeping with everything that has a heartbeat, you man-whore!" she shouts.

The cafeteria erupts in laughter. A few in the crowd whistle their encouragement.

Nicole sits and mutters, "God, I hate him."

I chuckle. "I think you just made your point."

She cracks a smile.

Luke leans back, smirking as he looks around the cafeteria. I frown in confusion. I check my tray to see exactly why he looks so smug.

"You stole my food!" I say.

He turns to me and shakes his head. "How do you know it was me? It could've been anyone."

I shake my head. "Why else would you have that look on your face?"

He shrugs. "Maybe because I am currently loving life . . ."

I narrow my eyes at him. "Admit it—you stole my food."

"I would never admit to something I never did."

I growl and stand. "I'll be back. I'm going to get some food," I say before heading to the lunch line.

Once I reach the line, I turn my head and see them both talking. I curiously furrow my eyebrows.

What could they be talking about?

After grabbing my food, I walk back to the table and overhear Nicole say, "You have to do it soon. You don't want to disappoint her."

Just as I reach the table, she looks up at me and smiles before getting up.

"I'm going to the bathroom," she says.

Before I can even react, she walks off, and I furrow my eyebrows at Luke. "What were you two talking about?"

He shrugs. "Nothing special."

Before I can push him further, his phone rings. I frown at him, and he shows me the screen to see that it is his mom.

Perfect timing, Bree . . .

"I'll be back," he says and walks towards the cafeteria doors. My frown deepens.

What are they hiding?

*   *   *

"Hey, Grace! How was school?" Eve asks as I walk through the door that afternoon from school.

I shrug. "Fine, I guess."

She furrows her eyebrows.

I arch my eyebrow at her, and she pats the seat next to her. I let out a sigh and drop my bag, walking over to the couch to sit next to her.

She puts the popcorn beside her, turning to me. "Why do you look so down?"

I shake my head. "I'm not."

She rolls her eyes. "Very funny. Now, tell me what's wrong."

I let out a sigh. "It's just . . . well, at lunch, Nicole and Luke were talking while I was getting some food, and they looked very serious. When I got back to the table, Nicole made up an excuse to go to the bathroom, and when I asked Luke, he said that it was nothing. I just feel like they are hiding something from me."

"Maybe they are . . . or maybe they aren't."

I look at her, a bit perplexed. "What is that supposed to mean?"

Eve shrugs, a smile on her face. "It could mean anything . . . but it could also mean nothing at all," she implies, the smile still on her face.

I let out a frustrated sigh. "Tell me—"

"Look in your bedroom," she tells me almost immediately.

I scowl. "Why?"

She lets out a groan. "Don't ruin it. Just go and look."

My scowl deepens. "Don't ruin what—"

"Grace, don't make me drag you up there myself."

I purse my lips and get up from the couch. I make my way to the stairs. I glance back and see Eve watching me with a wide grin on her face. I roll my eyes and walk up the stairs.

Why do I have to look in my room? What could possibly be there?

I walk into my room, and in no time, my frown disappears as a smile makes its way onto my face. I look at the beautiful purple dress and grab the note that is resting on top of it.

To Gracie,

I know this is last minute, but I have a reason. I forgot about the dance. Yes, that's my reason, and hopefully, you can find it in your heart to forgive me for my stupidity. Also, you're probably wondering how I got your dress size—don't worry, I didn't sneak into your room and look at your clothes. I asked Eve to check for me. I hope you like the dress, beautiful.
See you tomorrow night.

-L. P xx

I smile and drop the note on my bed. Before I can even touch the dress, my phone goes off. I dig it from my pocket and see Luke's message:

> *Damn, I forgot to ask . . . If you are free tomorrow night, will you go to the dance with me?*

My smile widens, and before I can type a reply, my phone buzzes again:

> *I mean, I already know you're going to say yes. How can you reject this beauty?*

I let out a laugh and grin, typing my reply:

> *No.*

> *Think you're meant to reply with yes, Gracie.*

> *No, I meant no.*

> *Okay, whoever I am talking to right now, hand the phone to Grace.*

> *It is me. I am saying no.*

> *You're joking, right?*

Before I can send my reply, my phone begins to buzz like crazy.

> *Ha, you're probably joking . . .*

> *Please say you are!*

> *If you are being serious, I swear to God, woman . . .*

While reading his last message, my phone rings. I let out a laugh and answer the call.

"Please tell me you're joking," Luke says.

When I continue laughing, he groans.

"You're joking, aren't you?"

I stop laughing, holding my chest to steady my heart. "Yes, you moron! Of course, I will go with you."

He sighs. "I totally knew you were joking."

I let out another laugh.

Sure you did, Luke.

CHAPTER FIFTY-FIVE
Wink at Her So I Can Prove My Point

I look at myself in the mirror and cannot help but let the smile crawl its way onto my face. Nicole stands behind me, smiling and looking proud of what she has done for me.

My short, dark purple hair is curled to perfection, and with the little amount of makeup she has put on me, I am honestly stunned. My pale complexion, which has been for a while now, is more toned. My emerald green eyes are shining brightly as I look myself over, proud of Nicole's work. The knee-length purple dress that Luke bought me is nicely hugging my curves. Good job, Luke.

I look at the black flats I had stored in my wardrobe for a while and smile. I look myself over once more before turning around to thank Nicole. My smile widens, and I pull her into a hug.

"Thank you, Nicole. You did an amazing job," I say.

She flips her straight brown hair over her shoulder. "I know I did."

I let out a laugh and look at what she is wearing: a simple black dress that goes down to her ankles. It is strapless, which shows off her incredible collarbone and toned skin. Her brown hair is straightened, and the bruise that was on her eye is covered up with makeup. You can see it a little if you are up close, but from far away, she still looks as beautiful as always. I don't know how she does it, honestly!

"Wow, you two look stunning," someone says.

We both break apart to see Bennet leaning against the doorframe with a small smile on his face. I walk over to him and give him a hug.

"Thanks." I crack a smile and pull away from him. "Did you ask Eve?"

Bennet nods. "Why do you think I wasn't here yesterday afternoon? I was packing," he says.

A grin spreads across my face. "Remind me to thank Eve when I get back."

I turn around to look at Nicole, shyly focusing her gaze on the floor.

"Nicole . . ."

She looks up at me.

"Ready to go?"

She nods.

I look back at Bennet and see him smiling at her. I cannot help but roll my eyes. "You haven't even been here for a week, and you're already attracting girls."

Nicole clears her throat. I turn around and look at her, a grin still on my face.

"If you're talking about me, you are so wrong," she says.

I raise my eyebrow at her and then look back at Bennet. "Wink at her so I can prove my point."

Bennet does, and quickly Nicole's cheeks turn a slight shade of pink. I grab her hand and pull her out of my room, rolling my eyes.

"And you said that I was wrong," I say before she can say a word.

Eve sees us and beams with delight. "Oh, you two look absolutely breathtaking!"

I let out a snicker. "We know, we know."

"You two aren't leaving until I get a photo," she says before she sends Nicole and me on our way to the school dance.

*　　　*　　　*

As Nicole and I walk towards the gymnasium where the dance is being held, the memories of last year's school dance flood into my mind.

"Now, for the moment we have all been waiting for . . . ," Ember grins proudly.

I cannot help but let out a nervous sigh.

"The choir is now going to perform for us in front of the whole school!" she shouts.

The crowd begins to go crazy—clapping, shouting, and whistling. I know they are not cheering for the whole team; they are cheering for one—Nicole.

As the curtains draw open, the choir starts to walk into the light. I find myself walking behind everyone, and suddenly, before I can even comprehend what is happening, I trip over something and fall flat on my face. My dress flips, revealing my underwear to the whole school.

The students begin to laugh, and when I find the courage to stand up, I look at the person who tripped me on purpose.

Ember.

"Hey, are you okay?" Nicole asks, bringing me out of my thoughts.

I nod, waving her off. "Yeah, I'm fine. Just thinking about things."

"Don't worry about Ember. She said she isn't coming tonight," Nicole assures me.

I bite my tongue. And that is supposed to make me feel better? That only makes me more suspicious! Maybe she is plotting something against me.

"Oh, I guess that's okay," I lie.

"You bet. Now, you go and find your boyfriend while I go and retouch my makeup," she says before disappearing.

I let out a sigh, standing in front of the gymnasium doors. I push the thoughts away from my mind and push the doors open. I look around and gasp in disbelief.

The place looks amazing! Pink and purple streamers are everywhere, and balloons are spread across the ceiling. A few tables are set to the side to make enough room for the dance.

God, why am I even here? I ask myself, looking at the few people who are sitting at the tables with cups in their hands. I let out a sigh and shake my head.

"I can't do this . . ." And just as I turn around, I bump into a hard chest, making me stop in my tracks. I look up and blush in an instant.

"Oops . . . sorry," I mutter.

Luke lifts my chin so I can look up at him. "You can do this, Gracie. I'm here."

"Thank you," I mumble.

He rubs my back. I look up at him and notice a smirk on his face. He leans down and brings his lips next to my ear, kissing it. I close my eyes, my blush still on my cheeks.

"You look beautiful, by the way," he whispers in my ear, making my face feel pretty hot at his every word.

His smirk widens.

"S-so do you—I mean, you don't look beautiful, I'm just saying—wait, I'm not saying you don't look beautiful because you are, but you look more—sexy!" I squeal out, feeling my hands start to shake.

He tilts his head and grabs my hand, pulling me out of the gymnasium and into a classroom, closing the door behind him.

"Breathe," he says with a grin.

"Why?"

"Because you're going to need to—"

Before he can even finish his sentence, he grabs my waist and pushes me against a table, his lips crashing on mine. I place my hands behind me so I don't fall back and kiss him back, a small smile on my lips. Now, I regret not taking a breath . . .

CHAPTER FIFTY-SIX
Luke . . . Isn't a Player?

"Thank you, seniors, for performing that amazing dance routine for us!" the principal says, clapping with the rest of the students.

The clapping goes on for about five seconds until it dies down.

"Now, we are going to have the slow dance for everyone!"

Everyone starts to stand up from their seats, walking to the middle of the gymnasium. I notice some people sneak out instead, and I cannot help but chuckle.

Typical.

As I stand up from my seat, Nicole comes rushing over to me, pulling me aside. "Guess what I heard?"

I furrow my eyebrows. "What?"

She grins. "The evidence William got from me paid off. James was arrested for the murder of your dad, for kidnapping you, Bennet, and Luke, and for his abuse towards me."

"Really?" I gasp.

She nods.

I wrap my arms around her in a hug, smiling happily at the news.

"Oh my God, you don't know how much this means to me."

She giggles. "I'm just glad I could do something to help," she says, pulling away from me.

"Thank you, Nicole."

She squeezes my arm before walking to the middle to dance.

Suddenly, Luke grabs my hand and drags me to the dance floor, where half the school has already gathered. A slow song, like in the movies, begins to play. He wraps his arms around my waist, pulling me closer to him. I wrap my arms around his neck and rest my head on his shoulder, smiling.

As I look around, I notice a few people are doing the same, and when I see Nicole, she sends me a small, genuine smile. I return it, and she nods before turning to her date, whom I don't recognise. Not so far from them, I see her ex, Derek, glaring at them with his arms crossed over his chest.

"What are you thinking about?" Luke asks, his voice quiet.

I shrug and close my eyes, his cologne filling my nose. Wow, it's not that bad.

"Nothing special," I reply.

He chuckles. "Oh really? So I don't count as special?"

I open my eyes and raise my eyebrow at him. "Not everything is about you, Luke. Remember that," I say with a smirk.

"That's harsh, Gracie—really harsh." I know he is only joking by the tone of his voice and the smile on his face.

When I lean my head back on his shoulder, a million questions start flooding my mind, but the one that sticks out the most is the one I asked myself before I left the house.

"Hey, Luke, how did you manage to choose this dress for me?" I chuckle.

He raises his eyebrows at me. "Don't you like it?"

I shake my head. "No, I do. I just don't know why you chose a dress like this. Usually guys go for really short dresses that show a lot of skin," I say, hiding my grin.

He lets out a chuckle. "Knowing you, you'd probably throw it away if it showed too much skin. Besides, I'm a gentleman."

"Well, other people don't think that."

He breathes out a heavy sigh. "People call me a player, yes, but that's only because of what happened one night when I was drunk."

I look at him in shock. Luke . . . isn't a player? Is that what he is trying to tell me?

"What happened?" I ask, the music still making our bodies sway.

He looks down at me for a brief second before looking to the side.

"There was this one girl, and she was like a queen to everybody. She was gorgeous, powerful, and she always knew how to spread rumours around like wildfire. You see, I was at a party, and she forced herself on me. I was drunk, and I didn't know that she was drunk too. After the party, the next day at school, everyone was saying how I took advantage of her, even though it was her who forced herself on me. Of course, no one believed me, and that's when people started to label me as the player of the school," he explains quietly.

"Where was I, and how come I didn't hear this?"

"I think this was when you and Randy were dealing with your own stuff, so you mustn't have paid attention. I'm not sure."

I nod, but I furrow my eyebrows. "Who was the girl?"

He lets out a sigh, closing his eyes. "You wouldn't believe me if I told you. No one does," Luke mumbles.

I frown and stand on my toes, pressing my lips to his before pulling away. His eyes open, and he frowns at me.

"I will believe you, Luke," I whisper.

He sighs again. "If I tell you, you don't go confront that person."

I nod.

He bites his lip and closes his eyes again. "Nicole."

*   *   *

The time flew by quickly, and now, it's the end of the night. Everyone is leaving, and a few people are packing away the tables and chairs.

Luke and I are sitting on the stage, though, just watching everyone. Our hands are holding each other's, and I'm leaning my head on his shoulder, keeping my gaze on the balloons on the floor.

"You know what's funny?" he asks.

I look up at him, a small smile on my face. "What?"

He looks down at me, a smile on his face. "I wasted my breath blowing up half the balloons, even though I knew they weren't going to be used." He chuckles to himself, and I let out a laugh.

"That's not funny. That's just sad."

Luke stops laughing and looks down at the floor.

"Oh," he mumbles. "That is sad."

I chuckle. "Told you so."

He stares at me without saying anything, and neither do I. I look into his blue eyes and notice the sadness in them.

I still do not say anything, and when his lips meet mine, I can't help but close my eyes.

God, I love him so much.

He pulls away and tucks a strand of hair behind my ear. "I love you."

"I love you, too."

Before we can say anything else, the gymnasium doors open. A guy raises his hands in the air.

"Fight outside!" he screams and runs back outside. Everyone stops what they are doing and bolts to the scene.

I look over at Luke, and he nods, jumping down from the stage. I do the same and grab his hand again.

"I wonder who is fighting who."

I shrug. "I don't know for sure, but my bet is on Derek and the guy who was holding onto Nicole tonight."

For a split second, he looks down at me with wide eyes.

"Really?"

I nod, walking out of the gymnasium with him. "If looks could kill, that guy would've died in a heartbeat."

"You've got to be kidding me!"

We run to the scene. When we reach the entrance, the crowd of students has formed a circle. Someone chants Derek's name. My guess was correct.

I deserve a medal.

Luke calls my name, and I run to him, grabbing his hand. He pulls me through the crowd. And without any warning, someone hits my stomach, making me wince at once.

Before I can give the person a piece of my mind, I find myself in the circle with Derek, Nicole, and her date.

I watch as Derek throws a punch at the guy, but before Derek's fist hits his face, Luke jumps in and grabs his hand, stopping him. I look over at Nicole, screaming at Derek. The guy raises his hands lazily, blood rushing out of his nose.

"Don't do this, Derek. You could kill this guy," Luke warns him.

Derek growls, pushing Luke away. "That's exactly what I plan on doing!"

The crowd goes wild.

Nicole notices me and runs over to me, holding onto my arm without saying anything. She continues screaming at Derek, who is making his way over to the guy again.

"Derek, stop!" Nicole screams, but of course, he does not listen.

Derek releases another full swing punch, but Luke jumps in, so instead of hitting the other guy's face, Derek hits Luke's head.

I gasp in disbelief.

Luke immediately gets knocked down onto the ground. Without hesitation, I run over to Derek, and kick his balls.

Nicole runs to her date and grabs his arm, fleeing the scene.

I rush over to Luke, who lies unconscious on the ground. I crouch down to him, tears beginning to form in my eyes. "Luke, get up," I say, slapping his cheek.

He is not moving. I grab his hand, looking up at the crowd.

"Call the fucking ambulance!" I scream.

The crowd quickly gets their phones out and starts making calls. I look down at Luke and shake his shoulder.

"Luke, get up!" I yell, hoping he will wake up. I grab his head and place it on my lap, stroking his blond hair out of his face.

"Luke," I say weakly. "Don't do this to me."

Tears are already streaming down my cheeks. I grab his arm and place two fingers on his vein, hoping to feel the pulse. His pulse is slowing down. My heart begins to race, and I run my hand over his lips. "Help is on the way, Luke."

Help is on the way . . .

* * *

Nicole quickly walks over to me, concern written across her face.

She received my message then, I think to myself as she takes a seat next to me.

"I'm here, I'm here."

"What is happening to my baby?!" Bree screams at the lady behind the counter in the hospital.

"Answer me!" Bree shouts. My tired eyes witness her fists banging the table.

"I don't know, ma'am. Just take a seat and—"

"I don't want to take a seat! I want to know how my son is doing!"

Nicole holds onto my hand and watches Luke's mum. "He will be okay, Grace. He is a fighter."

"That's what everyone keeps telling me," I mumble and stand up.

Nicole frowns at me.

I wave her off. "I'm going to get a drink."

She nods.

As I walk past Bree, I cannot help but notice how broken she looks.

"He will be okay."

I rub my eyes and walk down the hallway towards the machine, scanning the selections. I click for a hot chocolate and watch as the cup begins to fill. As I wait, I glance to my left and spot Bennet and Eve approaching.

I grab my drink and walk over to them.

"Hey," I mumble.

"Are you okay?" Bennet asks.

I shrug. "I would lie, but there is no point. The person I love is in a hospital room with doctors who aren't saying anything to us. So, to answer your question, I'm not okay."

Bennet pulls me into a hug, aware that I have a hot drink in my hand.

"Everything is going to be okay," he tells me before pulling away.

I let out a sigh and bite my lip. "Just . . . stop saying that," I say. "Everyone is saying that, and I'm on the verge of breaking down."

Eve places a hand on my shoulder. "It's okay to cry, Grace."

"Yes, but I have spent an hour crying. I'm done crying. I'm just going to hold it all in now."

She sighs, removing her hand from my shoulder.

Suddenly, Bree let out a scream.

I turn around to see the doctors finally leaving the room where Luke is. Bree runs up to one of the doctors and grabs him by the shoulders.

"How is he? Is he okay? Can I see him?" she asks in a hurry.

I walk over to her, standing by her side as we wait for the doctor to say what he has to.

The doctor lets out a sigh and runs a hand through his hair. "Are you his mother?"

Bree nods.

He turns to me and raises a brow. "And you are?"

I hold onto my drink, looking up at the doctor. "Girlfriend."

He looks over at Bree and points to the room where he came from.

"We will give you five minutes with your son. He is still unconscious, but you may spend those minutes with him if you wish."

Bree quickly runs into the room. I turn to follow her when the doctor stops me.

"We prefer you see him after his mother."

I let out a sigh, nodding. I step away and take a sip of my drink.

The doctor walks back to the room and closes the door so no one can enter.

I take a seat next to Nicole.

Bennet leans against the wall in front of me and runs a hand through his hair.

"I hope everything is okay," he says quietly to Eve, probably thinking I could not hear him. "I mean, for Grace's sake," he adds.

"Same," Eve mumbles.

Before I can take another sip of my drink, another doctor rushes into Luke's room. I get up from my seat and hear Bree screaming as she steps out of the room. The door closes behind her just as she collapses to the tiled floor, tears falling down her face.

I rush to her and stop when the doctors say, "Clear!". My eyes widen, and my hands begin to shake.

"I hope everything is okay."

"Everything is going to be okay."

"He will be okay, Grace."

Suddenly, the door opens, and the doctors run to the reception desk. They ask for something, and when they hurry back to the room, the doctor we spoke to stops them.

"It's no use," the doctor mutters. "He's . . . gone."

EPILOGUE

It has been a week since Luke died in the hospital, and to say that I am broken is a huge understatement.

I feel like my heart has been ripped out of my chest, stomped on a million times, and then thrown back to me, leaving me to fix it all by myself.

I haven't talked to anyone since that night the doctor uttered those two words—final words. My world spun, and my hands dropped the drink on the floor, followed by my body. Nothing felt real after that. Even now, it still feels like *he* is here, holding my hand and making me smile like no other person ever has.

It just doesn't feel real.

Eve and Bennet have been trying to get me to leave my room—to do something other than sleep, stare at the wall in complete darkness, and cry. But my body will not let me do anything. It is not that I do not want to, it is the fact that I just cannot. It is like the devil has wrapped chains around my legs and arms and tied them to the bed, so I cannot do anything but grieve in my own way.

A few people have tried to contact me, but I ignored them all. Bree has even attempted to reach out. A part of me wants to speak to her, but an even bigger part of me warns me not to. I do not think I will be able to keep it all together while talking to the mother of my deceased boyfriend. I just cannot do that.

The only reason I have come out of my room today is because of Luke—his funeral. I know he would have wanted me to stay strong, so I guess you could say I am doing this for him.

I look at myself in the mirror and breathe out heavily. "I can't believe it has come down to this," I mutter to myself, looking at the black dress that stops just above my knees. I wore this dress to Mum and Dad's funeral, and now . . . Luke's.

My heart clenches as I let my thoughts go back to Luke. Every time I try to think about something else, my mind just has to go back to him. I cannot even try to sleep without thinking of him.

He is always just on my mind.

"Grace," Bennet calls from outside my door. "We have to go," he informs me softly.

I let out a sigh, running my hand through my hair. It is time.

"Okay . . . ," I say quietly.

When he is no longer in sight, I look at the phone that Luke bought me. I bite my lip.

See what I mean? Everything in this house, everything that I own, every person I see . . . they all remind me of the person I love.

Luke Peterson.

I let out a sigh and walk over to my door, grabbing the handle with a shaky hand. I turn the handle and pull the door back before stepping outside. The bright light from the windows downstairs makes me close my eyes for a brief second, my eyes adjusting to the brightness.

After a moment, I open my eyes and blink a few times before making my way down the stairs. I know I probably look like I have not slept in days—but I have. However, whenever I am awake, I only cry.

Eve notices me walking down the stairs and comes over. "Hey."

I send her a wave. "Hi."

My voice comes out raspy. I let out a cough to clear my throat and look up at her, smiling down at me.

"Uh, I decided to move the trip to my hometown until next month because of . . . everything," she says.

"You don't have to do that . . . ," I say quietly.

She shakes her head, waving me off. "But I am. I know you're not ready for any interaction with anyone, and I'm not going to force you. I can wait till you are ready."

Nodding, I cannot help but look down at her obvious baby bump.

"Where is Bennet?" I ask.

Eve points behind her. "In the car. You ready to go?"

I nod.

She walks towards the front door, and I walk out of the house, closing the door behind me.

I am so not ready for any of this.

*   *   *

"My s-son was the most bright, c-cheerful, happy boy, and that's what he would've w-wanted us to remember him," Bree finishes.

The people in the church just stare with pity in their eyes. She then makes her way down the stage and towards the seat next to me. She wipes away her tears and lets out a heavy sigh.

"It's your t-turn, Grace," she says weakly to me.

I gulp, gathering the palm cards in my hands as I leave my seat. All eyes are on me, but I try to ignore them as I make my way to the podium, breathe out a sigh, and place the palm cards on the glass, adjusting the microphone.

I look up at the crowd and see everyone waiting patiently for me to speak, knowing that it may take me a few seconds to collect myself.

The truth is, I am not collected—and I never will be.

They just do not know that.

I bite my lip, look down at my palm cards, and look back at the crowd. Before I know it, I find myself speaking into the microphone, reading the cards.

"Most of you don't know . . . but that's okay. I am usually known as *the nobody* at my school, but one day, one boy made me feel like I was somebody."

I let out a shaky breath and close my eyes, the image of *him* appearing in my head.

"L-Luke Peterson," I say quietly. I open my eyes and bite my lip.

"The day Luke approached me, I was confused. Why would somebody like him want to help someone like me? From that day, though, I slowly began to see the real side of him—not the side they saw. Luke was always smiling, and when I was with him, I couldn't help but smile too," I say, flipping the card to the back and reading the next one.

"Luke will always be someone that stays in my heart, along with my parents, and no one can change that. Some of you might have different perspectives of Luke, good or bad, but during the few months that I spent with him, the side that always stood out more was the one where he was always willing to put himself second . . . something that will stick with me forever," I say, holding back the tears that are threatening to fall.

I suck in a breath and close my eyes, lowering my head a little to try to calm my racing heart.

"Luke . . . was everything to me, and no one may have known this, but he showed me that even though you might be stuck in a deep, dark hole, you can always find the light. To me, Luke was my light," I say, turning to Luke's coffin.

"I'll miss you, Luke," I say quietly, gathering my cards and walking down the stage. A few people clap, and instead of going back to my seat, I walk straight down the aisle and out of the church.

Suddenly, without warning, the tears fall from my eyes. I drop to my knees on the grass, pulling my hair.

"Why, Luke, why?" I mumble.

The door opens, and Eve stands there, frowning.

I wave her off and lower my head again.

"Please . . . just leave me alone."

She crouches down, takes something out of her pocket, places it in front of me, and kisses my forehead.

"Luke told me to give you this," she whispers quietly before walking back to the church.

I hold back a sob and look at the folded paper. I grab the paper and unfold it.

The words Dear Gracie come into my sight. I bite my lip and suck in a deep breath before reading what is on the piece of paper.

Dear Gracie,

If I am not here anymore, you can continue to read this. If I am, though, just stop, tear the letter, and throw it in the bin because there is no reason why you should be reading this if I am still alive. That would make everything awkward when I see you.

I asked Eve to give this to you if I don't make it, and if you are reading this now, make sure to thank her.

Okay, you are probably crying your eyes out while reading this, but everything will be okay, Gracie. I'm so sure of it. You know how I know this? Because when I first met you—the day when you were leaning against the lockers crying—I knew you were strong. I know you still are. You are so strong, Gracie. Don't let anyone tell you otherwise. If they do, call them gorillas. That's the best way to do it.

Moving on to the serious stuff, though, what Nicole and I were talking about that day at the cafeteria was about my condition. She is the only person I felt like I should be telling it to. I know we have had our rough times, but that's in the past now, and since you and she are like best friends now, I felt like I had to solve the conflict between the two of us.

Anyway, Nicole was saying that I had to tell you about what I had, and so, I am writing it to you now because I just can't find it in myself to tell you in person. You would be too stressed out with everything, and I didn't want to add that to your list. I know that makes me a coward, but I am telling you now, and that should be enough . . .

I have . . . well, had cancer.

I was diagnosed with glioblastoma multiforme. It is a tumour that grows in the brain and affects the spine. Two years ago, the doctors said that I would probably have around fifteen months—but lucky me, I earned an extra few months. A few months before I met you, I was having seizures and blurred vision. I kept it to myself, and when my father died, I just lost the courage to tell my mum. I couldn't tell her that her son was on the verge of dying too. So, I told the person who I thought could help me—Nicole.

She knew a few doctors in her family. We settled our past, and she agreed to help me. Well, who could say no to a dying seventeen-year-old, right? I met up with her grandmother every Tuesday and Thursday for some lab tests. I was keeping it all from my mother, but I begged her not to say anything to anyone. Just like Nicole, she wasn't able to say no and kept it a secret. I also think that the money I've been stealing from Daniel's stash helped to keep her mouth shut.

Then, just last week, Nicole's grandmother had told me that with the number of seizures I was having, I didn't have much time left. So, I planned everything out. I would take you to the dance. I would tell you I loved you. I would never leave your sight. I wanted everything to be perfect that night.

But anyway . . . skipping the sad parts—I love you, Grace. You are honestly the best thing that has happened to me, and if it weren't for Daniel, I wouldn't have met you—the beautiful girl with purple hair, and your future children should be grateful that they have a mother like you, because you have been through so much.

You have to tell them stories about us, though. Stuff your future husband. I don't care. He can go kiss my butt if he has a problem with me.

Well, I'm going to leave this short because I have to leave to get to the dance tonight. I never wanted to end it this way, but life hates me, so . . . what can you do?

I may have saved you from jumping, but I guess you can't save me from falling.

I love you, Gracie. Don't miss me too much.

-L .P. ☺ ♡

The tears continue falling, but what makes the small, sad laugh escape my lips is the tiny smiley face and the love heart next to his initials.

The End.

BOOK YOU MIGHT ENJOY

LOVE IS BLIND
Tara L. Declan

Romantic. Tragic. Everlasting.

If you love young adult romances that'll leave you in pieces from authors like John Green, Nicolas Sparks, and Jamie McGuire, you'll definitely fall head over heels with Love is Blind!

"Even fairy tales have their struggles."

What happens if one day everything you had and worked for are taken away in an instant?

Payton Jennings has been breezing through classes and acing them. But a day that started perfectly fine day ended in a gruesome incident. A rage out of pure jealousy has targeted one of the school's most famous students and opened fire.

Reece Collins' life is something one can consider as perfect. He is rich, smart, handsome, famous and generous. It, therefore, shocked the whole school when he was shot point-blank, leaving him blind. And just like that, his popularity and his friends vanished as well.

Except for one— Payton.

Lost in the darkness and the fear of not being able to stand back up again, Payton helps Reece realize that there are bigger things that are bound to happen and that everything happens for a reason.

How will Reece cope with the incident that changed his life forever? As a person with a troubled background, how will Payton overcome her insecurities to help Reece overcome his fears? And will Reece and Payton prove that love is not about what you're seeing but what you're feeling?

Grab this eye-opening YA romance book and let it show you that what is important is indeed invisible to the naked eye.

BOOK YOU MIGHT ENJOY

OUTCASTS
B.D. Fresquez

How can he act so calm and collected after he just stole my first kiss?

Riley Summers doesn't quite fit in the Fairfield High crowd. She listens to Led Zepplin and watches Star Wars—not your usual teenage girl favorites.

She has been fine with living in the fringes of her high school scene until Aiden Callaway, Fairfield's infamous rebel hunk, "kidnaps" her one afternoon. He eventually lets her go, but their time together is far from over.

Join Riley and Aiden on their senior year journey—a year of Star Wars movie marathons, a crashed wedding, a paint war, and something unexpected: a keen, growing attraction.

This might be your next favorite rebel-boy-and-nerd-girl romance. Grab your copy now!

ACKNOWLEDGEMENTS

I'd like to thank my sister, Brielle, because if I didn't tell her about this book, I probably would've left it unfinished.

I would like to thank my editors and agents for making this actually happen. It is a dream come true!

And I would like to thank my readers, as it is you guys who have stuck by my side since day one.

Thank you.

AUTHOR'S NOTE

Thank you so much for reading *Saving Gracie*! I can't express how grateful I am for reading something that was once just a thought inside my head.

Please feel free to send me an email. Just know that my publisher filters these emails. Good news is always welcome.
talesha_mitchell@awesomeauthors.org

Sign up for my blog for updates and freebies!
talesha-mitchell.awesomeauthors.org

One last thing: I'd love to hear your thoughts on the book. Please leave a review on Amazon or Goodreads because I just love reading your comments and getting to know you!

Can't wait to hear from you!

Talesha Mitchell

ABOUT THE AUTHOR

I'm an average teenager who doesn't like coffee. Yep, hot chocolates for me! I have loved writing ever since I was little and have dreamed for so long to make writing a career for me.

Anyway, I've got to leave this short as I am currently craving Cookies & Cream ice cream, and in the mood to binge-watch some movies!